I0600214

Mads
Vol. 1 A Cash City Omegaverse Story
Shasta de Leon

Smith Book Investments

Dedication

To the grumpy folks. I see you. Understand you.

I am you.

Copyright © 2025 by Shasta de Leon

All rights reserved.

No part of this publication may be reproduced, distributed, or transmitted in any form or by any means, including photocopying, recording, or other electronic or mechanical methods, without the prior written permission of the publisher, except as permitted by U.S. copyright law.

The story, all names, characters, and incidents portrayed in this production are fictitious. No identification with actual persons (living or deceased), places, buildings, and products is intended or should be inferred.

ebook ISBN 979-8-9996433-1-5

Paperback ISBN 979-8-9996433-4-6

Book Cover by KILLDERA

Edit by Cupid's Inkwell

First edition 2025

Contents

Introduction   VIII

Prologue   1

1. Insurance   7

2. Corruption   14

3. Soirée   20

4. Lilac   25

5. Limerence   30

6. Rut   34

7. Post Traumatic Stress   40

8. The Beta Profile   44

9. Mating Ceremony   50

10. The Interview   54

11. Urban Lounge   63

12. Little Momma   69

13. Pack Lead   76

14. Omegas Love Gifts   80

15. Turn Down For What   86

16. Rejections   90

17.	Second Interview	95
18.	Third Party	103
19.	Mickey	109
20.	Pressure	117
21.	First Date	124
22.	Bleach	132
23.	Romancing	139
24.	Working Lunch	145
25.	The Faircastle House	151
26.	It's Happening	159
27.	Pack Life	169
28.	A Look Within	173
29.	Slinging Pies	178
30.	Hard Read	188
31.	Face the Music	197
32.	The Phone Call	201
33.	Fate Calls, Alphas Answer	210
34.	Marked	215
35.	Tea Break	220
36.	Full Moon	223
37.	Courting Gift	235
38.	Virgin Alpha	240
39.	The Scent of Her	244
40.	Places, Everyone	249

41.	Preferences	253
42.	The Last Meet-Cute	261
43.	Pack Soto	266
44.	Roundtable	274
45.	Sunday Candy	281
46.	Exit Interview	289
Epilogue		297
Afterword		299
About the Author		300

Introduction

Mads is a follow-up duet to the Ondine duet. Ondine Vol. 1 & Vol. 2 are not necessary to read before Mads, but there are some characters and situations first introduced in Ondine that are the focus in Mads.

Previously on Cash City Omegaverse...

Below is a brief summary of Ondine Vol. 1 & Vol. 2, and how it pertains to Mads's story. Be warned: spoilers ahead.

Ondine is an omega who went into contract with Jake Meier and his two alphas, Sebastian and Shadow. They run Meier Protections Group, a security company in Cash City. After being subjected to an unwanted scent test by local gangster Lee Man-ho, Ondine fell into a devastating bond sickness.

While being treated, Ondine found her scent match, Shadow's half-brother Freddie, and bonded him. Afraid of losing her, Jake Meier found her crush, Arnie, a beta, and blackmailed him to bond with the Meier pack, ensuring Ondine would choose his pack even though she had a scent match.

Mads was Arnie's roommate.

Two beta men who lived together who own a lot of aquariums. This is when we learn that Mads dated an omega without her alphas' permission, and they assaulted him. This happened off-page.

In the final chapters of her story, Ondine finally confronted her parents, asking for the deed of her childhood home so she and her new large pack could live together more comfortably. Her parents abandoned her in that house when she was 12, never living with her again. This confrontation included Ondine learning that her parents missed her graduation from Fair Castle University because they were too busy courting an omega. The omega, Acadia, is Ondine's age, a nail in the coffin of reconciling her relationship with her parents.

Ondine bonds with the Meier pack, and the six of them move to their new country home.

Ondine's story ends happily ever after, but for Mads and Acadia, it's just beginning.

Prologue

1 year ago...

Mads thought they had to be done with him. Both alphas were out of breath as they circled him from above like two prehistoric vultures circling their prey, hovering on a column of hot air shooting up from his broken body. He didn't want to continue to lie here in a tight ball trying to protect the soft parts of his body with his limbs, but it was out of his control.

The Dougherty brothers were twins and bonded alphas. They were in their late twenties, with soft jaws and pale faces. They had trouble growing facial hair, and yet one of them was still trying for a mustache. It was patchy and thin. The brothers wore blue jeans and white t-shirts, and it appeared as though they shared clothes between them.

The mustached one spat on Mads and called him the same thing he'd been calling him since they first drove him off the road.

"Bastard. Fucking bitch. If you think you can take our omega from us, then you have another thing coming."

He could have sworn he saw Nancy in the cab of the truck that chased him over this bridge.

The Dougherty brothers drove their own truck out to hunt down Mads, not bothering with anonymity. It was a gaudy, current-year

Dodge Ram 2500 that had to have cost them as much as most people's mortgage payment. Running down Mads didn't scratch the body, and thank god, because it was a custom paint job—pearl white.

The truck had struck him with the chrome bumper, causing his body to fly into a hidden slope off to the side. The Dougherty brothers exited the vehicle to continue the assault with their heavy boots and leather lined knuckles.

They came prepared to beat the shit out of him.

And for what?

Mads didn't know their omega wasn't allowed to date other people. Shit, he thought she was as free as he was. But Nancy had deceived him. Making him an unwitting pawn and loser in whatever game she'd been playing. Did she plan to make her bonded alphas jealous? He didn't know, and yet he asked himself this as they rushed up on him.

The alphas grasped at whatever part of him they could get their meaty little fists on. The non-mustached one sunk his hands into Mads's hair, fingernails scraping against his bruised scalp, then yanked his head back like a doll. The other used the opportunity to punch Mads square in the face, breaking his nose upon impact. Mads heard the sound of breaking bone before he felt the pain of it. Non-mustache Dougherty brother wanted his chance to punch Mads too, but didn't let go of his hair to do so. This time, Mads flew back from the force, skidding on the gravel. The alpha laughed, wiping Mads's unattached hair off on his pant leg.

"You're just a pretty boy that our omega wanted to fuck, you know? That's all betas are good for anyway, a quick fuck. We should just keep you as our whore since you are too weak to be of any good. Useless and weak!"

One of them found a piece of rebar, about three feet in length, off in some concrete rubble, and when he returned, they took turns beating him with it. Each powerful blow resulted in fractures along his body, splitting the skin and cracking his bones. Mads wanted to fight them off, but being thrown across the road by that lifted truck earlier had put him at a disadvantage from the start. Every blow had to be accepted. Mads thought that each hit would be the most he could handle, and then another would follow, making him a liar.

His body lay sprawled out across some construction rubble and the gravel filled road. If he had had control, he wouldn't be twisted at the waist with his legs upside down and his face towards the danger. But he didn't have control. He could just barely move his head to the side. When he did, he saw the brother with the mustache sweating profusely and out of breath from exertion, his hands resting on his knees while he was hunched over.

It must be tiring work, beating a man.

For their last hurrah, his less tired brother jumped into the air and landed on Mads's thigh, crushing his femur under his steel-toed work boots. The pressure and force cracking his femur bone was like the earth cracking in two underneath your own feet. There was a vibration powerful enough to kill a man that snaked its way up his entire body and back down. His teeth clacked and tasted of metal. It felt like God himself had dolled out this punishment with his combined powers of life and death.

It caused Mads to pass out for a time, and when he came to, the truck was gone and he was alone. Every breath was a painful pull, and he knew his ribs were broken. The sun shone down on him, burning his skin, adding insult to injury. Mads lay in the dilapidated part of town, next to the bridge, until the sun went down.

Earlier that day, Mads had been thinking of going to a river casino with some friends over the weekend, or turning them down to see Nancy again. He had been thinking of asking his boss for a raise and was going to look into ways to do that more effectively. He was thinking of buying another fish for his tank, even though it was out of his budget. But lying on the ground, none of those futures existed anymore.

It had been ripped from him.

All the lives he was going to live were gone. And he was empty, and so was his future. He knew he didn't want to die, but this was a death, too. Blood ran over his eye and down his neck, carrying with it a single tear.

Mads realized two things at once: he could no longer feel most of his body, and if he was going to be rescued he'd need to do something about it. He would need to alert someone, anyone, that he was there and he was alive. He moaned and raised his voice. By the time someone found him, a runner out for a late night run, Mads's voice was hoarse and nearly gone.

"Hey man, are you ok?" The voice of a young man came out of the darkness. "Oh fuck, are you alive?"

The runner called an ambulance and stayed with him until the police arrived.

Mads didn't recall all the details that had happened that night, and most things had to be told to him later by the police, who pieced it together from the reports of the first responders and the evidence of his own injuries. The whole attack was from 3:10 pm to 3:25 pm. He laid near the road until 9:00 pm, when the runner heard him yelling and found him. The timeline didn't make sense to him. He thought the attack lasted hours, not a measly 15 minutes. His recollection of the details was lost. But what his hindbrain did remember was how the alphas made him feel: Powerless. Out of control. Defenseless. Weak. They taught him that, if motivated enough, any male alpha can destroy, almost completely, everything. *Alphas* equal *danger*. Alphas *were* danger.

Stay away.

At all costs.

destroy, almost completely, everything. *Alphas* equal *danger*. Alphas *were* danger.

Stay away.

At all costs.

1

Insurance

Mads

I 'm not really supposed to be buying a coffee right now, but I'm celebrating. It's been over 13 months of absolute fucking hell, and today I'm getting good news.

I set myself up in the middle of the café with my journal and my phone, and my chai tea latte. I flip through my entries from this last year, seeing the scribble that has been my life. How hopeful I was when I first met Nancy. How she lit a fire inside of me. And then how it burned me up from the inside out.

Her two alphas, Case and Morris Dougherty, did not know about me, and when they found out, they were not ok with me sleeping with their omega.

I guess omegas aren't supposed to be collecting beta boyfriends.

I'm a beta, what about 80% of the population's designation is. The rest are alphas, and an even smaller percentage are omegas. Omegas are often women, and only an omega can give birth to an alpha. They travel in packs, for reasons I don't understand. Maybe because there are so few omegas? So they have to double up, triple up, to all get a chance to be with an omega—who's to say? I never bothered them. I guess until I thought it would be ok to take Nancy out on a date.

I'd been warned about alphas, but I ignored the warnings. What was the worst they could do? I'm a man. They are men, at the end of the day. I didn't fear them. But I definitely do now.

Nancy approached me while I was flying my drone at the park by the river. She was so interesting and real. She was a flame and I was a moth.

I asked her out immediately. Her alphas knew about us, or so I thought. She mentioned she had two of them, brothers, and she hated them. I didn't ask questions. Honestly, I didn't even know how to ask to not offend her.

She and I went out several times over the course of a month. I took her back to my apartment, told my roommate to get lost, and we slept together. I figured if she wasn't supposed to be sleeping with other people, then she wouldn't have launched herself at me as soon as we walked through the door. Right?

These alphas, the brothers she supposedly hated, ran me over with their car. They beat me, shattering my femur. I was in a coma for two months and in the hospital for six months.

Now, I have to walk with a cane.

I'm in constant pain.

Nothing is the same.

There's Mads before the accident—hilarious jokester always looking for a good time, and Mads now—recluse and forlorn jackass no one can stand to be around.

I can't even be in public long. I start to get anxious that I might see an alpha. Or have to interact with one. It sends me into a complete tailspin.

The medical bills started coming in before I even woke from my coma. All my savings were eaten away those first six months. I moved in with my mom, and I needed a medical bed and medication, and all this goddamned equipment. The insurance only covered a fraction of the cost. My mom works two jobs to try to pay for everything and keep us afloat.

But today everything changes.

My settlement against the Dougherty pack is dispersing soon. My lawyer texted and asked for a call today.

It should be enough to pay the rest of my medical bills. Buy me a normal cane and not this shit one I got from the hospital (that I'm still making payments on). And pay my mom back for all the living expenses.

My old boss is calling me at 1:00 pm to talk about starting back again.

I'm going to get my life back.

My lawyer's number shows up on my phone, and I answer straight away. A smile I haven't felt in forever stretches across my face.

"Matthew, give me the good news," I say.

"I mean, it's good news for sure. The $250,000 is being dispersed today."

"Oh god," I breathe.

I wanted more, but this is totally fine. I've had a while to determine what I would do with this. It's not enough to pay back my expenses, but I start work again soon. This will help me get back on my feet. I need this money. It's the only thing I have been looking forward to for months. My entire life has been on hold until this is finalized.

"Yes, not bad," Matthew says in a tone that doesn't sit right with me. Before I can say anything about it, he goes on, "So, my payment will come first, and then the insurance company will take theirs. If there's any left, it will be sent to you by the end of the week."

I grab my thigh as it flares up in a strong ache.

I can't safely describe the pain in my body. It feels like there's some-one sawing down through my bone. An invisible demonic being with manic energy, just ripping and tearing my muscles, and bowing and bending my bone in an unnatural way. It feels like the world got moved into the background, and this pain is all foreground. Sometimes I can focus past the pain, to the background. Other times, like now, I can't.

"I'm sorry, but I don't understand," I say between my teeth, hold-ing back my reaction to the ache. I don't want to take more of my meds. The ones I took this morning should be good for another hour.

"Yeah, so, in this case, your settlement will be used to pay back the insurance company for what they covered on your medical costs."

My voice is harsh as I raise it to say, "I'm sorry, that doesn't make any sense. I've been paying my medical expenses."

"Right," Matthew says in his lawyer voice, no longer using his friendly voice. "You've been paying what they haven't covered. Your settlement is going to be used to pay back what the insurance covered."

"You keep using the words 'pay back'. Don't I get 'paid back' for what I've been covering?"

"Look, it's not great, but this happens. Do you know how much they've covered this year?"

My leg flares up so bad I think I'm going to pass out.

"Matthew, I've paid nearly $60,000 in bills! I think it's upwards of $300,000 that insurance covered! Are you saying all of my settlement is going to the insurance company?"

"Well, no. I'll be taking $10,000 before it goes to them."

I hang up the phone, grab my leg with both hands, and try re-ally hard not to scream. A sound comes out, but it's muffled by my clenched jaw. The pain is so intense. It always feels like a version of the pain I felt in the hospital, when my body was bloated from the saline, and the drugs were wearing off. But out here, there's no button to press. There's only the pain and the big wide world around me.

I toss my journal in my backpack, throw away my $7 coffee, and limp out of the café with any dignity I may have left while leaning all my weight on my fucking cane.

But really, I hope I get hit by a bus on my way home and die this time.

I'm joking.

Mostly.

I get to the apartment and I sit at the bottom of the stairs. My mom and I are on the second level. They look like rooms at a motel, all looking out over the parking lot. The stairs are metal and janky. We still can barely afford this place. I stretch out my leg as it involuntarily shakes, and I try not to pass out. *I'll breathe through it. I'll get through it.*

I try square breaths, and when that doesn't work, I do triangle breaths.

Fuck.

Fuck!

I'd been relying on the settlement. And it's gone. There's nothing left. The fucking insurance and lawyer bled me dry.

Pack Dougherty wasn't wealthy, so my lawyer talked me into a realistic amount. $250,000 sounded good at the time. I didn't know there were sharks in the water.

My phone rings an alarm since it's time for my call with my old boss. I hop on Zoom on my phone, and when the screen shows my face on camera—I look like shit.

My usual light brown hair looks dull and stringy. I haven't been able to see a barber. I've just had my mom cut it when it gets over my ears. My face is ashen white. I haven't spent any time in the sun. The lines between my eyebrows are deep, probably from holding in the pain. My lips are tight and smaller than usual. I should have shaved. It's been a few days.

I often find myself staring at myself in a mirror or in pictures, since my body has changed so much, it's like I need to memorize it again and tell myself that's me in the mirror. I'm six foot even, but I don't hold myself up straight anymore, and I found people don't refer to me as "tall" like they used to. I don't wear anything stylish, or risky. Like today, I am in some dark gray chino pants and a pale gray, lightweight sweater with the sleeves pushed up. I'm wearing some new sneakers my mom got for me at the shoe store she works at. I told her I needed something practical, something that will take a lot of wear on them since I walk to more places than I choose to take a car.

"Mads!" My boss says, hoping to see the old Mads. The smiling, full of life guy. I try to find him and bring him out, but it's not happening.

"Luke, how're you?"

"So good! So good! Are you outside on some stairs?"

"Yeah, I needed some air," I lie.

I used to never lie.

"Great, ok, well, good news, we can keep you on a zero dollar payroll for another month so you can stay on the insurance."

"What?" I don't hide my surprise.

"Yeah! One more month. It'll give you enough time, I think, to find something."

"No, Luke, I want to come back. I'm ready. I thought that's what we were discussing."

"Oh, I apologize that there was a misunderstanding of our call today. We've backfilled your role, and I don't have the budget for two of you guys. Plus, it's probably not a great fit. You'd have to come in every day. There's a minimum physical requirement. It's not very accessible."

I tune him out. They aren't going to let me come back. They never were.

I turn and throw up off the edge of the stairs. The camera picks up everything.

"Fuck, are you ok? Oh my god."

I end the call and lie back. Vomit on my chin. My leg is outstretched and shaking.

My only thoughts are how my vomit tastes like chai tea latte, and I'll never be able to have another one as long as I live. Which, at this rate, will not be much longer.

2
Corruption

Acadia

This is absolutely ridiculous!

I'm so worked up that I have to stand up and pace. My heels click on the marble floor. Everything in this place echoes. Glass walls. Metal furniture. Open ceilings. All the outside walls are windows. All the workers wear white business suits. It's creepy, but I've painted myself into a corner.

I'm 24, almost 25, and I'm ready for a pack.

You'd think omegas would be treated better at a place called the Alpha-Omega Placement Institute.

Until now, I tried to avoid registering with them.

I knew how corrupt and unfair their system is, but I thought I could still work the system and find a way to do this on a level playing field.

But this place is more complicated than I thought.

I opened myself up to be courted two years ago. I thought I finally found my pack. The Whitehorse Pack. An older couple who had been together most of their lives. Both alphas. How fucking cool is that? And I was so intimidated by Bianca. She's beautiful and had this air of power. Cornell was so openly kind to me. They talked about buying me a house. I had a minor heat with them. They'd been courting me for over a year until I decided to go into a contract with them. A contract to court. Which is very common, and expected, with omegas.

At the time, I was willing to look past some of our issues. I didn't want to judge them by their age or designation. So I overlooked that I was still needy after nights together. I needed to buy one of those fake alpha cocks with a knot to use after we hooked up. I also kept it from them because I was worried they would think they weren't good enough.

It didn't even occur to me that *my* feelings on the matter were important as well. I was too busy being the caretaker of their feelings of inadequacy that may arise that I gave no credence to my feelings of being embarrassed my two alphas left me wanting.

It was embarrassing! For me and for them. We live in a society that is designed around omega satisfaction. It's the whole reason alphas and omegas form packs—because omegas are needy little things.

Actually, thinking about it, it wasn't embarrassing to buy the fake cock from the sex store. It was not that at all. The blue-haired woman with a thick nose ring and tattoo stars across her nose that looked like rainbow freckles, described each cock to me with impressive detail. She even pulled a smaller one out of the package that vibrated, and touched the tip with my nose, so I could feel the difference in settings. And when I got home later, it was her that I imagined trying it on me in some fantasy where she was just trying to sell me more toys, and I was trying to pretend this was just good service.

It can't be good when you have two full-grown alphas courting you, but you actually imagine a beta store clerk when you masturbate?

But that wasn't the only red flag. When I met their daughter, that was too much for me to continue to justify.

I tried to overlook her age, just a year younger than me, and I tried to overlook the fact she wasn't even told about me until I waltzed into that café. I tried to be ok with everything.

But I wasn't.

I left the café where we met, in tears. I sat in the back of a city cab bawling, thinking about their little beta daughter being left all alone at 12 years old.

Their daughter had said things to them that didn't match up to what they told me. They said she was a very independent girl and did so much better when she was at boarding school. But that wasn't the truth.

They left their kid at their summer house and never really saw her again. I can't think of Bianca or Cornell Whitehorse without thinking about that little beta girl, a suppressed omega, being rejected by her parents. Or her discovering she was an omega so late in life and having no one.

I couldn't imagine doing that to your own child.

And then I thought, what if I had a beta daughter? What if my alphas didn't want her? I bawled my eyes out for hours about that too. My nonexistent future child.

I dissolved my contract with them and registered with the Institute.

Now I have a whole new set of problems. I told them I wanted a pack with a beta. Even now, my lip quivers thinking of my future beta daughter, and I want to make sure my pack would never reject her. I need them to accept a child of any designation. If they already had a bonded beta, then perhaps that means they wouldn't be prejudiced against them.

It makes sense to me.

I mean, to be fair, omegas rarely give birth to betas. But they still do. And I would be damned if I bonded someone who would have a problem with that.

The problem is, at the Institute, I've only been presented with two options.

Two.

Thus the pacing.

Finally, my caseworker's manager comes into the office.

"Acadia," she says, and gives me her hand to shake. "I heard you have some feedback?"

She looks like she's planning on pissing me off. She's another beta, just like my caseworker. They look like the same person, just twenty years between them. They both look at me like they want to cajole me.

But I will not be cajoled!

"Feedback...right. Miss Angeline here has given me two packs. Two. I've been registered with the Institute for a month now. And just today all I've seen are two files. On two packs."

"I believe that's correct, yes. You want a pack with a bonded beta. We have two options here for your consideration."

I smile tightly. "There's no way, excuse me, on this green earth, there are only two packs available for me. That's outrageous."

"Have you looked through the files? Maybe before you reject them, we could go through them together and properly vet them."

She isn't listening to me at all. On purpose.

"Can you really stand there and admit there are only two packs that meet my criteria?"

She gives me some bullshit speech that lasts a really long time about how the process (does not) work. She says they take into account everyone's preferences and lifestyle. They match the alphas and omegas with the highest level of discernment.

Bullshit.

"No, absolutely not. You and I both know these two packs have preferential treatment. I want all my options."

She offers to go through them with me and sell me on them.

"No, I want all my options. I want all available options. Now. That's possible. And I want it. I cannot believe I have to keep asking."

She huffs before giving me her same speech all over again.

But this is bullshit and I will not stand for it.

What if I were like most omegas and was easily agreeable? I would be absolutely taken advantage of.

Both of these options are shit.

When her speech is ending, I say again, "This is not how this is going to work. You will give me all the options, and I will decide who I'd like to interview and possibly let court me."

"No, you don't know how this works."

"Ma'am, let me propose an option," Angeline says to try to calm the situation down. "You can attend the Quarterly All-Pack Soirée tonight. It's for unassigned packs and omegas to meet organically. What if you do that while we take a second look at our algorithm?"

"Why was I not already invited?"

Miss Angeline and her manager look so guilty. It's because I was being pigeonholed into these two options, that's why.

I'm going to rip this place to shreds, I've decided.

But until then, maybe I'll go to the soirée. I need a pack. My heat is coming up, and at this rate, I may have to book a room at a Heat Clinic.

I usually take heat suppressants. But they need several weeks to come into effect, and I stopped taking them when I thought I was bonding the Whitehorse pack.

They send me off with the information, and just for the drama of it, I push the two files I'd been given into the trash. The same files had been emailed to me, as well, so it's only a symbolic gesture, like flipping the bird.

Which I do as well.

3

Soirée

Locke

We are running late, and it's Oscar's fault as usual. He spent way too much time ironing our shirts. He made sure we wore matching suits, well, his idea of matching. Kol's assigned color is emerald. I'm gold. And Oscar gave himself a deep burgundy red. So, he's got us all done up in our colors. Kol is in a green suit, and Oscar is in a solid red suit. I'm in black with gold paisley detailing.

It's all just so much.

Also, Kol needed to masturbate before we left. So we all had to wait for that to finish.

We didn't particularly mind. Oscar views it clinically, like a solution to a medical condition, whereas I was admittedly turned on, but we didn't have time for both of us to masturbate.

We finally arrive at the Institute, and there's a valet at the entrance of their building. The front is a high-rise office building right in the middle of downtown Cash City, but it hides a massive garden and pond beyond its doors.

Oscar carefully vets the valets until he finds the one he trusts the most with his Lincoln Navigator. I'm nearly jumping out of my skin to get a move on.

I get out of the car first and adjust my fitted black suit, running the palms of my hands over the sides of my long blonde hair. I have it slicked back tonight and I don't want the strands to fall down. Kol is out of the car next. He's taller than me and has short, brown hair. He's got this 'handsome devil' look. Strong jaw, clear eyes, and just enough scrub on his face to make the ladies pant after him. He's broad shouldered and fit. He comes up to me and fixes a stray hair, and then pats me on the cheek.

I playfully slap him away. He laughs as he dodges my attempt.

Oscar tells the valet how exactly he wants his car handled, then gives him the keys along with some cash. Oscar is our pack lead. He's from Colombia and has a Spanish accent. His aura is strong, and I enjoy being around him when he lets it out. To me, Oscar looks like a stone-cold killer. He's handsome with a full head of thick, dark hair and tan skin. He has some gray on the sides, just enough to give him that "papi" look. His mustache is thick and gorgeous, and he keeps it well trimmed. When you can get him to smile, his mustache curls up and it's reward enough seeing that. He adjusts his gold cufflinks and joins us at the curb.

Three alphas. Three desperate men. Oscar gives us an encouraging smile, and we finally enter.

We make our way to the back of the building and out the grand doors to the gardens. Within them is a grove where there is a small building with columns and massive windows, which is where the event is taking place. We walk through the grove, where they've set up games like corn hole and badminton, so the alphas and omegas can get to know each other. We walk into the open-air building, and thank god there's an open bar and catering. Thank god because I'm starving.

I was too nervous to eat lunch, and then I was too nervous to do anything about it later.

"Fucking hell," I mutter when I see who is all here. "It's a total alpha-fest."

I get us drinks from the bar, and Kol gets me a plate of some food. Mostly sweets, because he knows me so well. We take up a spot in the center. Kol picked the spot out last time, saying it would get us the most attention.

And we stand there. Like jackasses.

The party moves around us.

It's not a party full of people who know each other or have anything in common at all. The only thing we have in common is that we want a pack. We want an omega. Which oddly does not give anyone enough to talk about. So it's quiet except for a string quartet playing somewhere.

We stand and we wait and we drink our drinks. I get us a second round—we stand and we wait and we drink our drinks.

"This is our third soirée," Kol eventually points out. "There was the Sweetheart Soirée. The Speed-Dating Soirée. And now whatever this is. Quarterly All-pack? What does that mean? We've been accepted into the Institute for months now and haven't even met with an omega for placement."

"Well, we did meet that young Chinese girl…" I try to point out, but Kol cuts me off.

"She was 19! I figured an omega would be young, but come on. Can she at least be in her twenties? If we wanted an omega just barely of age, we should have just stayed in Salt Port."

Oscar agrees with him. Oscar is 34 years old. I can see him not wanting a young omega. Kol is 29. I personally don't mind a young omega, but I'm also the youngest at 24.

Our only preference for the Institute has been that they don't require a long courting period. We haven't been matched to a single omega. This entire process feels like a scam.

We've been desperately seeking an omega for months. We moved to Cash City recently because our chances of meeting an omega would be higher. Its demographics and stats for O/B/A population and omega safety are the best in the country. They have the most Heat Clinics per capita. The omega citizens here are the most educated and highest earning. It was founded by an omega for fucksake! Orrin Cash was an omega, and he designed all the public services around omegas.

Oscar puts his hand on my shoulder, reminding me to relax.

Maybe I should have masturbated too. Just to calm down a little.

I scan the room for the millionth time.

I can be impatient.

But I'm sure we will find someone.

Or maybe it'll never happen, and we will never be with an omega, and I'll lose my brothers and never be happy and die.

I close my eyes and breathe deeply.

We are near the bar and catering tables inside the gallery, where there are descenters in the air. You can walk out to the outdoor gardens if you want to open yourself up to scenting.

None of the omegas do that. They all stay here. I think they are all worried a wayward alpha will get too close and try to scent them. I don't blame them. We are all gigantic, desperate fuckers. Oscar reaches down and gives my hand a quick squeeze. He knows how desperate we are.

The first soirée, we tried to hide our desperation. Kol thought it would scare any omega away. But by now, none of us care. We *are* desperate. We are running out of time to be chill about it.

Kol has pointed out all the omegas that are here. There's the male omega we saw last time. Oscar is straight. I'm open. And Kol is just too in love with women to deprive him. So we introduced ourselves, but we didn't get our hopes up. This time he looks at us and I give him a nod and a tip of my glass. But that's it.

He's surrounded by smiling alphas, so it's not like he's in want of our attention, too.

I squeeze Oscar's biceps and tell him I need some air. Kol takes my place at his right side, and I take off to the garden.

It's pretty much empty out here. There's a corn hole setup for anyone who likes to make an omega play corn hole in a cocktail dress.

There are bushes carved into weird shapes. Pathways and trees with raised flower beds. There's a pond somewhere. I don't know, I just need to breathe. The event ends in an hour, and I am so afraid it's another bust.

I find a stone on the ground, pick it up and toss it once in the air, then catch it in my palm, holding the smooth rock tight in my grip. I go searching for the pond I found last time. I bet I can get this rock to skip across it.

I'm not paying attention, so I nearly walk right up to a woman looking out over the water. I stop and back up before she notices me.

She's lost in thought. The moonlight bathes her in silver. She sighs deeply. Like she has so many worries. A warm summer breeze moves over the water. Oh my god.

Oh my god.

I gasp, and my hand goes to my heart.

Her scent.

Like lilac blossoms warmed in the summer sun. It rips through me while simultaneously healing every last part of me. My mouth opens and her scent is everywhere. I'm drowning in it. *A scent match.*

4

Lilac

Locke

The alpha in me demands I *take*. It wants her. It's the most uncivilized I've ever felt in my life.

She's wearing the fuck out of a little purple cocktail dress. I want to rip it off of her and claim her in the mud of the pond.

Her hair is black like a raven's feathers. She's not as short as most omegas. Thank fuck. I hate when they are too tiny.

What am I saying?! I'm already acting like she's mine.

I do *not* behave this way.

Just go up and introduce yourself. Just walk a few steps and say something.

I lift my foot to try to obey, but instead I take off in the opposite direction.

Stupid. Stupid. Stupid.

No, not stupid! I need my pack. I can't do this without them. There's an omega out here who is my scent match! She's probably all our scent matches! She has to meet us at once. I don't want her to favor me over them. If I meet her first, she may! What if it's only me that's her scent match? What if Oscar doesn't like her? I can't leave Oscar.

He's so particular. He doesn't accept just anyone into his life. But I love him. He's mine.

They have to accept each other.

And Kol. What if she doesn't like him? He's lived a long life. He has a lot of skeletons most younger men might not have. What if she can't accept him? The alpha in me roars in anger that I've left her.

I bust into the gallery, sweating through my suit entirely. My hands are red from holding them in tight fists with the stone still clutched inside.

I run up to my pack, my eyes wild, but my voice is completely gone.

"Locke! Are you ok? What's going on?" Kol is worried, but I can't seem to form words to explain myself. His hands are on my shoulders, and he's trying to get me to look him in the eyes.

I can't. If I do, then I'll see how fucked everything is.

A scent match! I have a scent match! This can only be bad. Why would it be good?

Kol grabs me and leads us to the garden. Once out of the gallery, he pulls me to him and slaps my face.

"Owe, fuck that hurt!" I wince and hold my smarted cheek. The stone pressing into my face.

"You were freaking out. What happened?"

I take a few calming breaths before I answer. "I found a girl by the pond."

"You know we are here to meet a girl, yes?" Oscar points out. I narrow my eyes at him. English isn't his first language, and sometimes he likes to wield that against me.

"An omega. And I think she's my scent match. My scent match. Tell me I'm going insane, Oscar!" I'm freaking out again and he goes to slap me, but I throw up my hands to stop him.

"Kol, stop hitting Locke. Where is this pond? Let's go find her? Are you sure she's your scent match?"

I turn to the garden, but it suddenly looks dark and looming. I shudder.

Kol sees my hesitation, my fear, and he takes some pity on me. He takes my hand and pulls me away from the gallery.

"Where's the pond, Locke? We'll handle everything else. Just take us to the omega."

He gives me a reassuring look. Oscar takes me by the arm on the other side, and they both pull me forward. I don't resist, but I don't exactly lead the way. We eventually find the pond, but the girl is gone. I'm both relieved and disappointed.

Less afraid now, I walk up to the spot on the shoreline where she stood. Her warm lilac scent is still here.

Oscar and Kol go searching around for signs of her.

"What did she look like?" Kol asks.

"Like a dream."

"Locke, please answer the question," Oscar barks at me. It's not an alpha bark. He would never do that to me. I'm sensitive to them. But I can tell he needs me to give him the answer, clearly.

"She was about 5'9". Violet-colored silk dress, with an open back and ruffles on the bottom. Short black hair. Pale white skin. She seemed worried. She was lost in thought."

"Chinese?" Oscar asks. There's a large population of Chinese people in the city, so it's not a strange question. They just want to get an idea of who they are looking for.

"I think she was white. American. I didn't see her face too well. She was turned away from me. And it's dark out here, as you can see."

I rip off my suit jacket since that warm breeze is back and I'm still sweating like a madman.

"Why didn't you..." Oscar starts to say, but cuts himself off when he sees me bend over my knees and drop my head, trying to breathe through my mini panic attack. "Ok, Locke, you need to calm down."

"What do you think I'm trying to do?"

"I could always slap him again," Kol says while gesturing at me. I'd give him the finger, but I need my hands to keep steady. He chuckles at me.

Oscar walks all over and around the pond. He looks contemplative and focused, but doesn't say anything.

A scent match.

How is this even possible?

We make it back to the party and my pack mates fan out looking for her. I don't look for her. I'm petrified we may actually find her.

I go to the bar and stare at the options. Wine? That'll give me a headache. White wine? That's too sweet and it will make my tummy hurt. Whiskey? That's Kol's drink. I can't take Kol's drink. Tequila? What am I, underage?

"Can I have a vodka cranberry, please?"

I throw a fiver in the tip jar and walk away with my drink. Oscar and Kol come back to me.

"I've left a voicemail with our case worker, Angeline. I told her to call me back."

I shake my head, about to keel over.

"You didn't..."

Oscar cuts me off. "No, I didn't say anything about a scent match. Until we know for sure, I'm not saying anything. We'd get kicked out of the Institute for falsely claiming a scent match with one of their omegas."

I nod my head, happy we are on the same page.

We stay until we are ushered out and I'm drunk off vodka crans. Kol has to practically carry me to Oscar's Lincoln. He tosses me in the back and I lie on the seats, aghast at the events of the evening.

5

Limerence

Acadia

There's not a single beta at the soirée. I know I'm at a place called the Alpha-Omega Placement Institute, but come on. Betas make up 80% of the population. And designations aren't predictable.

How weird would it be if I just went up to people and asked, "If you had a baby, and the baby was a beta, would you love and care for that baby your whole life?" I mean, I *will* ask any potential pack this question eventually, but I just don't see a lot of alphas being genuine about their answer. It's obvious what the right answer is.

At least to me.

And what someone is willing to say out loud and what they'd actually do are two different things.

Bianca and Cornell may never have set out to reject their daughter. I'm sure they were happy to just have a baby. She was probably very cute.

The thing is, I was a 12 year-old girl once. We stop being cute little kids at that age. If your parents don't already love you unconditionally, things get real.

And I'll be damned if my future 12 year-old daughter is anything less than loved and adored and taken care of.

I decided to leave the event. I ordered a car back to my apartment, a co-op for omegas and their handlers. Most units are shared with several assigned omegas. I'm an "older" omega, so it's just me and my handler, Maria, in our unit. She's an omega in her 70s. Her pack is all gone. She's been an omega handler for eight years now. I'm her third omega.

She's very protective of me.

I come in and put my keys in the bowl.

"Acadia, you're back!" She declares. She has a margarita in her hand, and she's wearing her aquamarine moo moo. She's drunk.

Typical.

Don't let the flaming red hair and giant toothy smile fool you. Maria is very strict with me. I'm surprised she isn't giving me a dressing down for going to the party without security.

She believes that omegas should wait until bonding before inviting alphas to a heat. She also believes nose rings are for degenerates, and omegas should never get tattoos. She knows about my nose ring (kinda hard to hide it), but I have successfully hidden the little omega symbol on my upper thigh from her.

But, you know, she's kind of funny and she genuinely cares about me.

"Heya Maria, how's your evening?" I ask casually.

She launches into the story of her evening. The show she's watching, the drama with another omega handler here, the diet she's trying, and the state of the poo in her cat's litter box.

I nod along with her details while removing my shoes and earrings. Eventually, she takes a breath so I say goodnight and rush to my room. She stands outside of it and chatters on for another ten minutes while changing into my soft clothes.

She needs to just walk away.

I'm alarmingly horny and I'd like to turn on some music and have some alone time with my fake cock. I really don't like going this long without getting laid. I've just been so upset that it didn't work out with the Whitehorse pack. I was all in.

Until I wasn't.

Maria is still chattering away, so I get on my phone to check the omega courting app. It's just as dry and depressing as usual. And no packs with betas.

Huh.

A thought comes to me.

Maybe I should download a dating app *for* betas. What if my problem this whole time is I should be *dating* a beta.

I've never dated anyone before. Omegas don't date. They get courted. But who cares about traditions?

Renewed with my new and clever idea, I leave my main bedroom for the secondary room attached. I fling myself into my nest, which is just a glorified walk-in closet with slat doors, and research the best beta dating apps. There's one with no texting, only video calls. Sounds kinky. It's called "At First Sight". That is the corniest thing I've ever heard. I find another one called "Beta On You", which also offers video calls but is largely for meeting betas. Jackpot.

There's an option to hide my designation, which I kind of love. It levels the playing field.

I say my name is Cadi, which is pronounced the same as Katie.

I upload some pictures. One of me having drinks at a nice bar wearing a low-cut top, another of me in a linen dress sitting under my window surrounded by my plants. I like to sew, so I have one of me behind my sewing machine. I don't know what to put for "Looking for..." so I just say "having fun!" I try not to overthink it.

My card stack gets bigger and bigger with beta men who want to match with me. I go through about twenty profiles before I switch over to the side where I can "like" them first. The very first one is a man named Mads. He's cute. So cute that I giggle and change position in my nest like it will help me see him better. He has these prominent curly lips, deep inset eyes, a proud nose, and black hair. His body is out of control. How is this man a beta? There's a photo of him in swim trunks that I screenshot. Just looking at him is making me wet. I change positions again, but this time on my stomach.

Is this guy even real?

His profile is so funny and lively.

I read it fifteen times. He's 27, so only three years older than me. As opposed to 24 years older than me, like the Whitehorse pack. A lot more normal.

He has honey-brown eyes that have this beautiful amber color, like they are lit from within.

I decide to message him asking to connect.

It's all voice notes, no text.

I clear my throat, "Hello, Mads, I'm Cadi. I love your profile. You are so cute. I'm looking for..." don't say a beta. Don't say a lifelong commitment with babies and sex and merging bank accounts, "Someone to spend an evening with. Let me know if you are free."

Yeah, that works.

Oh my god.

I then prop up the phone with Mads's profile pic, and I take care of that aching need between my legs.

6
Rut

Kol

My whole life I've been hungry. I look at every new situation with one goal—make it bigger and better. Everything can be improved, you just have to locate the assets and build on them. It's how I ended up in the Soto Pack.

I saw Oscar Soto and knew he would do so much good in the world. I wanted to be with a man like that.

And Locke is the funniest man I know. Not on purpose. He's just a mess and I enjoy it. I've been able to focus on him enough to get him his own real estate license just like me and make a lot of connections. Not a lot of money. That's my job.

Locke keeps saying he wants to be a "house alpha" (a term he's made up), and I will rue the day if that ever happens.

We arrive back at our Cash City rental exhausted and frustrated. Locke is his usual mess, but this time for good reason, and Oscar is quieter than normal.

Not me. I'm fucking keyed up.

A scent match.

I wonder if she's mine, too.

We have to get an omega, and soon, so it didn't even cross my mind that we could have a scent match out there. I was willing to compromise on so much in order to find an omega, and now there's a possibility I won't have to compromise a damned thing. Scent matches are everything to an alpha.

She'll be exactly what I need.

Or what Locke needs.

All three of us have our reasons to be this desperate, but mine is the most shameful.

I've gone into ruts.

It's something feral alphas do. It's like an omega's heat. Where the alpha must fuck and fuck so much they pass out. And it can last a day or more. It started happening a couple of years ago, but now I'm down to falling into ruts nearly every month.

Oscar has done a lot of research, and I'm on hormones and supplements, but it doesn't completely solve the problem. An omega would fix me. As shitty as that is to ask of someone. Her heats and my ruts would go in sync, and eventually my ruts would taper off in intensity.

But until then, I'm pretty much constantly thinking about sex. I'm almost always bricked up. And I have to yank my dick morning, noon, and night.

It makes starting my real estate business in a new city so easy.

Oscar can't get a job either. And Locke wants to be a house alpha (again, I have to stress that this is not a real thing). So my pack is bleeding dry.

And if we court an omega, there goes the rest of our savings.

But a scent match!

My god.

Courting her would be a dream.

Fucking her would be like fucking a goddamned angel.

Locke knew moving here would be a good idea. It took convincing Oscar, through facts and data, but here we are.

Oscar is on the phone with the case worker, Angeline. It's on speaker. We are gathered in the living room of our apartment downtown. It's on the first floor and only has two bedrooms. Locke and I share a room. It's a nice place, but it's nowhere near what we are used to lately.

"Angeline, thank you for taking my call this late on a Friday night," Oscar says, letting his panty-dropping Spanish accent fly.

"Oh, it's no problem, Alpha Soto. How can I help?"

"We met an omega tonight at the soirée. However, we were unable to get her name. Can you be of assistance in connecting us?"

"Oh my goodness! That's so great to hear! I love when these things work out."

Locke is worried. I can feel it in our bond. He's got great instincts, so I don't question it. Something has got him feeling this way.

I get his attention and he shakes his head. He doesn't want to tell me.

"Can you give me any details about the omega?"

"Yes, she's tall, for an omega. She was in a violet dress. Short black hair."

"Oh! Like shoulder length or like a pixie cut?" She asks. We turn to Locke, and he answers, "A bob."

"Oh! I think that's Acadia. It must be. Did she have green eyes and a silver nose ring? Also, long acrylic nails?"

Again, we defer to Locke, who shrugs his shoulders.

This new description drives me absolutely wild. The alpha in me loves it. Green eyes? Nose ring? If she has even one tattoo, I'm screwed.

And long acrylic nails. I can see them now wrapped around my cock, her pert mouth...Oscar smacks the back of my head.

I guess he could feel that.

"I believe that's her. Can we be connected with her? We'd like to court her, formally."

There's a long pause.

How did Locke know? Dread floods the bond from all three of us.

"So here's the thing, Acadia has a preference. And I'd love to circumvent that preference, but it's a dealbreaker."

She's choosing her words carefully. What kind of preference? We are the most basic alpha pack there is. We've watered ourselves down and wiped our histories so we fit most omega's preferences. How did this happen?

"Would it be an imposition to tell us this preference?"

"Well, it's kind of out of the ordinary. She wants a pack that has a bonded beta. Male or female. But they need to be bonded and registered."

I've never seen Oscar with his mouth hanging open in shock before, but this did it.

That...is...definitely out of the ordinary.

I mean, I've seen packs with bonded betas before, but to specifically ask *for* that is so odd. I could see an omega saying they *don't* want that before I'd ever see this.

"Why?" Locke speaks for Oscar. A rare occurrence.

"You know I cannot say. But it's a dealbreaker. Like I said. Now, because I like you guys, I will tell you this, but it didn't come from me. You don't have the ranking in our system for visibility to a lot of our omegas. But with her preference, you'd be able to get on her list. But you would actually need to have a beta."

We are holding our breath.

I fucking knew it! I mouth to my pack. I knew there was some fancy ranking system putting wealthy or connected packs above ours. I knew it was all a big fucking joke! Fuck this fucking place!

Oscar puts his hand on my shoulder to calm me down.

"Ok, we are on it, Angeline, thank you for the tip. The next call you get we should meet her preferences. I expect that's all we will need to do in order to get an interview, correct? We are highly motivated to start courting her."

"Call me as soon as you have a bonded and registered beta, and I'll get your file in front of her. Ok?"

We agree and end the call.

Oscar is the first to speak. "I'm going to get a drink and start researching this. I can't..." and then he takes off to his room.

I grab Locke by the back of his collar and drag him to our room. I sit in a plush armchair and tell him to go somewhere I can't see him.

He's rolling his eyes at me and grumbling, but I can tell he doesn't really mind. Our bond hides nothing.

"Ok, Locke, describe her to me again. Don't leave anything out." I unzip my pants and reach inside to stroke my hardening cock.

Locke grumbles and sits down on his bed. "Fuck you, Kol."

"Was she wearing heels?"

He takes a deep breath and I can feel him getting into that headspace. "Yeah, black ones. Like all the girls her age wear. She stood still with her arms loosely crossed in front of her."

"And how did she smell?" I get comfortable and lay my head back, closing my eyes. I pull my cock all the way out and speed up my tempo. I'm so sensitive tonight.

"Lilacs. In the summertime. Like being a field of them. It was like a gift or a magical experience. It hurt, actually, to fully take her all in. And then it was like a drug with that wave of oxytocin."

I groan, but try to keep it quiet. I know this is weird. I know it. But do I care? Not really.

He continues to tell me about her. How forlorn she looked. The moonlight in her hair. Her hips and waist, and her exposed back. I then start picturing what her face might look like. A nose ring and green eyes. In my mind, I give her tattoos. Blue jays, roses, and skulls. Tattoos fit for an omega in the Soto pack. We are bonafide now, but we weren't always.

She's going to be our queen.

And then I come, and it rips up my leg, causing my muscles to spasm. I cry out in pain and pleasure. Cum whips over my stomach and some parts of my shirt. Fuck, Oscar is going to be pissed he has to send this to the dry cleaner.

Locke kicks the back of my chair and leaves the room. Hopefully, to get a drink.

7

Post Traumatic Stress

Mads

Telling my mom that we aren't getting the settlement is nearly as bad as when I was run over by that car. She's better than me. When I give her the news she takes only a minute or two to be silent, and then she gets up and makes us some bread and butter sandwiches.

Then I tell her about my job.

She needs three minutes to accept that.

I bury my face in my hands in shame, but she tells me to stop it and eat my dinner.

"I'm going to the library before it closes so I can apply to some places. I wasn't looking because I thought it was a sure thing getting back on with my old place. I have a great resume. It shouldn't take long. And since I'll no longer need all the time off for physical therapy, I'm sure I'll get something."

"What's going on with physical therapy?" she asks in her thick Dutch accent.

"We can't afford it, mom. And I can just do what they taught me at home."

She sighs and lets it go. For now. She's tired. I'm tired.

I spend the rest of the day in the library applying to everything under the sun. I've been an executive assistant at my last two jobs, and I'm not looking to expand. I like getting an office together with the right systems and procedures. And I'm really good at rallying everyone and setting such a good tone. Or at least I used to be.

I have my MBA, and so my role isn't greeting people or getting coffee (I still often do those things). It's more like narrowing down internal system strategies or presenting a dozen options for financial spend.

At this point in my career, I should be taking on an actual leadership role, but it's never interested me.

The library closes at nine and I wait for the bus for over an hour before I resign myself to walking home. It's over a mile. A quarter of a mile and 30 minutes in, I find a bench and sit down.

I don't think I can keep doing this.

I'm in front of a bar and decide fuck it. I'm going to spend some money on a beer and pretend I'm a normal person.

I hobble up to the door and the bouncer doesn't look at me twice. All the seats at the bar are full, so I find a booth and slide in.

I wave the bartender over by holding up my cane. She's an older woman, and she comes over quickly.

"Hey, usually at this hour on a Friday night I'd ask you to come up to the bar to order, but I see you are limping like a dog."

I cringe at that statement. I know I can't hide my limp, but I'd really prefer it if people didn't tell me to my face what injured animal I resemble while walking around.

On more than one occasion, I've had people pull over their car, as I was walking along the sidewalk minding my own business, to tell me they could take me to the hospital since I clearly was in distress. Convincing them this is just how I walk leaves me so angry and overwhelmed, and then they don't know what to do with all their "good will". No one wins.

She doesn't notice me cringe or the headache she's suddenly given me, she just goes on, "Good on you snagging this booth while it's open. What can I get you?"

"Any specials? $5 beer?" Sometimes they have Heinekens for $5 at the bar I used to go to with friends, I think. It feels like ages ago.

"Yeah, I'll get you something. $5 you said?"

There's no $5 beer. I hold my tongue, too poor to have any pride, and I nod. She leaves and comes back with a stein of a Pilsner. She confirms it's $5 and I hand her $8. She rushes off to help the actual customers filling the place.

People are looking at my booth with covetous eyes. This was a dumb idea. I shouldn't have come.

I'm not even halfway through my stein when the door opens and five full-grown, jacked alphas come into the bar.

I know they don't look like the Dougherty brothers, but my body doesn't seem to care. My breaths are gone. Too fast and I'm not getting any air. Is my throat closing up? My hands don't have any blood in them. I forget where I left the handle of my beer, so when I dart out my hand to grab it, I just knock the whole fucking thing over.

My vision is blackening around the edges.

The alphas come up to my table.

I think one of them is asking if I need help or maybe they want my table or something, but all my brain hears is "Oh look, the little bitch beta thinks he can fuck around with an omega and keep his balls."

My arms fling to the sides, and I try to get out of the booth. I stumble and fall to my knees on the open floor. I can't find my cane.

Someone pulls me up from under my arms, and when I'm on my feet, my head tips back, and my eyes meet an alpha. He's a foot taller than me.

"Hey, man, are you here with someone? I can go get them?"

I know fear is leaking out of me. I can't help it. I manage to shake my head no and then tear my eyes away from his. I have to get out of here. My hands start groping the empty air for my cane. One of the other alphas figures out what I'm looking for and gets it for me. But all it means is I'm completely surrounded.

As soon as my cane is in my hand, I lurch out of there. I must look like a psycho hobbling back and forth, barely making any headway, trying to run out of a bar. The bouncer thankfully opens the door for me and I'm out.

The warm summer air welcomes me, and I get my first breath in.

I keep going down the block and all the way home. My leg is completely inflamed to the point I have to go to bed with my jeans because I can't get them off. At least the day is finally over.

At one in the morning, my phone pings and I ignore it.

8

The Beta Profile

Kol

O scar spends the entire weekend evaluating plans for getting a beta. He has several profiles of betas he imagines would be good fits for us. One of the features is "cute" because he wants to make sure Acadia likes him. He actually has no idea why Acadia wants a beta in her pack. None of us do.

So he might as well be cute.

Oscar is also considering a female beta. He says she may help with my rutting problem.

The whole point of the beta is for Acadia. Not me. I tell him this, but he waves me away.

Again, we are going on very little information on what kind of beta this little omega is looking for.

While he did that, I went over applications for a personal assistant. I assumed Locke was going to take on this role when we moved here, but it's just not the thing for him. He's more of a start a project and abandon it kind of guy.

I'm building a real estate portfolio from nothing out here and it's to the point I need to hire someone.

Amongst the applications that have come through in the last week, there is this hotshot MBA guy. He's been the EA to two CEOs in the last three years. Why he's applying to be a PA to a real estate investment company, I don't even know. I absentmindedly click on his LinkedIn profile. When his picture comes up I think, "ha, he's cute." And close out. I don't need some business bro PA. I need someone who can drive all over town. Make financial projections. Comp reports. Manage my schedule. Send paperwork. Print documents. It's the work of someone who's careful and smart. Not someone trying to buddy up with CEOs.

I reach out to three applicants and ask them to use my link to schedule a call.

By the end of the day, Oscar has upgraded his research and planning to a giant corkboard on the wall by the kitchen table. Locke is staring at it like it's a Jackson Pollock painting. I just shake my head at it. It'll make sense in an hour, I'm sure. Oscar's mind is like a machine.

Not one applicant gets back to me or schedules my calendar. I get back on my laptop and send out three more emails.

I'm looking at two properties in the late evening and I drag Locke with me. He has great initial feedback on spaces. It's all from his gut and he can't explain his reasoning, but he's usually right in the end.

The first property he loves. It's a row of rentals. All filled with tenants. The doors lead out to a tight alley downtown. They got together and built a garden between two of the units.

Locke says it won't be a moneymaker, and they would be better off turning it into a co-op. I give them my card and say if they want consulting, I can do that for them. It's better than a new landlord.

The second property is a restaurant. Locke smells the grease before we even make it inside. We figure out later that the exhaust system would need a total gut job. More money than it's worth.

I get home late and still have no responses on my personal assistant job. I'm sure by tomorrow, one of the six will respond back. But as a little Hail Mary, I send an email to the hotshot.

What's the worst that could happen?

He's the only one who responds and he schedules me for my next available slot. Mads De Vaan. Oscar dresses me in green slacks and a plaid dress shirt. No tie. His corkboard looks orderly. There's one side for beta traits and how they would work best with the four of us, Acadia included. The other side is options for meeting a beta. My favorite is "pool tournament at local bar". Like, where did he think of that?

Before I leave, Oscar stops me. "Kol, it's been a couple of weeks since you've been with anyone. Are you doing ok?"

Oh, I was hoping to avoid this conversation. But Oscar, being the closest thing to my current physician, and being my pack lead, I have to be honest.

"No, not really."

"Maybe you should stay out late and find some relief."

I sigh deeply. "I can't."

"Why?" He has to know.

"I would. I need to. I am jacking off like four times a day now. I know. But ever since Locke said she's a scent match..."

I can't say it. My inner alpha thinks she may be my scent match too, or maybe even just *my* omega. The idea of going out to a club or a bar and picking up some woman to fuck feels so wrong. Like I'd be cheating on her.

"But if you go too long..."

"I know, Oscar. I know. But I can't anymore."

"I want you to just consider it. I don't want to meet her and then your pheromones scare her. You can get really intense."

I look down in deference. I understand what he's saying. I do.

All three of us have our issues and reasons we needed to leave Salt Port, our home, and I'm no exception.

I blow out all the air from my lungs. And I nod. I'll go out. After my interview.

"I'm going to take the interview here in the kitchen. I don't want to go to that café nearby. Is that ok? I suddenly don't want to leave."

Oscar understands. He gathers his work and takes it to his room.

The hotshot is right on time to the video call.

He looks so different from his LinkedIn photo. His cheeks are hollow. He has dark circles under his eyes. His smile doesn't reach his eyes, and he no longer has black hair. It's a mousy light color.

"Hello, Kol," he says with a strained voice. Is this guy ok?

"Hey, Mads. Thanks for the opportunity to talk today."

We get started, and he's got great responses to my questions. His history and track record are so impressive. The projects they've been having him do are really inspiring. I could see myself needing to give him the same complicated projects, and knowing he'd be able to take it and run with it makes me feel great.

"Have you ever managed real estate portfolios before?"

His answer makes me feel like an idiot for not paying close enough attention to his CV. He's handled larger portfolios than I ever have.

"Alright, let's talk compensation. What're you looking to get?"

I'm getting a buzzing feeling in my stomach. I can see so much potential working with him. I wouldn't keep him as my assistant for long. I'd set him up to be a partner. The only reason I'm not suggesting it now is because he is being very clear about being an assistant.

"I need $5,000 a month. Can you make that happen?" Is he joking? I think he's joking. He sees the look of confusion on my face, so he goes on. "It's just what I'm looking for. Is that something we can work towards?"

"That's $60,000 a year, Mads. Is that how much they've been paying you to do this at those large companies?"

I know he's a bit offended because his curly mouth goes noticeably straight. "By the time I left, that's where I was at."

I think they were paying him in peanuts.

"Mads, I would pay you that just to manage my calendar, and Google does most of the work. This job starts at $90,000. But with your experience..." I shake my head, "I'll send you over an offer. You can look through it. There's no health insurance right now. I'm just getting started here in Cash City. So I'll make sure there's language about how I have additional pay to cover you getting personal insurance."

"Um..." His professional image cracks, then he puts himself together. "Cash is king. That's fine."

"Let's meet in person to go over some details." I don't miss him visibly wincing. "How does tomorrow for lunch sound? You pick the place. Send me a calendar link with the address."

When I end the call, Oscar slides into the chair across from me.

"Why do you look like that? He seems like a good hire."

"I just got a weird feeling he's not ok. Like personally. He looked like he's aged so much from his profile picture. And at times, he kind of had a kicked puppy look. I don't know. There's a lot of potential there. And he's very familiar with Cash City. I'm sure we will be able to get out of this rental by the end of the year. Get Acadia a nice place. I wonder what kind of house she wants. Something on the river? Maybe in the foothills or mountains?"

"Let's just focus on today. Are you going out?"

I look out the window.

"Yeah, I'll go out tonight." I will go out and try to pick up a woman. All the while, my omega is out there, just out of reach.

So fun!

9

Mating Ceremony

Mads

I lay my head on the counter and feel the cool laminate on my hot face. The interview went well. Kol seems like a good guy. A bit aggressive, but at least it wasn't directed at me. He's clearly an alpha, his shoulders were massive. How am I going to have lunch with him tomorrow? Or work with him?

I'm going to shit myself.

I send off the calendar invite to a pub and grill to meet Alpha fucking Soto tomorrow for lunch. How on earth am I going to pull this off?

I better pull it off.

$90k a year? Everything he was saying I'd need to do is an absolute cakewalk. I could take his funds and build his portfolio in my sleep. I could give him three options and a secret fourth option.

I leave the stool I'd been sitting on and go crash on the couch. I've never been paid more than $45,000 a year. This is life changing.

And then I pull up that fucking dating app, At First Sight, I forgot to delete. Well, I did delete it, but I didn't shut my profile down. The other day, I got an email that I had a message on the app. So, I re-downloaded it.

And there it was.

A voice note from a very pretty, most likely not real girl.

Almond eyes. Smattering of freckles across her nose. Black hair. Silver nose ring. A body to get lost in.

I would imagine it was fake but the voice note she sent was so...genuine. And charming.

But she was leaving that message for the guy in the profile from 13 months ago.

Not the shell of a man I am now. The broken husk. I'm three bad days away from the grave, not even in the same plane of existence as this girl.

I listen to her message again. Just to remind myself what life used to be like.

And then suddenly, my finger accidentally presses the video call button.

Fuck!

How do I hang up?! There's no option to hang up! It's all grayed out! The phone rings loudly. *Briiiiiing*! *Brrrriiiing*!

And then she picks up.

Good thing I'm in a decent shirt. And I'd done my hair for the interview. I sit up.

She looks beautiful. She's beautiful.

"Hello?" She says, and I am done for. Oh no, this is bad. This is so bad. She looks confused by me. Just like Kol did.

"Your hair," she says. "It's not black."

I chuckle with insecurity. "Yeah, sorry. I used to dye it. It's this dry blonde color usually."

"Oh," is all she says.

And then I keep talking because I'm so nervous. "My friend is a hair stylist, and she said I'd look good with black hair. But I let it grow out this year and haven't dyed it. She said black or white is my color. Not...this."

She nods and we go silent.

"Yeah, I'm sorry. I haven't been on the app for over a year. I thought I deleted it."

Her eyebrows bend in together. "Oh, I don't know how this works. I've never used a dating app. Did I do it wrong?"

"No! I did it wrong. And now you've seen a profile with year old photos. What's," I take a deep breath, "what's got you on an app?"

"I kind of wanted a date."

"A date? And have you gotten a few?"

She blushes and it makes me relax.

"No, I matched with you. I've been waiting for you to respond."

Oh my god, she's so cute.

I'm not going to tell her she can match with more than one person. That would not help me at all. Suddenly, I'm feeling emboldened.

"I could take you out on a date. Would you like that?"

I suddenly remember the last time I asked someone out was Nancy. My stomach churns at that.

She giggles and drops her head out of view of the camera and I get a look at her surroundings. I knew she was outside, but there are all these women behind her wearing very nice dresses and men in suits. When she pops up in view, I notice the baby's breath flowers in her hair and she's got quite a bit of makeup.

"Where are you?"

"Oh," her voice trails off, and she has a guilty smile on her face. "I'm at a mating ceremony."

"A mating ceremony! And you took my call!"

"Well, I wanted to talk to you. But hush, the omega is about to walk down the aisle."

Oh my god. And I hear it. The music swells and Cadi turns the camera to show a small, little omega in a sweeping white dress holding bouquets of flowers, walking down an aisle towards an altar with four male alphas.

Good fucking god.

She turns the camera back to her, and she gives me a funny smile, and I can't help but laugh.

She puts her finger to her lips to tell me to be quiet. And then I watch most of the ceremony as she makes silly faces, and I try not to laugh.

She clearly thinks mating ceremonies are weird. She rolls her eyes at all the corny bits—in a subtle way, of course.

Packs don't often have a big ceremony. If they do it's often just a reflection of weddings.

She does get a bit misty-eyed during their vows, but who wouldn't?

I haven't smiled this much since before the incident. My cheeks ache. When it ends, she tells me her phone number, I write it down and we end the call.

I text her and tell her I'd like to take her out.

I'm halfway in love with this girl already.

I take my pain meds and I'm out of it for the rest of the day.

10

The Interview

Kol

My two ridiculous pack mates trail behind me on my way to the interview with Mads. Locke asked if he was a beta, and when I said I thought he probably was, he declared we should bond him. A guy we've never met. Who I'm trying to hire.

Oscar, the level-headed leader, agreed. He didn't agree to *bond* him, but he wanted to get a good look at him and consider it. He said that betas meet at work all the time. I think he needs to stay off dating articles for now.

Oscar keeps asking me questions I have no answers to. Like what his type is. How tall he is. If he's single.

I remind him that these are highly inappropriate questions, and he just looks at me like I'm the ridiculous one.

Locke asks me what his hobbies are, and I think I'll actually ask the beta this.

We show up to the pub a full twenty minutes early, and yet my eyes lock with Mads the moment we enter. They go wide in fear that he tries to hide it. He's already seated, and we come over to join him. He doesn't stand when we approach the table, and his eyes keep falling away from me. On the call, he was a lot more confident. I think bringing my two gigantic alpha pack mates was a bad call.

We are scaring the guy.

And more than usual.

"Mads! It's nice to meet you in person. You're early!" I say with a light tone.

He gives me a tight smile and looks back down at the table. I look at Oscar and Locke, who are both emoting worry.

"It's nice to meet you, Alpha Soto," he replies with a shake to his voice.

"Hey, I'm sorry to bring my pack along. I'm realizing now it's a bit intimidating." Oscar and Locke pull their chairs back and sit a good distance away so it doesn't look so aggressive.

"This is Oscar Soto. He's my pack lead," I say with a smile. Mads ignores us both. His shoulders are practically to his ears. "And this is Locke. He's my pack mate. He used to be my PA, but he's terrible at it."

Mads doesn't even give me a pity laugh.

"Here, I brought this to show you." Mads slides a Manila envelope across the table. "You mentioned on the call you were going to look at that commercial property on Mansion Park. I pulled some comps and history. I made a projection on if you were to rent it, based on historical data, or if you wanted to restore it and sell it. There's a tax relief for selling to certain organizations, so I included what that would look like." I'm absolutely floored looking through the packet Mads made for me. It's so well organized and clear. Oscar gets a giddy feeling, so I slide it to him. He loves a good data report. Especially well summarized.

"Personally, I think it's a good investment if you have a solid plan and don't hang on to it for too long."

"Yeah, I would be inclined to agree. This is incredible, Mads."

He still can't look at me. The server brings him a Coke, and we tell her our drink order.

"I'm very excited to work with you, but you seem kind of over qualified to be honest. Are you thinking of getting your broker license? You'd kill it."

He just shakes his head but doesn't answer. I noticed his hands flex and grip, like he's trying to calm down.

He closes his eyes and takes a deep breath. "I'm sorry, I thought I could do this, but I don't think I can."

Oscar sits up straight. He's so confused and worried about this behavior. As am I.

"What do you mean? I'm sorry if it was inappropriate to bring my pack."

"Yeah, I...Here's the thing. I was assaulted a little over a year ago by a pack of alphas, and I have trouble being around them. I'm going to actually ask you all to step away, so I can exit this bench and leave."

None of us react, we are in too much shock. Finally, Locke stands and grabs Oscar and they leave right away. I don't, though.

I stay.

His words do something to me.

"Mads, thank you for trusting me with that information. I'm so sorry that happened to you."

"I'm also disabled. From the attack. I have trouble walking or standing for long periods. I use a cane." He's saying these things like they are reasons to turn the job down.

My heart hurts for him, and my pack mates return the same feeling from wherever they've gone off to. They are 100% still listening in because both of them have boundary issues.

We haven't always been pacifists. All three of us have had issues with aggression. I can remember at least twice I took my fists to a beta male.

So, I can't sit here and pretend what happened to him was just a couple of bad apples.

Alphas are this way.

We do this.

No wonder Mads looked so different from his profile picture. I even thought he looked like he'd aged significantly.

I cast my hand out over the table and lay it palm side up.

"Listen, we don't have to meet in person to do this work. Do you have a laptop? You can work from home and we will do this all remote. If you can visit some properties we can go at different times. We'd probably be too busy anyway to always be working together."

"I don't have a laptop."

I notice the tremor in his body. He's turned completely away from me.

"Ok. Send me your address and I'll send you the equipment you need."

I feel this deep-seated need to make this work. Like I can't let him go.

That's he's mine.

I can't let it show. I have to be a "beta" about this. But I do feel like he's mine. My possessive side is growing and I want the names of the alphas who did this to him. I want to make them suffer for what they did to him.

I bury those feelings deep.

"Are you serious?" he asks, and meets my eyes for a moment.

I pull my hand back.

"The job is yours. My offer is already in your inbox. Once you accept it, I'll send you the equipment and it's a done deal. What kind of person would I be if I told you that you needed to hang out with my pack in order to have a job? Your trauma and disability aren't factors here...or rather, I'm just trying to say I'll accommodate them. No problem."

"Why?"

Because you're mine. But I don't say that because there are plenty more reasons.

"You're the best candidate. You are dedicated. Your work is exceptional. I'd be lucky to have you."

We sit there for a moment. All our drinks sit untouched.

"I'll look over the offer."

I tip my chin. I don't want to leave. I want to stay here with him. I don't want to let him go either. The alpha in me is pacing its cage. It's got its eyes on something it wants.

But I am in control.

"If you have questions about it, give me a call. I expect a response by tomorrow. I'll go settle the bill. Stay and have lunch, on me. It was nice to meet you, Mads. Take care—"

Before he can respond, I stand and go see the server to leave her my card on the tab. I tell her to make sure he eats something.

He's not going to do that but I thought I'd try. I can already see him getting out of the bench. His cane is one of those aluminum ones you'd see at a hospital. It's ugly as sin. He sees me looking at him with disgust and I hide my expression. Fuck. I just didn't like his cane. He should have a better one.

Before I mess anything else up I leave. Oscar and Locke are waiting for me on the sidewalk outside.

We take off down the street but after a block I turn around. I want to see him leave the pub.

"That was wild," Locke remarks, his floral shirt is unbuttoned, and it whips around in the wind. Clouds edge across the sky, casting us all in gray shadow.

"Yeah," I agree.

"I don't think we will be able to bond with him. I was initially thinking we'd pitch it like an extension of his job. But...with his trauma. There's no way," Oscar thinks out loud.

Finally Mads leaves the pub. He walks like he needs immediate medical intervention. His limp is severe and his whole body is rigid. I have to hold myself back from chasing him down the street. the wind whirls his untidy, light brown hair wildly.

"Those alphas did that to him? He said it's been a year?" Locke sounds just as possessive and angry as I feel about the situation. Our feelings definitely match.

"Yeah, but it's not our problem. Let's not make it worse for the guy. We will find a different beta."

"We need to find someone now. Today. We are running out of time. Oscar is running out of time. I have no time left at all. You ran out of time long ago," Locke unhelpfully points out.

I grit my teeth.

I'm perfectly aware that we don't have time. It's like a chant I say to myself all day, every day.

"Locke and I will go back to the board. You need to go find yourself some relief, Kol. I don't want you back until you do."

"I'll go out tonight."

If we were back at Salt Port I'd have more options. Old friends. Old hookups. Places I could always get lucky at. Cash City is still so new to me.

The same with finding a beta.

We may have had a chance of finding a willing beta in the Salt Port.

But that's not an option.

We are still staring at Mads as the sky darkens even more with the impending storm. He stops and leans up against a building, out of breath. The three of us start walking toward him, about a block away, and when he starts back up we continue to follow him at a distance. We don't say why we are doing it. We just do.

If he were an alpha and we were showing this behavior, we'd all come to the same conclusion—he's pack. But we don't say anything. And we don't bring it up. Because he's a beta who cannot even be in the same room as an alpha.

He's not ours.

We get back to our place eventually, soaked from the rain, and Oscar points to the kitchen table where we all take up a seat. Locke removes his floral shirt, and rings it out over the plant on the center of the table.

"What do we think?" Oscar asks.

"I want him," Locke immediately replies.

I groan and throw my head back. We just said we would let him go! Where was that energy?

"We can't have him. He nearly had a full blown meltdown just being near us. Please, we have to leave him alone."

"I don't know, Kol. He matches a lot of what we are looking for." Now Oscar is betraying me.

He looks over his corkboard.

"He's unattached. Our age. Acadia simply wants a beta and he's a beta. He's going to be a great assistant to you. Having a pack member be in your company is a benefit. Locke is attracted to him..."

"Hey!" Locke shouts.

"Don't deny it, Lockey, we all felt it."

He pouts. He is the newest bonded member and sometimes forgets that there are no secrets here.

"And this report he made for you? It's fantastic. I can't stop looking it over."

I take my packet away from my pack lead.

"No. I'm saying no."

"Saying no, and yet you are already courting him. You tried to buy him lunch. You are getting him a laptop. This whole job offer is a courting gift."

I'm aghast. I have to grab at my chest because I'm so offended.

I didn't realize it, but he's right.

The bastard is right.

I'm courting the beta.

"I don't know if we have a choice anymore, though, Kol. Let's be real. At the end of the day, we are alphas with natures we can't deny. We can all feel it. He's ours. Any other choice from now on would upset our base selves," Locke so casually points out. Like he isn't saying the most significant thing.

I know what they are saying, but I also want to protect Mads from this fate just as much as I want to ensure it happens.

I leave the table to go get ready to fuck something tonight. Like I'm a goddamned animal.

At least the rain has stopped.

Later, just before I head out, Oscar calls my name. Locke looks at me with a miserable little face.

"It's ok," I say to Locke and go to Oscar at the kitchen table. In front of him lays a leather muzzle.

I try to avoid staring at it, but it's like a black hole that the entire house is slowly sliding into. I know it has to be done. If I bite someone while I'm in rut, it would ruin us even more than we are ruined now. My alpha has a tendency to take over and since it's been a while...there's a good chance of it happening.

Oscar sighs and stands up, taking the muzzle with him. I turn my back to him. We are the same height, so when he comes up behind me he can easily pull the muzzle around my face. He secures it to the back. I put my hands up and make sure it's sitting right. It doesn't go under my chin. It kind of sits below my lips and at the top of my nose. It cinches in on my cheeks and jaw. It's comfortable. Oscar pats it as well, ensuring it's secure.

I turn back to face him and we just look each other in the eyes. He's a good pack lead. He does what needs to be done. Our safety is important to him. He knows this is humiliating. He knows. But we both know it's necessary.

11

Urban Lounge

Acadia

While I had one of the best phone calls in my life with Mads, and he texted me later, he still hasn't actually asked me out. Am I missing something? Do I need to...plan a date and then tell him to take me on it? Do I give him my schedule? What does, "I want to take you out sometime" mean to betas?

I've worked myself up into a frenzy.

I was hoping he'd ask me out for tonight. Since it's Thursday and they do $2 shots at this really fun dance club that I like to go to, Urban Lounge. And, there are always tons of betas! I love dancing. And I love a good deal.

But he hasn't written me back in days.

Fuck it. I'm going to take myself to the club. My omega friend, who I used to do things like this with, just bonded her alphas. So she's no longer available. But I can just go by myself.

No big deal.

Except for all the omega kidnappings lately. But I'll be fine.

I spend a couple of hours getting myself into my pretty little lavender dress, blowing out my hair, and doing a full glam makeup. My nails are long and sparkling black from the last time I was in the salon.

I order a car and escape before my handler sees me.

When the car pulls up to Urban, I already know it will be out of control. People are all over the streets. There are food vendors and sports cars parked out on display. I stride up to the bouncer, cutting the line, and when he sees I'm an omega, he gives me a soft smile.

"How's the crowd in there?"

"Hardly any of your kind, if that's what you're asking."

"Alphas?"

"Too many," he replies with a smile. He moves out of the way so I can enter. I do have some privileges in this world, and being a young, single woman who is also an omega, getting into clubs is one of them.

"There's a cover tonight for most folks," he tells me as I pass him.

"A cover? For what?"

"Delta Delta Delta is the DJ tonight."

My mouth drops open. Delta 3 is one of my favorite EDM groups. Oh, this is going to be good.

The club is out of control. It's standing room only even though there are two levels out here in the main area. There are three bars with half a dozen mixologists at each one. Blue and green lights flash so everyone is shadowed and grayscale. The music is amazing, but it sounds like Delta 3 is just playing club music right now—remixes and mashups. Maybe they will do their own stuff later. I'm dancing while waiting to get my shots. I'm going to take two right away.

And I do.

Followed up by a third.

God, I feel good. I'm whisked away with the energy of the crowd and I've completely forgotten myself.

I find myself hours later in the women's restroom asking a team of beta girls, who look like beautiful goddesses, what a man means when he texts, "I'd like to take you out sometime," and I get very concerning answers.

The bathroom is flooded with gorgeous women, all helping me work through this conundrum.

"You should just ask him what he means!"

"He means he'd like to ask you out, but he has a girlfriend!"

"Men are so stupid."

"Men just want the princess treatment. Don't respond."

"Tell him you don't have plans this weekend and see what he says."

"Block him!"

The consensus says to block him. But I don't want to do that. It's at least nice to know none of us really know what Mads means. But at the same time, that blows.

Me and two of the girls, who are cousins, go up to the bar for gin and tonics. We are laughing and dancing and they introduce me to their boyfriends (much to my frustration as I really thought one of them was hitting on me), who are very polite. But kind of ugly.

The lights are moving along with the beat of the music. My g&t tastes amazing. And I feel so damned good. Delta 3 begins their actual set. Their EDM music makes you feel like falling in love with strangers or getting into bed with your best friend. It makes you feel like everyone is here on this planet just to love and be loved. I drink the rest of my drink and set it on the bar top, then turn to enter the main dance crowd.

And that's when I see him.

The most handsome man I've ever seen in my whole life. An alpha. He's far away and amongst a crowd on the dance floor, and yet I still know he's totally my type.

He's so tall and broad. He has dark hair that's long in the front and falling in the most sexy way, and totally shirtless. He's absolutely delicious, and I must have him tonight.

The omega in me will settle for nothing less.

He turns and I see he's wearing a face mask. It's leather and looks kinky as fuck. Oh my god, are all my dreams coming true?

He's grinding on a blonde girl and it's everything in me not to rip her hair out. I've never felt more possessive in my life. I'm not sure what to make of it. I get closer and closer to him, dancing to the music and becoming one with the crowd. Eventually, I make my move, I turn into him so our fronts are pressed together, and I place my hand delicately on his chest. When I have his attention, I twist so my ass is pressed into him.

He does not need any more clues.

He's got it.

He places his hands on my hips and feels me sway along with the beat. The music is frothy and fucking sexy as hell. His dark jeans provide great friction against my bare thighs. His hands are perfect—large, strong, and demanding.

And we dance for what feels like half the night.

Some bright lights take over the dance floor during a bass drop, and we both get a good look at each other.

He bends down and buries his face in my neck and hair.

"An omega," he purrs.

I squeak at his gorgeous deep voice, muffled by the mask. What I wouldn't give to hear him say my name while I was riding him for my life.

I grab his face and pull him to me. I say in his ear, "I'm just here for a good time. Don't get all alpha on me. Can you be chill?"

"Oh, I can be whatever you want me to be, little momma." And he squeezes both ass cheeks. And I let him. Because it's helping. I'm horny as all hell, and I need this. I need this. I need a mindless mess-around. I'm pressing myself into him, and he's matching all my energy.

For the last year I'd been dating two older people. I was the picture of maturity. We talked about having a child, and always did the math on how old they would be when the kid grew up. We went to all the fine dining places. We talked about retirement portfolios a lot. And I just want to be young now, please. I want to hit on girls in bathrooms. Get drunk. Wear a skanky dress.

I want to fuck this stranger.

And as soon as possible. We get moved along with the crowd as we grind and dance into each other. We work each other up in a frenzy, and I don't know what to do next, but something has got to happen next. I lift a leg to his hip, and he holds it up and presses his hard cock right to my pussy. We have way too many clothes on.

Something no one would agree with me on if they saw my outfit.

Our eyes latch, and time slows down for a brief moment. He's so fucking beautiful. I didn't know people came this pretty. He leans in, the leather of his mask touching the shell of my ear.

"You're panting, little momma. Do you need some relief?"

I nod, and he feels the motion.

He drops my leg and takes my hand, and then leads me off the dance floor. I'm a puppet entirely under his control.

I'm only faintly aware that he's leading me down some corridors and up some stairs and around a corner and then finally through a door. Darkness greets us. I'm only focused on this tall, gorgeous alpha when we are finally in a small, dark space. Just him and me. His hands on my body.

Actually, his hands are on my thighs, pushing my dress up to my hips.

The faint thump of the club music can be felt through the wall he has me pushed up against.

His whole body is screaming at me to be fucked, and I would like to oblige. He finally finds the edge of my panties and in the smoothest move ever, he's got them completely off of me, pocketing them, and then arranging my leg on his shoulder, as he kneels before me.

Just before he does anything else, he looks up at me in the dark and asks, "Is this ok?"

"Please yes, do whatever you want to me. Please, alpha."

His body trembles at my words, and he presses his mask onto my bare pussy.

12

Little Momma

Kol

She smells like a floral dreamscape. Her pussy is godly. I've never been this keyed up in my life. I toured Urban Lounge months ago to possibly buy out the current landlord. So, I knew about this little unused office on the second floor, and knew that if you jiggle the handle just right, you could get it open.

And yes, at the time, I notated it in case I wanted to fuck someone in it.

I think about fucking someone all the time. It's a noise in my head that I can only turn down but never off. Most women satisfy the noise for a little bit, but to have a real honest to god omega in my arms—that's the ideal.

All roads lead to an omega for an alpha. I let the animal in me come out to play. An omega is everything to an alpha. All her sounds and tastes and reactions were designed to kill me.

And I'm fucking dead on arrival.

I have two fingers in her pussy and my muzzle pressed firmly to her clit. She rocks herself over my face, and I make sure she has a lot of friction to work with. I hope I die like this, face buried in omega pussy.

I wish I could rip this thing off and shove my tongue into her.

I lead her on, chasing her orgasm, until she explodes above me. Her fingers gripped my hair.

I ease a finger from my left hand into her ass. I don't let off of her clit. I want a second orgasm. And a third and a fourth. I want her fucking wrecked.

She loves it. Her noises are getting louder as I lead her through another one.

"Stop, please, I want your cock. I want your cock inside of me," she begs.

Nothing compares to the way an omega begs. I cannot deny her, even to increase her pleasure. I pull out of her, pushing the fingers that were in her pussy under my muzzle and into my mouth. Then I graze her whole cunt with all four fingers on my right hand, and stick them back under my muzzle, chasing the euphoric taste. Memorizing it, for when all this ends.

I turn her around and push her front into the wall, then I pull my hard, aching cock from my jeans and line it up on her swollen pussy entrance.

This will end, though. This will end, and I'll never have her again. Because my packmate Locke has a scent match, and it's Acadia's wet cunt I'll worship for the rest of my life.

A primal whine rips out of me.

Don't think about that.

How can I ever let this omega hurt my pack? She fits perfectly in my arms. Her smell. Her cunt. The way she moves. Perfection. But so wrong for me.

I sink into her slowly, because I need to memorize this. I'm going to stroke myself to this memory for a long time. Her leg shakes as I push further and further into her.

I bend my body so that I cover her completely. My hands come up to either side of her head, resting on the wall.

"How does that feel, little momma?" I say in her ear, my voice strangled just like my cock.

She makes a similar strangled noise to match.

And then I fuck her.

I fuck her like this will be the only time I get to fuck her, because it is. She pushes back on me, wanting me further and deeper and harder. I'll give her anything she wants, and how lucky am I that she wants me?

If there wasn't a scent match for us, this beautiful, sexy woman would never actually want more from me anyway. An alpha who suffers from rutting is often put away. We lied in our documentation to the Institute about my medical condition. If they were to check the records in Salt Port, then we'd be screwed.

A rutting alpha is a broken alpha.

Oscar tells me I can manage if we bond with an omega soon. That it won't get worse, and I can even cure myself of it. He takes my blood weekly. I take whatever pill he gives me. And the noise is still there.

"Please, alpha, I want your knot," she cries into the wall. Her hair is wet with sweat, her arms are shaking, and she's already come with my finger on her clit and my cock rutting into her.

Under normal circumstances, I would never knot an omega in a nightclub, but this will buy me even more time.

And I don't have a choice. The omega I'm currently deep inside wants it.

We will figure out the consequences later.

I've been holding back, so it's only a matter of giving in before I'm coming inside of her tight, perfect cunt.

I stroke her back and sides, calming her, relaxing her. I brush the hair away from her face, and push my knot in.

This is it. This is all I ever fucking needed.

My heart beats in my ears, and it aligns with the beat of the music from the club. 140 bpm.

I wrap my arms around her as her body goes limp, and while we are connected, I keep her on her feet.

My muzzle rests on her neck. My teeth aching to be pressed into her flesh. Saliva pools and drips down my chin.

I turn us so we are leaning up against the wall on our sides. I pull her up and into me, so her head flops back on my shoulder. My muzzle runs back and forth across her neck.

"So beautiful, so sexy."

She's doing that omega thing where she gets all lethargic and pliable when she's knotted. But I need her to stay coherent, because I'm not done with her.

"Little momma," I rumble into her ear. "Don't you leave me just yet. I still want to play with you."

She rolls her head off of me and tries her best to come back to the land of the living.

"Being knotted is not the end. Did you know that in this position, both you and I can just keep coming? Over. And over. It doesn't take much."

She's lucid now. Her hips rock back into me.

"I usually just fall asleep," she murmurs.

"Well then, the alphas you've let take care of you are all losers, little momma. Let a real man take care of you—"

She does not think that's cheesy at all, which just goes to show she's ready.

I position us so she can lean forward across my arm, my hand on her neck. Then I use my other hand to pet her clit, bringing her back to the brink. My knot is firmly in her, but I can still fuck her like this. I just need the right leverage. As soon as her hands shoot out to hold her up using some sort of furniture (it's pitch black in here), I find that friction.

"Oh my god! Oh my god! I'm coming. I'm coming already," she screams.

And I'm coming too. I see phosphenes on the edges of my vision because it's so intense.

She's panting and growling and muttering.

One more.

My hand reaches out, groping the thing she was using to hold herself up. It's a chair. I turn us and sit down, bringing her onto my lap. Her legs outside of mine.

"One more," I grit. She's not going to make it. Her slick is running down my legs. I gently play with her tits, rolling the nipples gently in my fingers, her dress pulled to reveal them. One more.

She leans forward, putting her hands on my knees, so she can fuck me herself.

"Good girl," I groan. She's a good fucking girl.

And then she rips me to shreds. I'm coming into her for the third time. My spent trapped inside her with my knot.

"Fuck!" I can't even tell if she's coming again because I lose all my senses.

I grab her around her waist and keep rutting up into her. I'm lost. I'm gone. I've left this earth.

Eventually, I'm aware my face is pressed against her back. And I'm coherent again.

I'm satisfied. The noise is gone. I'm spent and used up.

I listen to my heart rate slowly lose count with the beat of the music. It takes about twenty minutes, and my knot slowly loosens.

I'm so lost in this feeling of peace, it doesn't register that she's removed my arms. Then she pushes off of me, my knot down enough she's able to unattach us.

My cock is suddenly sensitive to the air and elements. My pants are somewhere.

Cum runs down my thighs.

But when I look down to search for my pants, the omega takes off out of the door.

She's gone.

She left me.

Fuck.

I find my pants and leave the club. We were in that room for over an hour. Good fucking god. I'm covered in her cum and pheromones. I can't go home like this. Locke will strangle me.

As I walk down the empty city streets, I rip the muzzle off of me, having to snap the leather strap in two. I throw it into a trash can. Along with her panties. I can't keep them. I check into my gym. It's 24 hours and expensive as all hell. The beta at the front desk doesn't smell anything on me other than liquor, smoke, and sex. I use the showers, scrubbing myself raw. I buy some pants and a zip-up hoodie from the beta to change into, then I toss my clothes into the trash on my way out.

I stop at a corner store for a sports drink.

I need to lie down.

I get back home around 3:00 am. Oscar is waiting for me on the couch.

"Did you find someone?" he asks me. I nearly roll my eyes at my pack lead, but I remember myself.

"Yes. An omega."

Oscar stands and comes to smell me. I did a good job cleaning up. He makes me open my mouth to show there's no blood in it. I do it, but only because I think he mostly wants to see my sharp teeth. He notices my gym branded outfit and nods.

"And how do you feel?"

"That's a hell of a question, alpha."

His hand comes down on the back of my neck, and he forces my head down. He also bends his head down, and we push our foreheads together. It's an old mating gesture alphas do with each other. It makes me feel all warm and fuzzy inside. Like he loves me.

"Tell me."

"I feel amazing. And guilty. And calm. And like I did something very wrong that I hope Locke can forgive me for."

He lets up and steps back.

"He knows what you needed to do."

"And how does he feel?"

"Anxious. But I'll take care of it."

I nod. Oscar pats my cheek affectionately. I finally leave for my room to find Locke asleep.

Small mercies.

13

Pack Lead

Oscar

I march myself to the Institute the next day. Everything is taking way too long and going oh so wrong.

We've been in this city for months, and we are only inching closer to our goals. I knew Locke and Kol were manipulating me into the decision to leave Salt Port, but they presented a great case. First, Locke's troubles with Legs O'Bannon. Then Kol's medical problem can only be solved with an omega. All three of our problems can be solved with an omega, and we were blacklisted in Salt Port.

It wasn't Kol's fault for getting us blacklisted, or for even getting us into this mess, despite it being a direct result of his actions. While we were at the O'Bannon packhouse, Kol took a shine to Locke. I could feel his desire in the bond for him. Not a sexual desire, they've never been that way with each other, but the kind alphas have for their packmates.

Kol bit Locke, suddenly, and without warning, in front of everyone, with a bonding mark. The women screamed. I tried to pull them apart, and Legs O'Bannon was angry enough I thought he'd execute us right then and there. I dug us out of that mess with a bargain. Which is why this is so important. It's important for them and for me to get an omega.

I've spent the last twelve years working towards my PHD. I have a fully completed residency, but I can't get hired as an unbonded alpha. My three-alpha pack doesn't count when you are an OB-GYN, specializing in omega births. Even if I'm damned good at what I do.

I'm trying to get a research position, and even then, I've been turned down time and time again because of administrative bullshit.

My omega patients never minded.

My residency proved that.

But my designation makes it impossible for me to do my work.

I'm not complaining. The only complaint is that I thought that by now we would have an omega, so it wouldn't be a problem. I've been specifically told by two major hospitals to apply again when I have a bonded omega.

I walk into the building holding my gift in front of me like the offering it is. Angeline greets me, despite me arriving unannounced. She takes me up to the meeting room near her office.

"Alpha Soto, what can I help you with?" She asks cheerily.

"I'm here to ask you to give this courting gift to Acadia. On behalf of the Soto Pack."

She gets a weird look on her face. She's going to say no.

I slide the blue box across the table to her anyway. Inside is a silver chain necklace with a pendant. Lilac blossoms are cast on the polished silver pendant.

"We are in the process of courting a beta. We hope to have him bonded soon. I don't want the natural timeline of these things to ruin our chances at making our intentions known to the omega."

I can't tell her we think she's a scent match in case she accuses us of lying to get to the omega. They will remove us from the whole Institute if we make a claim like that just to see the omega.

But I'm hoping the little lilac blossoms will communicate to Acadia that she's special to us.

"I'll see what I can do. But this is highly irregular. If she did end up getting this, most likely I wouldn't be able to tell her who sent it unless she chose your file."

I nod in understanding. Though I'm pissed.

We've been paying monthly for access to the Institute. Not to mention the exuberant application fees. It feels like we are constantly getting the runaround. And the worst part is, Cash City has the best placement center in the country, so this is the best they can offer.

I remind her again I'd like Acadia to receive this right away. That it's important.

"I understand, Alpha Soto. I do."

And since I'm here and have her at my use, I ask, "And do you know *why* our girl wants a pack with a beta? It may help us with our process."

She bites her lip.

"You know I shouldn't be talking about this, but to be honest with you, no, we do not. She is very serious about it. I meet with her today, and then again next Wednesday. I'd like to get your name to her by then. Is that something you can do?" She's whispering and leaning close to me. Like she's telling me a secret.

"You'll give her the gift today?"

She sighs, but nods her head.

"Then I'll have a beta by Wednesday. It's done. I appreciate your hard work and dedication you have to the placements you handle, Miss Angeline."

She doesn't seem to enjoy my compliment when I am asking her to go against her company's policy.

She doesn't offer her hand, and neither do I.

She walks me out, and I make sure she has the box in her hands.

14

Omegas Love Gifts

Acadia

M y walk of shame is more like a sprint of shame. I run all the way home in my heels and dress, covered in cum.

I can't get my keys to work, and it wakes Maria, who is very concerned about my state. She tells me more omegas have been kidnapped this week. Which isn't true. There was one, but she was not kidnapped, she just went missing for a few hours.

Maria is also quite the gossip, so I'm pretty sure come morning, the whole complex will know what I walked home looking like.

"Acadia, we have the morning walk with all the omegas in just a few hours," she reminds me. The unbonded omegas go for group walks through the park in Chinatown twice a week.

"I know, Maria. I know."

We have a whole squad of personal security who walk with us.

I hop in the shower and reluctantly wash away my alpha.

My alpha, he is not. But damn if I don't feel like I dreamed him into reality. I've never kept going after being knotted like that. In one dingy, dark room at a night club, this man had me coming more than even during my partial heat I had with the Whitehorses. It was short due to my medication, but it didn't make it any less real. I was an omega in need of a lot of orgasms. Alpha females are notorious for making an omega climax. It's kind of their whole thing. And yet...

Maybe Bianca wasn't living up to her reputation. She was nowhere near the level club-guy was.

I find myself stroking my pussy to the memory of the smells and sounds of club-guy. He called me "little momma," which I have to admit was perfect.

I groan and stop myself.

I know for a fact Maria can hear me in here.

Sighing, I finish washing him away and get myself to bed. Like a proper omega who has to wake up in a few hours for the omega walk.

The walk goes fine. The gardens are beautiful. I'm not even hung over. A good fucking will do that to an omega. I do drink two lattes, though.

Omegas are not supposed to drink caffeine. It's really bad for you. I literally don't care right now, though.

I go to my appointment at the Institute. I'm wearing a periwinkle suit, in hopes I can feel powerful enough for another battle.

Angeline looks...awkward. She keeps flitting her eyes around to see if we are being watched. We are in a meeting room near her office. The walls are all glass, so if anyone did want to look in, they'd be sure to see us.

She's so cute in her matching pink suit. She looks like a Barbie doll with her long blonde hair and polka dot tights. She's young, but she's married. To a male beta. Not that I'd want to pursue someone who works here. Oh my god, Cadi, get it together. Besides, all her fidgeting is driving me up a wall anyway.

"Angeline, you are bugging the hell out of me. Do you have something you need to tell me?"

She sighs and then leans in close, lowering her voice. "You've caught the eye of a pack. But they don't meet your criteria. The pack lead, who is a very handsome older Latin man with a mustache that would make your mother weep, gave me a courting gift to give to you."

"Tell me more about this mustache," I tease. She rolls her eyes at me.

"He has an accent, too."

"Girl, I need more than facial hair and an accent. But show me the gift."

I love gifts. I am an omega after all.

She looks around again to see if we are being watched, then passes a small blue box under the table.

I put it on the table and open it, openly. Because Angeline's cloak and dagger bit is cute but not my style.

It's a silver necklace.

Silver is something given to feral alphas to subdue them. But it's also given to omegas as a show that they control the alphas. I pull it out of its case. There's a sterling silver pendant with little flowers cast on it.

Lilacs.

I look up at Angeline.

"Where did I catch their eye?"

"The soirée."

Hm. Interesting. I wonder why they didn't make themselves known. Alphas are usually always making their presence known around me. I'm an unbonded female. They are larger than life. I missed an entire alpha...and his pack. That's not right.

"How big is his pack?" I ask, my voice a little soft and faraway, as I look over the gift.

It's so shiny. It is lightweight and delicate. The metal clinks beautifully on the chain as I pass it through my fingers.

"Three alphas. All male. They just moved to the city. They are quite motivated to get an omega."

I put the necklace back in the box and snap the lid shut.

"Well, thank you for the gift. But, you'll have to give it back to him."

I slide it across the table. Angeline puts her hands up.

"No, I won't touch it. I shouldn't have even given it to you. I know they don't qualify. But he was quite insistent. Do with it what you please."

I take it back. I have to admit I'm kind of glad to have it back. What does that say about me? Do I have no convictions?

I open it up again and run my finger over the bloom's edges. It's such an interesting choice. It could have been diamonds. Or gold. Gems and jewels. Heart-shaped whatever.

This is...classy. And it feels like it has a message.

"Acadia?" Angeline asks.

"Hm?"

"I shouldn't say this," she lowers her voice, "They are courting a beta right now. The alpha who brought you that."

"They're courting a beta, and they want to court me?"

She chews on her lips, but just nods.

Angeline's boss comes swirling into the room, and I hide the box. I don't want to get her in trouble.

We get started going through three, yes, only three, more files. I'm barely paying attention. They have their profiles on a big screen and are pitching them to me. But my mind is elsewhere. It's on the club hottie from last night. The mind blowing fucking.

This whole process is the worst. Will any of these options blow my back out like the alpha from last night?

There's a pack photo with some alphas that all blend into each other. This guy works as a CEO/CFO/CXO. This guy loves golf. This guy rock climbs. Oh, this man looks interesting. He plays hockey. I can't muster even a single ounce of interest.

And then, because everything has to be so ill-timed, Mads texts me.

I'm reminded I should have a pack courting me soon, so I can invite them to my next heat, as I excuse myself from the room.

I really shouldn't be entertaining a single beta.

I should go back in and see if hockey-guy likes sushi or tacos.

> Hello, Cadi. Are you free tonight? They have an outdoor movie playing at the Riverfront Park. I thought we could go together.

I stare at the screen, willing myself to be calm. Mads asked me out. For real this time. I wish I could show all those girls from the bathroom so we could squeal and jump up and down together. Instead, I'm in this hallway in this cold building. I look through the glass wall at Angeline. I bet she'd squeal and jump up and down with me, but her evil older twin would not approve.

I look back down at the screen.

> I've never been. It sounds fun. Meet you there at 8?

The movie won't start until dark, which will give us an hour to find a spot and talk.

> It's a date.

I turn and do a very quiet and itty bitty squeal and jump up and down. And then I return to the room where I'm shown pictures of alphas and given information that means absolutely nothing to me.

One of the packs has a female alpha, and I get the shivers when they talk about her. I think about Bianca's apathetic behavior towards her daughter, and my stomach sours, and I frown through the rest of the meeting.

15

Turn Down For What

Mads

I decide it's less scary to ask a pretty girl out on a date than to accept this job offer from these three alphas, so I do that first.

Then I stare at the job offer I printed out at the library. It's good. It's too good.

I can't put my finger on it, but it feels like there's a catch.

I read through every word so many times I have it memorized: $98,000 a year. End of year bonus.

Why would he say $90,000 in the meeting but offer me even more? Especially when I asked for $60k.

A little voice in my head says, 'He doesn't want you to say no.'

I don't want to view him as an alpha, but this feels like dirty alpha behavior. Like he's treating me like an omega. Oh my god.

Oh my god.

Is he courting me?

No, that's stupid. Alphas court omegas. And other alphas. Not betas. Fuck, this is why I can't deal with these people. They are so extreme. If he wants me as his employee, and wants me desperately enough, he'd court me. He's already asked me if I prefer Macs or Windows. He's going to buy me a whole setup.

What if I offend him? Look at his omega wrong? Deny him? Will he break my jaw?

I have to end this now.

I log back into the computer at the library where I've been all morning and email Kol Soto.

I tell him that I appreciate his generous offer, and I'd love to work with him, but I am respectfully declining. I wish him luck in filling the role.

I hover over the send button. I should call him and tell him over the phone like a man. Give him the opportunity to hear this from me and not read it in his inbox.

I log out of the computer and gather my things. I exit to the gardens on the terrace of the library. It overlooks the river and it is rather peaceful out here.

I call Kol and he answers on the first ring.

"Mads! It's great to hear from you. I almost called you myself."

I huff out a laugh. Alphas. One step away from mania.

"Of course. Alpha Soto, I," he cuts me off.

"Kol is fine. None of this alpha stuff. Just Kol."

I sigh heavily. "Kol. I apologize that this isn't the news you want to hear. But I cannot accept your offer. I wish you all the best in filling this role. You deserve someone really great, and I'm sure you'll be very successful in Cash City."

Silence. I look at the phone to make sure the call didn't drop.

"Kol?" I eventually ask.

"Yeah, sorry, I'm having trouble understanding. Can I get some feedback? Is it the offer? I can go higher..."

"No, that's not it. It was more than generous. More than..."

Oh, this is not going great.

I adjust my leg out straight. I'm sitting on this uncomfortable bench with wood beams instead of slats. The edges of the beams are digging into my butt.

Kol's voice levels out to a penitent tone. "Was it because I brought Oscar and Locke to our lunch? I'm so sorry I did that. They can be kind of nosey."

"Yeah, you said that. To be honest, yeah, that was alarming."

I don't know what else to say, and Kol seems distressed.

We sit in silence, and it spurs me on—

"And since I'm being honest, your behavior is worrisome. You seem really set on me joining you. I have a lot going on. I just need income and health insurance. And I'd prefer to keep my distance from alphas. I know that's shitty to say. Hopefully, with insurance, I can go to trauma therapy and work out some of my problems."

"Ok, yeah. It's not great to hear. Alphas can get possessive and single-minded when they want something."

He's being vulnerable, and I'm being honest, and it's snowballing.

"And you want me?" I ask slowly.

He clicks his tongue. "We all do."

I suck in a breath and stand up, like I need to run. *We all do.* Meaning his whole pack. They want me. This isn't a job. I knew it. I knew they were being weird. We are no longer talking about me being employed by him, but bitten and bound for life.

"I'm sorry, Soto. That's not going to happen. Find another man to bite. And stay the fuck away from me."

I hang up the phone and consider tossing it off the roof into the river.

Oh my god. I did not think he'd confirm my irrational thoughts. Kol wants me. His pack wants me. They might not let that shit go. Is this worse than being targeted by a pack? Fuck me, it feels like the same thing.

I turn off my phone completely, afraid he'll call back, and then take the elevator to the ground floor. I need to go home and take my meds so I can go on my date later. That's where my head needs to be at.

And I need to keep looking for a job. A normal one. Not a front for a lifelong commitment to psychopaths.

16
Rejections

Locke

I gently take the phone out of Kol's shaking hand. He's having trouble breathing. He's sitting at the kitchen table with his laptop and papers, and rolled up housing plans, in shock.

I make sure the call ended, and then I set it down on the table. I heard everything. I heard the fear and resolution in Mads's voice as he told my pack mate to fuck off. Kol's eyes are darting around the room. It's usually me panicking, so this is new and exciting.

I go to the sink and fill a bowl with cold water, then dump some ice in from the freezer. I come back to the table to find Kol gripping the edges of the table with white knuckles. I push aside his laptop and replace it with the bowl.

"Dunk your face in, Kol," I command, putting a little alpha bark in it so he knows I'm serious.

This morning, I crawled over to his bed and sniffed him from toes to skull. Whatever he'd gotten into, he'd cleaned himself up entirely before coming home. But I know he stepped out. I know he fucked an omega.

His whole body was relaxed in that bed like he'd actually slept and didn't just toss and turn.

I couldn't help being upset. And disappointed. Acadia is ours. She's the only omega for us. As soon as I found her I knew she was ours, and we needed to be loyal to her.

Why couldn't Kol have found a beta to fuck, at the very least? Why an omega?

And now? Now he's lost our beta...

Kol dunks his head in the cold water and stays in it so long I think he is trying to drown himself.

Oscar calls Kol's phone, and I answer.

"Oscar?"

"My bond is flooded with Kol's feelings."

"He's fine." I wait for a second, and finally, Kol comes up for air, water flying all over the table. "He's fine. Mads turned the job down."

"And Kol didn't convince him?"

"Well, he caught on that it was probably going to be more than a job. He told Kol to leave him the fuck alone. He said, 'Find someone else to bite.'"

"I see. I was headed home, but I'll go see what I can do."

"Yeah, I understand."

"Send me the beta's address."

"Ok. Will do. Goodbye."

I set the phone down on a side table.

"Oscar wants to go talk to him."

"No." Kol lurches up. "No! We cannot hassle this man."

I push him back down onto the chair. He's not going to intervene. I have no more time left. If we don't find Acadia, Legs is coming for me.

"Mads is ours!" I hiss.

With his face and hair dripping wet, he says while his voice rises and rises, "Everything is a mess. Oscar can't get a job. I'm going to have to institutionalize myself soon. And Legs is going to fuck us all over in the end. We're absolutely fucked."

I don't react. I understand the situation. And I understand we can't let Mads go. The moment I saw him sitting at that table with that pathetic look on his face, I knew he was mine. His curly lips carry all his real thoughts. I watched his mouth the whole time, and every single thought of his was portrayed there first. Made me want to kiss him to see if I could feel what he was feeling.

"We have not made one right move in years!" Kol yells. "What makes you think our judgment should be trusted!"

I turn my head away. Done being yelled at. I've been yelled at my whole life. Legs made sure not a day went by I didn't get a dressing down or a good beating. I don't need this from someone who says he loves me. Not again.

"I'm sorry, my brother." Kol drops all his ire and approaches me. I try to deny him, but he pulls me into a hug anyway. He says he is sorry into my hair.

"He's ours. Acadia is ours. I know it."

He nods to placate me.

Legs O'Bannon is coming for me. He has a man trailing me every time I leave this apartment. It's Mickey he's got out here. He's mean as a dog, and vigilant too.

Legs was my guardian, and I grew up in that pack house. He has a daughter, Aurora, and I always viewed little Ro as a sister. But when I was 18, he declared I'd bond her when she became of age. I'd bond her, and then let Legs decide all the other members of my pack. And then he'd control everything we did.

Like he controlled everything that happened in Salt Port.

Oscar and Kol thought bonding me with them would be enough to get me out, but Legs threatened their lives unless I went into an agreement with him. If I found my own omega before Aurora turns 19, then there's no more obligation to him or his family.

If I don't, then I belong to Legs and his privileged little daughter.

It sounded like a fair deal to me until he blacklisted my pack from every available omega in the state. I didn't realize how far his reach was. But when you supply all the illegal hormones and scent blockers in the state, and run trafficking for arms, flesh, and drugs—you can do quite a bit.

After months of struggling to find an omega while staying in our home, we left.

But seeing the Irishman in the corner of my eyes every time I leave this house, I know I'm never going to escape Legs O'Bannon. Thankfully, this city is run by Lee Man-ho, the Wong Clan, and the Nightingales. Several warring packs who wouldn't let Legs near their business in the city. We don't have their protection, though. If shit went down, we'd be extradited.

Kol looks at me like he knows I'm thinking about this shit. He knows how desperate we are.

We get Acadia, and that's it for Legs. He has no more hold on me. And it's bigger than just bonding an omega. She's my scent match. That supersedes law any man or mobster can make.

He can't even go back on our gentlemen's agreement. We all know he would weasel his way out anyway.

Aurora turns 19 in less than two weeks. On my 25th birthday. We share a birthday, my little sister and I. The girl who tied herself to me with her childish demands.

I let Kol go, and he walks away, locking himself in the room we share.

I walk up to the window out back and see the black town car Mickey drives. The silhouette of his head in the driver's seat. I'd go looking for Acadia myself, but I don't want to lead Mickey to her. And neither does Oscar. So he's told me to stay in the house.

I guess my dream about being a house alpha is coming true sooner than I thought.

17

Second Interview

Mads

I t takes the rest of the day for me to get home, take my meds, eat a bread and butter sandwich, shower, and get to the Riverfront Park. My leg is behaving today, which is weird. But it might just be the adrenaline from my call with Kol earlier that I'm still riding on.

I've brought a quilt blanket my grandma gave me for my birthday one year. It's big enough to be a picnic blanket. I counted the cash in my wallet carefully— $40. I truly hope I can get through the night with just that.

The whole way to the park, on the bus and transfers, and walking, I feel like I'm being followed. I keep looking around and I don't recognize anyone. But I can't shake the feeling.

I've got my cane in one hand and the blanket draped on my other arm. I also have a backpack with sparkling water and some cups. I stopped at a corner store for the drinks, crackers, and cheese. I used my card so I would still have the $40 in cash. I pray to god my rent clears tomorrow instead of today so I don't get an overdraft fee.

I try to think why I'm going on a date when I'm unemployed with no car. But I've been delusional before, I can be it again.

I actually thought I was going to be talked into accepting the job, that's why I asked Acadia out. I thought I'd be celebrating. But speaking with Kol only validated my fears.

I find a nice spot on the hill overlooking the docks. The movie is projected onto a screen on a boat on the water. I came here a few times with my old roommate Arnie, so I knew where I wanted to set up.

I also needed to arrive early, so I could set up without her seeing how fucked up I am. It's why I arrived early to my job interview. Getting into a chair is an ordeal enough, I couldn't have my potential new employer seeing that shit.

I lay down the blanket and get that prickly feeling on the back of my neck like I'm being watched. I sit up and lean on my cane as I scan the area. There are quite a few people here already for the food trucks and market. But no one looks like they are paying me any attention.

But what if someone is following me?

I shake my head, deleting any paranoid thoughts that want to take root.

I see Cadi before she even texts me to say she's here. She is way on the other side, near the bathrooms and the aid station. Where the playground is where little kids play. She's wearing blue jeans and a green shirt that shows off her midriff. Her hair shines in the waning sunlight.

The text comes in—

> Cadi: I'm here! Where should we meet?

She scans the area for me, the crowd making it difficult. She's taller than I expected. I suddenly lose all my nerve. Why the hell am I doing this?

I'm not the same flirty, fun person I used to be. I'm not prepared for this at all. Oh god.

But, at this point I don't have a choice, I text her back.

> Mads: There's a big tree on a hill. I've got us a spot underneath it. It's on the south west side.

She looks for the west first, then the tree. Then she puts her phone away and starts towards me.

Should I be sitting or standing? Oh god, I can't be sitting on the ground when she gets here. That's so pathetic. What if she wants to hug? Can't do that sitting down for the first time. Fuck. I make the terrible and awkward journey to standing. I'm out of breath, and I'm also sweating. Fuck me. Why am I even out of my house?

I think she doesn't spot me until I'm fully standing. I have to lean on my cane, otherwise I'll put too much pressure on my leg and it'll start to get inflamed. And I'd like to last the whole evening.

She is smiling ear to ear. A silver necklace dangles from her neck as she climbs up the hill to me. It's not until she's in front of me that my whole face falls.

Oh my god.

Cadi is an omega.

How on earth is this happening right now?

"Mads!" she greets me and comes up to me for a hug. I use my free arm to lightly pat her back and she comes into my space. It's a fucking awkward hug. She steps back and looks down at the quilt.

"This is nice," she says at the same time I say, "You're an omega?"

Her face falls, matching my own.

But she fixes her face.

"Yeah, I'm an omega," she says proudly.

I shake my head. Her cat eyes and freckles are just the same as they were on the video call, but her entire essence screams omega.

It's the pheromones.

"You didn't disclose that…" I say stupidly.

"No, I didn't think my designation would be a problem."

"It's not a problem," I say quickly. But it is.

"You use a mobility aid?" She's being careful not to be offensive but pointing out we both hid something.

I look down at my cane. Then back at the omega.

"I'm sorry that I'm a bit shocked. Can I ask some questions?"

We are both standing straight as rods. She nods.

"Do you have a pack? Alphas?" I look at her neck for bite marks. Her hand goes to her neck, hiding herself from me. I know it's invasive to ask.

"No, I'm unbonded," she thankfully reveals.

"And are you being courted?" She's gorgeous. And nice. And fun. I bet she has a mob of alphas after her.

I don't miss that she hides her necklace under her shirt before saying, "No."

I nod and we stand there in silence.

"I guess designation is important to you? It matters?"

I want to say that of course it matters, but I am no newbie when it comes to women. She's not asking me to be so honest that I'll end up saying something stupid. She's asking if designation is something I'll discriminate against her for. I shake my head.

"That's not what I'm saying, no. I'm just shocked. I'm sorry. Do you want to know about my disability?"

She shakes her head. "I don't care about that."

I look at my backpack with the drinks in it.

I could tell her I can't date an omega. That she should have told me so we could have avoided this altogether. I could tell her that omegas are lovely people, but they have alphas behind them. Like an angler fish, that dangles a pretty omega, but its jaws are right behind the lure. Ready to snap your bones into a million pieces.

But I don't.

I've never been one to tell a pretty girl no.

"Do you want a drink? I brought sparkling water."

She looks surprised, like she was listening to my thoughts but didn't realize I'd decided to be a reckless minnow making another terrible decision because of a pretty face.

I wonder if my other leg will get shattered and I'll have to wheel myself around town by this time next year.

"Ok, let's have a drink," she says, and I gesture to the blanket. Here goes nothing. I make my way into a sitting position, and she doesn't make any indication it's as embarrassing or awkward as it is to watch me do this. I wince and hiss as minimally as possible.

I lay my cane down and pull over my backpack. I packed two stemless wine glasses wrapped in a kitchen towel. I set the towel down and put the glasses on top. Then I open one of the sparkling water cans, filling our glasses with half each.

She finally takes a seat next to me.

"So, you've never been here before?"

She takes the glass I offer to her.

"I've been to this park countless times. I was here for the Women's March. The protest against Prop 12 last October. But never to the movie nights."

I raise my eyebrows. "Are you politically active?"

"You could say so. I just can't sit idly by. I don't understand how anyone can, honestly."

"Well, I've been here countless times too. For the skate park. Food trucks. Giant pumpkin regatta. Chinese New Year lantern festival."

"Sounds like we come here often—" she says with a teasing tone. "We should switch some time. I'll go to the lantern festival, and you can protest the insurance company's denial claim rates."

I laugh, loud. Fuck. "I'll be there. With bells on. With bells on my cane."

She smiles.

"This is nice. I was worried. But this is easy. There's nothing to this."

What is she talking about? I look around. This?

"Oh…" I say and place my hand on my face.

"What?"

"You've never been on a date, have you?" I ask. On our call, she said she was new to all of this. I thought she meant the app. Not dating.

"Don't tease me," she says, but her voice is light.

"Well, this must be the worst date you've ever been on."

"And the best. You can't screw up."

I laugh. Oh my god, she's funny. I can't even remember the last time I laughed this much.

She takes a sip of her drink.

"Well, I'll take that as a challenge then."

She smiles at me. Her smile is so warm.

I ask her about her day, and she tells me about her walk through the gardens with the omegas in her complex. Perhaps a single omega is better than a bonded omega. Maybe this will be fine. She asks about my day, and I tell her I was job hunting at the library. I'm worried my employment status will be another bomb, but she doesn't even react like it is. Eventually, I pull out the cheese and crackers, laying them on a board I brought from home. She's very delighted by our setup.

I take a quick glance around, and as I suspected, we have quite a few spectators. An omega and a beta on a very obvious date would do that. I just hope they don't bother us.

She eats everything I brought and drinks all the sparkling water. I look to the food trucks. Should I get her some more? I'm not sure I can make it down the hill and up the concrete steps to the trucks and then back before the movie starts.

The park is filled with people. Our blanket is butted up against folks on all sides as the evening gets later. The sun sets soon. I adjust my leg and my sitting position and inadvertently scoot closer to Cadi.

"My favorite show, if I'm being honest, is Love Letter Home Renovations. I know it's silly, but I watch every episode multiple times," she tells me after I asked what she likes to watch. It's a show where people write in asking for help with renovation projects. Celebrity home designers pick the most inspiring letters and come help them renovate.

"You're joking."

"I know it's cheesy, but I love hearing everyone's stories and then how they do the renovations themselves with their own money. The show people just help them make it all happen."

"Me too! I love Love Letters. I watched it every day while I was recovering."

"No way! What's your favorite one?!"

"The one where the couple always wanted a baby, but they couldn't have one, so they turned their nursery into three rooms."

"Oh my god," she grabs her chest and frowns. "Yeah, instead of turning the room into like a gym or office, they demolished three of the walls and gave the space to other parts of the house. That broke my heart! I cried!"

"I cried!"

She places her hand on my knee, and I don't notice at first, since we are talking excitedly about the show.

Eventually, I go to adjust my legs and I realize her hand has been there a while.

She also looks at her hand.

"Is this ok?"

I look up at her.

And it's too dark to see her details. Then the movie starts up.

"Yeah, it's ok. You're very beautiful, Cadi. And cool. Thank you for sticking around on this date."

She smiles and I smile back.

"Keep being cute and maybe I'll kiss you later," she says casually.

Oh, she's way cooler than me.

She removes her hand from my knee, and I reach out and grab it before she gets away. I interlace our fingers. She's sitting a bit far from me to make this comfortable, and instead of pulling away, she scoots close. So close she's leaning on me.

Oh wow, this is nice.

This is very nice.

We watch the movie like this. Her head eventually resting on my shoulder. I stroke her hand and fingers as the charming romance movie plays. I'm barely even paying attention to it. Every nerve in my body is just cataloguing all of Cadi's movements. Her sighs. Her shifting. She's a very beautiful woman. She has this mature face that matches her mature personality. It comes as a shock when she's being fun or funny because you'd think she was above that. But she's so cool.

An omega.

How utterly ironic.

18

Third Party

Mads

I can't remember the last time I felt like this, like I was floating peacefully. Existing normally with the pain in the background and only a pretty girl in the foreground. Before the final scene in the movie, Cadi sits up and stretches.

"I need to use the restroom," she says.

"I'll pack up and go with you."

She helps me gather the things into my backpack. I take forever to stand, and then I need a second to stretch out my legs from sitting for so long. I try really hard to ignore my stiff leg. And the people who are trying to see around me standing right in their way.

She helps me fold the blanket, and I take it from her. Then we head down the hill, going through the maze of people. My head is down, and I'm trying not to trip or fall on anyone. When we emerge near the bathrooms, Cadi gives me a little wave and goes on into the ladies' room.

I find a wall to lean up against. I set the blanket down on the ground at my feet.

I'm rubbing my leg and finding my breath, so I don't notice a man approaching me. He stands directly in front of me, and I continue to ignore him, thinking he just doesn't realize how close he is to me.

"Mads," the man says, and I nearly jump out of my skin. His voice is deep and commanding, I know he's an alpha before I even look at his face.

"Oscar?" I ask even though I know this is the alpha that came to lunch with Kol. His mustache is unmistakable.

"I'm so happy you remember me," his rich Latin accent shakes me to my core. He's standing so close to me. Adrenaline pumps through my blood, prepping me to defend myself. "Are you here with an omega?"

Fuck I see it all. The pain. The fear. The feeling of death closing in.

"Don't be so scared, beta. I'm here to talk to you about the offer."

I can't answer. My hands are cold. My eyes are wide. What is he going to do?

"Was it the price? Because that's just your wage. We can negotiate more if you need it. We take care of our own. Is there a lifestyle you are hoping to maintain?"

My eyes blink dry.

"What?"

"Tell me what we need to do to make this happen. We are highly motivated." He reaches out for my arm and I flinch away from him. He drops his hand.

"Make *what* happen?"

"You're ours, Mads. What do we need to do to convince you of this fact?"

We all do.

Kol's words echo around me. They are highly motivated? Oh my god. They aren't going to stop.

"I don't play these games. I'm a beta. I don't understand this. This doesn't happen."

"It happens. We recognize our own. And I recognized you, just as I did Kol and then Locke. Are you resisting this because we don't have an omega? Are you into omegas? We are working on that now."

I snap my mouth shut and look around for Cadi. Has she come out yet?

"You'll have to end things with this omega. Locke has a scent match, so that's set in stone. Don't worry, these things tend to work out."

End things with Cadi? Is he threatening me? He's at least a whole foot taller than me. A hundred pounds of pure muscle more than me. His hand could cover my face, and I'd suffocate in under a minute.

"So tell me," Oscar says, his words darker and more serious, "what do we need to do to make this happen? What are your demands? Your preferences? What is holding you back?"

I consider hitting him upside the head with my cane and running for it. But I can't run, and this cane would crumple against his giant head.

Nothing and no one can help me.

"Have I no choice here?"

He shakes his head slowly while maintaining eye contact.

"This is happening, Mads. So prepare your heart. And your demands."

"What will you do to me if I resist?"

Confusion falls over him.

"You won't."

He places his giant paw on my cheek and pats me roughly.

"I will meet you for coffee tomorrow morning, and you can tell me what you want. I'll have Kol send you the details."

He takes a few steps away before adding, "And end things with this omega. Tonight."

He walks away, and I can feel some of the blood return to my body. Apparently, my heart was holding it in.

Cadi walks up to me with a smile. But then she sees my face.

"Are you..." I pull her into me and kiss her. She's shocked and still, but then warms up to me. She kisses me back and then wraps her arms around my neck. I lick at the seam of her lips, and she opens up to me. I deepen the kiss. No goddamned alpha is going to tell me who I can and cannot date.

No goddamned alpha is going to claim me.

This has to be illegal. Stalking? Harassment? Something!

Cadi moans. My hand touches her midriff and I pull her even closer, her bare skin igniting a fire in me.

She pulls back to catch her breath.

"Damn, Mads, you can kiss."

The sound of my cane hitting the ground snaps me out of the haze. I bend down to grab where it fell, and I pick up the blanket as well.

"I just really wanted to do that."

"I don't mind."

We walk hand in hand to the drop off and loading zone to wait for her car she ordered. She said she didn't get a lot of sleep the night before and apologizes that she'd like to go home. She kisses me on the lips and leaves.

Once she's gone I look up the nearest police station and start walking.

"What do you mean you can't do anything?" I plead with the officer who stands before me in full regalia and a side piece. We are in the front lobby of the police station.

"Well, did he threaten you?" The obvious sarcastic tone is unbearable.

"He threatened to make me part of his pack whether I wanted to or not."

"He threatened to dark bond you? What did he say?"

I grit my teeth. I hate how I have to convince this man I'm in distress and need help. It's like he assumes I'm here to waste his time. Like I want to be at a police station at night, instead of at home.

"He just asked what he needed to 'make this happen.'"

The officer's eyebrows go up. He's hoping I see that there was no threat there.

I gasp, realizing there was something threatening Oscar said. "He told me to break things off with the girl I was on a date with."

"Did he say 'or else' or anything like that?"

I don't answer, and he sighs. Fuck.

"What about harassment? This could be considered harassment?"

"Ok, did you tell him to stop, and he kept contacting you? Did you tell him to leave you alone, and he didn't?"

I'm trying to remember, but I don't think I did. Fuck! I didn't even tell him no. It's almost like I want this guy to persist.

"I'm sorry, but this is ridiculous. I'm just a beta. I didn't ask for a pack of alphas to declare that I'm theirs. They don't seem to understand I'm not interested. I can't be the first sorry sap this has happened to?"

"Well, the police don't really get involved, but you can always hire private security." He gestures to a wall with a board. The board has flyers advertising private security and bail bondsmen. Meier Protection Group advertises ABO protections.

"I don't have the money for something like that."

"Some of them take on pro bono cases. Meier Group is known for omega protections..."

"I'm not an omega."

"But they are kind of treating you that way..."

I bite my tongue so I don't tell him to fuck off.

"Look, make sure you document everything. Be clear with your rejections. If they threaten your life or physically assault you, call us right away..."

I'm no longer listening.

They are not going to help. Hire private security! Can you imagine? I'm not a senator's son!

I don't know what made me think the police would help.

I let him finish up and then thank him for his time and leave.

I'm still holding the quilt on my arm, so when I get out to the street, I push the fabric into my face and scream.

When I get home, I run a bath. I sink into the water and try my best to purge myself of the Soto Pack.

I quickly text Cadi and tell her I had a good time. She texts back and tells me she did too.

A text pings from someone else, Kol, that reads:

> Meet at the Lexicon Café at 10:00 am tomorrow. Oscar said to be prepared for a proper conversation.

I drop the phone onto the bath mat and sink into the water. What if I drown myself before tomorrow? Would that make them leave me alone? Or would they insist I haunt them even in the afterlife?

19

Mickey

Locke

O scar returns home. He's thinking heavily about something, and it's pressuring the bond. Kol comes out of the room to meet us. I'd cleaned up the mess from earlier and made a soup that's on the stove.

My alphas both eat and wash their bowls, then come sit down for our nightly chat.

Kol looks disturbed. Oscar looks stressed.

"I met with the beta," Oscar lets us know.

Kol perks up.

"I believe he was on a date with an omega."

What the fuck? Is everyone being unfaithful to our scent match? My scent match. Our omega.

I swallow and push that insane feeling away. The beta doesn't know we are courting an omega. Or rather, we *want* to court an omega.

"Was she pretty?" I ask unfairly.

"Aren't they all?" Oscar says just to put me at ease. But no, that's not true. They aren't all pretty. "I didn't get a good look at her, actually."

I look at Kol, who won't meet my eyes. The omega he was with last night was probably gorgeous if he's feeling this guilty.

"Also, Locke, Mickey is going to be gone for a few days. I was down there chatting with him. He's said that Legs is not sending a replacement. Mickey will be back on duty on Monday."

Mickey and Oscar have a friendly relationship despite the fact Mickey would put a bullet in my head if his boss told him to, no hesitation.

"Is he off breaking someone else's legs?"

"Wow!" Kol shouts.

"What?"

"Alphas attacked Mads and broke his leg. I don't want you talking like that around him."

He's right, I didn't even think that might come off shitty. The fact that Kol is thinking about this is curious. Is Mads always on the top of his mind now?

"Are we even going to be around him anymore? Didn't he reject us?"

Oscar speaks up, "I told him to tell us what he wants so we can have him. We're meeting with him tomorrow to work out the details."

"And he agreed to that?" Kol asks.

"I didn't give him much choice." Oscar shifts in his chair. "Listen, we have to bond him by Wednesday. That's when Angeline at the Institute is presenting another set of alphas to Acadia. We have to be on that list."

"Bonded and registered," I say.

"Bonded and registered," Kol echoes.

"And since we will be Mickey free," Oscar says to me, "I want you combing Cash City for your scent match. Every time Kol and I step out of this house, we run into another omega. She's got to be out there.

I don't want to see you until Monday unless you've found her. Locke, I mean it."

"Yes, I understand."

We go over some other pack business, but our meeting wraps up quickly. I get my wallet and keys. I try very hard to keep my emotions steady.

Kol is drinking on the fire escape. I stick my head out of the window.

"What club did you go to? Maybe I'll try my luck around there."

He texts me the address to Urban Lounge. He doesn't say anything at all to me. I take that as a sign to leave.

On my own little journey to find Acadia.

I find myself at a late night café downloading omega courting apps. I swipe through the profiles looking for a raven haired woman named Acadia.

She won't be on these apps. I can feel it in my soul.

I go to a corner market and buy fruit snacks and little Japanese sodas, so by the time I reach the nightclub my blood sugar levels are high enough I won't pass out.

I can feel him following me.

It's our little game.

When I arrive, there's a whole street filled with party people. Clubs. Bars. Nice restaurants. Homeless people. Peddlers. Men making hot dogs. Hundreds of women in small outfits. Hundreds of men in baseball caps. It's hot and humid. There are even horses on the street.

I spot a few omegas, all surrounded by alphas. She's not here. I know she's not here. She's somewhere safe, sleeping.

I just know these things. Just like I know Mickey is done following me and wants to change the game. I head back to the alleyway courtyard. There are more clubs back here, and a smoke shop, but everything is more quiet. More intimate. No cops.

I light my joint and wait for Mickey to approach me. I offer him a hit when he finally sidles up to me.

"Locke."

"Mickey."

I look over at him. He's wearing a different outfit than normal. He's wearing his "Locke outfit". It's a gold soft t-shirt, black chinos, and shiny black shoes. He always wears gold when he wants to see me. I pick at the bottom of his shirt, and he smiles. He associates this with me, but tonight I'm wearing my own style: yellow and orange floral shirt, comfortable khakis, and a leather belt. The buttons are open to show off my chest hair and white tank top underneath.

"Are they asleep?" he asks about my pack mates. Oscar went to bed an hour ago. Kol is drunk. He won't notice anything. He won't notice when I shut them out from my feelings.

I didn't lie. Mickey would shoot me point blank in between the eyes if Legs told him to. He may hesitate, but he'd do it.

Mickey was hired on as a muscle years ago, but never got his chance with me while we were in Salt Port. He wouldn't get a chance ever, but we have an arrangement.

We don't love each other or anything.

He's not pack.

"Legs is getting anxious. He wants you back in Salt Port next week. He wants you there before her big birthday party. I've had to distract him twice from asking me to just throw you in the back of my car and drive you home."

"Home," I scoff.

"Is this home? You never leave the house. I should know."

I resist the urge to roll my eyes. Mickey is here to watch me, and he takes that very seriously. My stalker was assigned to stalk me. He's exactly where he wants to be.

When he told Oscar he would be "gone for the weekend," this was actually his way of telling me, "I want to see you."

He probably saw us acting differently. Maybe he knows we found an omega...

"Did you get us a room?" I ask as I finish the last drag on the joint.

Mickey goes beet red. He nods his head vigorously. I extend my hand as if to say, *lead the way, then*. Mickey is stocky. Funny looking face. Enthusiastic. When he gets red like this, he looks even worse.

He takes me to a nice boutique hotel on the corner, The Nightingale. We check in and get our room. He's nervous but hiding it well. I'm not nervous at all. But as the floors light up, taking us further and further up to the room, I feel guilty.

Mickey is a beta. An untrustworthy, nasty beta. He watches me with an obsession that I don't trust.

He'll never love me like Kol and Oscar love me. And they don't even touch my cock.

But he does seem to worship me.

"I saw Oscar go into a jeweler. I went in after him and got his order. A silver necklace for a woman. With a pendant. He walked that necklace to the Institute."

I grunt instead of replying. He didn't ask a question, so there's nothing for me to say. I knew it. He noticed us behaving differently, and now he's here to collect.

"I still haven't told Legs you all have been going to the Institute. You know if he found out, you'd be done here. He'd finish this. Take out Oscar and Kol. Take you to do your duty with little Aurora. He talked about making sure you are observed during her heats, so he can make sure you get her pregnant like you should."

He's reminding me that he lies to Legs about my activity. Like how we were accepted into the Institute. And now he'll lie about a courting gift.

If Legs found out we were courting an omega, he would stop it. By any means.

So yes, I mess around with Mickey to keep my pack safe from Legs. And they don't know a thing. They are safe and happy.

I try and fail not to think about Acadia.

Would she understand?

Am I even capable of doing this, knowing she exists?

But if I deny Mickey—for an omega, a scent match—he'll go right to Legs. His loyalty is known.

I shut the door, and Mickey grabs me and throws me up against the wall. His lips crash into mine, and it's everything in me to return the lust. But I just want my omega.

Mickey strokes my dick over my pants. And I think about Acadia to get hard.

It works, thank god.

"What do you want, Mickey boy?" I ask because I'm not in the mood to play around.

He bites my lip, and when it snaps back to me, puffy and red, he answers, "We have all night. Don't be impatient."

He gets on his knees and puts his hot mouth over my pants, onto my cock. I need more than a single joint to get me through this. Thankfully, there's a bottle of wine on the table with our names on it. Like we are on a honeymoon.

Oscar said he doesn't want me back all weekend, and Mickey will know if I don't go back home. I will have to be here all weekend. But there's no way I can keep this up for two nights. At least sober.

Mickey takes down my pants to my ankles and licks the underside of my cock.

I reach out for the wine, and thankfully, it's a screw top. I drink in three whole gulps of it and then pour some over my cock and balls for Mickey.

He loves it.

He *really* loves it.

I catch his eye and for a split second I see, instead, Mads down on his knees before me. Licking wine off my half-staff cock. Now that's an image I can use.

"Come on, beta, suck me like you mean it," I say to Mads. Not to Mickey. I never call Mickey by his designation, so it's a gamble. But it pays off because Mickey takes my now fully erect member all the way to the back of his throat.

"Fuck!"

He works me with his whole body. His hand on my balls. His whole throat squeezing my cock. He's moaning and undulating. It takes forever, but I keep imagining he's Mads, and I come. He licks up every last drop.

"Fuck, I love you calling me beta. That's hot."

I nod and go into the bathroom, shutting him out.

I don't look up at the mirror. I wash my hands and take off my clothes. Then I slowly open the bond back up so I can check in on my pack. Oscar is still asleep, but Kol is going through it.

I call him.

"Locke, it's 1:00 am," Kol says instead of hello.

"Yeah, I know, you just worried me."

He sighs. "Tell me it's going to be ok."

Kol trusts me so much, I wonder if I deserve it.

"It is. It already is. Things are ok, and they will be ok."

We sit there in silence, and I open up the bond even more. Dread and doom pass over to me.

"What're you doing?" he asks.

"I'm at a hotel. She's not out here. I'll try again in the morning."

"That's good. I'm so sorry about last night. About the omega."

"Hey, I have no leg to stand on. I shouldn't have shamed you. You were doing what you needed to do."

"Don't be so understanding when I felt your real feelings afterwards."

"Let me be a better person, Kol. I'm allowed to evolve."

He laughs, albeit a bit strained.

He tells me he should go, and I let him go. Then I look up at the mirror. My long blonde hair isn't even looking frayed. I look put together. My beard is trimmed. My eyes clear. I don't match how I feel at all. I leave to go join Mickey for the night.

20

Pressure

Mads

I consider not going to the café. I consider it while I shower, brush my teeth, iron my pants, and button up my shirt. I woke up this morning at 4:00 am because I suddenly had ideas on *if* I were to join a pack of alphas. All speculative, of course. I just accidentally gave myself room to have a little thought experiment.

I don't want to be bonded to a pack. Or whatever they want from me. But if I was forced to, then yes, I'd have some demands.

I decide to wear a tie.

And then I eat a bread and butter sandwich and take my meds. My mom is asleep. It's her day off, and she's sleeping in. So I'm being quiet as I get ready. We used to have a dog, and I almost fill the food bowl we still have out, out of habit.

Mr. Snoots died a few months back. I've debated getting my mom a new dog, but not while she's working two jobs. The plan was for me to start working again, she can cut back, and get herself a new companion animal.

I'm already out the door before I even let myself think too much on this. I decide to show up late. They can all see me hobble into the café like a fucking disaster. Maybe it'll make them change their mind and leave the broken man alone.

It's one of those cafés grandmas take their daughters to and discuss only proper things. I check in with the host, and he leads me to the table where all the alphas are. Oscar is the only one smiling. He tries to shake my hand, but I use my right hand for my cane, so there's nothing to shake. I turn and make my way around the table to the empty chair. I don't hide anything as I prepare the space for myself. Test the table to make sure it'll hold my weight. Then manipulate my body to get into the chair. All three alphas observe me with rapt attention. I sit and balance my cane against the table and the wall.

I give them a tight smile.

Yeah, fuckers, you really want this broken fucking toy to play with? Think again.

"Thank you for coming, Mads. I was getting a bit worried you'd stand us up."

I level Oscar a look like *let's not pretend I'm here on my own free will.*

The server comes over and takes our order. I order a cappuccino, a croissant with cream, and Eggs Benedict. I plan on eating it all too. Fuck these guys.

Locke keeps looking out the window, like we are expecting someone else. He's a bit unfocused. Kol won't look me in the eye. He's ashamed.

He should be.

I drink my coffee. Eat my entire giant croissant, and I ask for a second cappuccino.

The alphas have just ordered coffees and small dishes of bacon and eggs.

Finally, Oscar brings up what we are here for. "I'd love to hear about your preferences and conditions, Mads. If you've prepared them."

I wipe my mouth with a cloth napkin.

"What exactly are you asking? What are you asking me for? I need you to be clear."

It's Kol who answers. "We want to make you pack. Bonded and registered."

"With a bite?"

He snaps his teeth together and nods. He's as serious as a car crash.

"You'd be a full member. Access to our funds, data, and resources."

"For how long?" I get the reaction I want. Alphas think in terms of forever. It is a shocking question to them to assume otherwise.

"You'd be ours. Always," Locke answers. That surprises me. I haven't heard much from the younger alpha.

"Why me? And don't say it's some magical *knowing* that led you to me. I want a real answer."

Kol stops Oscar from answering by saying, "You're considering it, aren't you? Tell us what we can do to make this happen, Mads. Tell me."

I click my tongue and lean back. "I went to the police. They told me I'd need to hire private security to keep you from me. I can't afford that. So here I am, with very little options, considering this fucking insane path forward."

Then our eggs finally arrive and I eat most of my food silently. Kol takes deep breaths. He's definitely upset. It seems like he's upset because of what they are all making me do. He keeps looking at me with pity, and Oscar with scorn.

I wipe my mouth, and ask, "If I were to consider this, what can you do for me? Can you pay off my medical debt? Give my mom a monthly allowance so she can retire? Make me a partner at your company?"

All three alphas are nodding *yes* to everything I'm saying.

"I wouldn't have to fuck anyone, right? This isn't sexual?" They shake their heads. Locke is the last to shake his head, and I note that. "You said you are getting an omega?"

"A scent match," Oscar clarifies.

I don't know the details of scent matches, and I hardly care.

"Would I have to fuck her?"

"If you'd like, but she'd be the one to dictate our relationship boundaries. She most likely won't be happy about us seeing anyone outside of the pack. Intimately—sexually."

Cadi races through my mind. Their omega wouldn't want me seeing Cadi, that's what he means.

"Would I have to submit to you, Oscar, or all the alphas?"

"Just me." That's not normal. Betas are at the bottom of any pack. Even *I* know this. He's essentially saying I'd be on the same level as Kol and Locke.

I keep eating my food, and it's only on the last bite I realize I haven't once panicked about being around them. I know it's the power shift. I have something they want. But this anomaly is weakening. I look down, and my hand is starting to shake. The closer I get to losing my hold over them, the more panicked I feel.

"What about my condition?" I ask with my eyes down in my lap.

"Your physical condition?" Oscar asks.

"No, that I can't be around alphas."

"Mads," Locke says. "We all have our issues." He adjusts in his seat so he can lean in and make eye contact with me. "I go into complete shut down when an alpha uses their alpha-voice on me, or even raises his voice at me. Oscar and Kol are very understanding. I'm sure they'd be for you too. I will be."

Kol adds, "I have a severe rutting condition, Mads. I'm on medication and trying to manage it. Oscar and Locke help me every day with it. They'd never abandon me if it got bad either. They haven't so far."

I look at Oscar, who says, "I can't get work right now. My pack supports me, and I do what I can for now while we work together to solve this problem. You don't need to come to us healed. We have experience as a pack, standing together, broken as we are."

I'm stunned. My mouth hangs open. I actually had no idea what a pack was even for. Why alphas and omegas formed them. What the benefit was. I had no idea they helped each other like this.

"Are you...together?" Do they do this because they are all dating each other? I gesture between the three of them.

"No, we aren't like that in this pack," Kol answers soberly. He's not offended by my question.

I sit back in my chair and think.

Alphas form a pack and support each other like brothers. More than brothers. More than friends. They all know the best and the worst parts of each other. I know there's some deal with knowing each other's feelings or thoughts or something too. So they can't hide from each other. It's never sounded more...desirable.

We talk logistics for a little bit. They have a two bedroom apartment they are living in temporarily. They said the three of them will share a room to give me space. Once they bond to the omega, she will pick out the house we will all move to. That worries me a lot. They say I have to live with them after the bonding. We could risk bond sickness.

I ask about the likelihood that they won't bond with the omega, and they just answer, "She's Locke's scent match."

I can tell they aren't disclosing everything, but I can't really handle the information they are telling me now. I will probably need to process this all first.

"How long do I have to decide?"

Oscar answers, "We want to know now. As soon as possible."

"I need more time."

Oscar sighs.

Locke excuses himself to the bathroom. Kol and Oscar have their back to the window, so they don't see Cadi stroll past without a care in the world. My eyes go wide. I'd jump up after her, but...you know.

She looks inside absentmindedly and spots me. She does a double take. I wave and she waves back.

She's with a whole little crew of omegas. They are completely surrounded by security. She failed to mention her walks with omegas included armed security, or maybe I'm just too naive to realize they wouldn't be protected.

"Cadi," I say quietly. She keeps walking, so by the time Oscar and Kol look up, she's gone.

"Your date?" Oscar asks. He doesn't know she just walked by. This must be her neighborhood. I never asked, but it makes sense an omega complex would be in this area.

"You want me to cut off ties with her."

"Our omega may not like you dating outside the pack. It's best to not get attached until you know."

I rub my hand over my face. "The omega will decide a lot of this pack. Almost like she'll be pack lead."

It's bait. To see how Oscar handles being told he doesn't have all the power.

"An omega is the sun upon which her pack orbits."

Locke comes back to the table. He takes a long drink of his coffee. I want to know so much about the alpha. That's a weird feeling. Is this what they mean when they say they just know we are pack? Because of this ease, when we are together?

"This is what we are going to do," Oscar declares, and his alpha influence, his alpha aura, pushes out into the room. It bears down on me and everyone. Betas aren't immune to the alpha influence. It feels like being pushed down into a bow before a king. It's wholly unpleasant. "Mads, you will spend the day with Locke. You will get to know him. Tomorrow, you spend the day with Kol. And Monday, you spend the day with me. By Monday night, you should be ready, and we can bond and register you."

I'm upset about him using his influence. And I'm upset that it's not a bad plan. He wants me to actually get to know the Soto Pack and then make a more informed decision.

And they will, in turn, get to know me, and maybe we will all realize how stupid this is when we spend one-on-one time, and I'll be abandoned and can move on.

I'm thinking about it.

Oscar pulls back his influence as we all consider his plan.

"I'll go settle the bill. Locke, you stay with Mads for the day. I'll see you tomorrow, then."

Oscar and Kol stand. They don't offer their hands to shake. They just nod their heads to me. They hug their pack mate goodbye and leave.

21

First Date

Locke

The beta sits before me, unimpressed. In all his photos on social media he has black hair. This dusty brown hair is just not working for me. It's natural though. Oddly enough. His curly mouth holds all his emotions so if I want to know what he's thinking I just need to look there.

He's got a lot of thoughts.

"So, what do you do on a normal Saturday?" I ask.

He's no longer eating. I think he was eating so much because it was the only thing keeping him from having a PTSD episode. And good for him finding a coping mechanism. I look out the window. I don't see Mickey, but I know he's there. He followed me from the hotel to here. I had to wash myself twice to get off all the scents.

"Who's out there?" he asks me.

"Hm?" I feign ignorance.

"Whatever. I'm going to the pharmacy to refill my meds, and then to the library to continue to apply for jobs. You can do as you wish."

I stand up when it looks like he's going to stand up. It takes him a while. Fuck me. Watching him sit down was painful enough. Standing is just as big of a show. I give him my back and scan the café, ensuring no one is watching him. I don't need the beta bothered. I'd prefer to keep things simple.

He makes his way past me and I jump forward to stay ahead of him. I make sure the path is clear and then I open the door for him. He's a grumpy thing and doesn't even thank me. Though I don't really need a thank you.

Even though I don't know the way, I still stay ahead of him. I don't want anyone on these city streets knocking into him. I have to look back to see if he's changing directions. We get into a rhythm and I'm able to predict the way easily enough. I don't need to look for Mickey. I know he's out there.

It takes for fucking ever but we get to the pharmacy. We are in a completely different neighborhood by this point. It's been over an hour. He goes up to the window and I notice his limp is more exaggerated. The fucker could have told me where this was and I would have ordered a car.

Whatever. We will do this his way. He finds a seat at that machine that takes blood pressure and we wait for them to get his shit.

I stand above him. He massages his thigh. I could do that for him. But he'd probably lose his shit if I tried.

"Did you like your hair black?" I ask instead of 'can I kneel in front of you and rub your fucked up leg?'

He looks up at me. So brave.

"Are you stalking my social media?"

"Of course. You smiled a lot back then."

"Yeah, I was a fool."

I frown at him. He doesn't believe that. His lips twitch.

"Instead of applying for jobs at the library, something you don't need to do at all considering Kol has already offered you a perfectly good job, I could dye your hair. I'm pretty good at it. I bet this place has some dye too. Do you live around here?"

His eyebrows get all crinkly.

"You're not dying my hair, besides…"

His teeth clack shut.

I take a step away from him. Give him some space. "Besides what?"

He adjusts his leg.

"I kind of want to go the opposite direction."

"Bleach?"

He nods, but doesn't meet my eyes.

"I could do that."

He rolls his eyes, and the pharmacist calls him over for his meds. It's a lot of stuff—over $300.

I get right up behind him and ask, "How long does all that last you?"

He sighs as though I'm being so difficult. "Some of this will last all month. Others, a week. This one here, I'll need another doctor appointment before I can get it filled again. But I'm not going to be able to do that until I have insurance again."

I give him a look like I'm scared and horrified. And he playfully hits me with his shoulder on his way out the door. Or at least I hope it's playful. We get out onto the sidewalk.

"Please, god, I don't want to go to the library. Let me do your hair. You'll love it. And if you don't love it, then you can use it as a really good excuse to turn us down again."

"Tempting."

But he's slower than before. He walks closer and closer to the building until he stops completely and leans on it. I stand in front of him and then I mirror him by leaning too.

"Mads," I say.

"What?"

"I'll get us a car. We can go to your place. I'm really clean. And I'm very good. We could tone it to a really bright silver. Is that what you want? Platinum?"

He groans and closes his eyes.

I pull up the maps app and look for a beauty supply store. I put the address into the car share app, and a car is on its way. I have not heard him say no. He'll have to speak up if he doesn't want something. Like a good boy.

The car pulls up, and Mads is breathing heavily through his mouth. I think the guy is in pain, but I don't say anything. He doesn't resist me when I say our car is here. He gets right in. It's only a few blocks away.

"Where are we?"

"I just need some shit. Come on in and wait for me while I get it." He exits the car, and I do a real good job not trying to help him. The supply store has everything. The bleach. The toner. The bowls. The combs and brushes. I don't look over at Mads, in case I spook him and he stops me.

He's sweating a little. Maybe he'd stop me if he weren't on a swift decline. Am I a bad person for taking advantage of him like this? Oh, whatever, he's going to look great!

"Ok, now is the time where you actually give me your address so we can get the hell out of here," I say and hand him my phone so he can type it into the app.

"It's like a block away. We should walk."

"Fuck Mads, I'm debating throwing you over my shoulder. We can drive a block. It's not a big deal."

He can't reply. He's too busy gritting his teeth. He turns away from me and starts walking. And we walk forever. He's a fucking liar.

His place is so fucking far, *I'm* tired when we get there, and I have two functioning legs. Maybe he's trying to kill himself so he can't be bonded to my pack.

He calls for his mom when we enter the small apartment at the end of the walkway. She's not home.

It has carpet older than me. The walls are thick with white paint from the years of move ins and move outs. We can hear the neighbors on both sides watching TV or yelling at their kids. Mads pulls up an oak dining room chair and crashes into it. He adjusts his leg out in front of him and starts rubbing and stretching.

I want to help.

But I know better.

I give myself a tour. It's two bedrooms. But maybe a third the size of the place my pack has. There's a bathroom in the hall. It's too small for my alpha body. So I set up on the kitchen table.

"Can you..." he starts and then stops.

"What do you need?"

"Just the meds I brought home, I dropped them on the counter."

I walk over, grab the plastic shopping bag, and bring it to him. Then I go get him a glass of water.

He sighs and tries to stand up.

"Ok, I get it. You are so strong and brave and independent. Just tell me what you need."

He growls a little. Like a beta would. It's so cute.

"I have to take these with food. I need some bread."

There's a loaf of white bread on the counter. I pull out a plate and put a slice on it. "You want butter?"

He nods and I butter it. There's a little blue butter dish right here, so I'm assuming this is something he does often.

"Two slices. Please."

I slide the finished plate to him, and he puts the slices together like a sandwich and eats them like it's his job. Then he proceeds to take four different pills.

I'm utterly fascinated, honestly. If he ever lets me take care of him, I could do such a great fucking job. He'd barely even notice. This takes so much mental energy. No wonder he hasn't smiled since I've known him. This shit is exhausting.

I find a towel in the hall closet and bring it over.

"Ok, I'm bleaching your hair. This is your opportunity to tell me to stop. Because as soon as I mix this bleach, it's going somewhere."

He levels me a look. A challenge. But says nothing.

"Ok, just sit there. Don't be difficult. If you can manage."

I lay the towel around his shoulders and get to work.

It's late, and Mads is showering. I'm guessing, based on the stool in the shower, it'll be a while, so I step out of the apartment. I walk down the walkway and sit on the steps.

Mickey joins me like he'd been waiting for this opportunity.

He looks pissed off.

"I'm going to ask you once, and I want a full fucking answer. We aren't playing 20 questions here. If I want you to jerk me around, I'll take my pants off."

Oh yes, he's pissed. I look to the sky for strength. A tornado of seagulls spirals above us in the pink sky.

"Are you courting a beta? Is the Soto Pack courting a fucking beta?"

As the smart man I am, I keep my mouth shut.

"What the fuck are you thinking? You are behaving so unbelievably *bad*. I thought moving here was to find an omega so you could fulfill your stupid agreement with Legs! We are weeks away. Days even! And you are in there for hours with a beta! Are you trying to hurt me? Is that what this is?"

He's yelling way too loud, so I stand up and grab him by the collar, pulling his face to mine.

"I don't work for you. You aren't special. My actions have nothing to do with you. Get that through your fucking skull! How I choose to spend my last few weeks of life has nothing to do with you. If I want to court a beta, I will court a beta."

"Fuck you!"

"Fuck you, Mickey!"

"You do everything wrong, Locke, and I have to watch it! You get involved with Oscar Soto. Who's a weak, bitch-ass alpha! You flirt with a rabid alpha, and he fucking dark bonds you! And now, Legs has no choice but to kill them to get you back. And who do you think he's going to make do that?! And now you are screwing around with some cripple beta…" I drop one of my hands so I can wind it back and punch him in the face. He doesn't react. He takes it. Like a good goon.

But he does spit right into my face.

"Are you in love with him?"

"I'm not in love with you—"

His hands grab my shirt and haul me closer. He's going to kiss me. I push him away and hit him until he releases me.

Mickey peels his lips into a cruel smile, laughing, and then gestures behind me. Fuck. Fuck!

"What the fuck is going on?" Mads asks from behind me.

Mickey spits at my feet, fixes his clothes, and then tries to walk away.

"Are you going to tell him?"

"You're dead either way."

I can't have him telling him a moment too soon. We are so close.

"Meet me tonight. Same place. Please, Mickey. Please."

Mickey is a fucking sucker. He loves this.

"Fine."

"Go now. I will meet you there soon. Go!"

Mickey chews on his tongue, giving me the dirtiest look like I am absolute scum, and then leaves.

I turn around to face Mads, who's on the top of the stairs looking down at me. His white hair is still a bit wet but looks fucking awesome. He's not leaning so hard on his cane.

"What's going on?"

"Nothing," I mumble.

"Who was that?"

I think he actually wants to know.

22
Bleach

Mads

I try so hard not to let him see the goosebumps erupting over my entire body as he works on my hair. His hands are both strong and gentle. He's confident in his movement. I have to suck in my lips so I can keep from...making any weird noises. He wraps my hair in plastic and we wait.

I don't know why I'm letting him do this.

I did want my hair done, and he did offer. I'd been considering bleaching it for a while, but I just couldn't afford it, and it seemed like a waste. Having Locke do it did make sense.

He keeps looking out the window like someone is right outside.

Locke has me lean forward over the sink while he uses the sprayer to rinse me. Then he puts the toner on.

I tell him I'm just going to take a shower so we are no longer on top of each other. Touching everywhere. Everywhere it doesn't matter.

I don't take long. And when I come out, he's gone.

The front door is unlocked, so I go outside to see where he's gone off to. That's when I see him and another man embracing. Or fighting. They look like lovers. Angry and sexually charged.

"...if I want to court a beta, I will court a beta!" I hear Locke shout.

"Fuck you!" the other man spits at him.

I stand there in horror as I hear things I couldn't have come up with in a million years.

He's fighting with a beta. A rough looking beta. He looks like a gangster. The gangster talks about Kol and Oscar getting killed. And then he asks if he's...I can't even say it. He's *in love* with me?

The man eventually spots me and leaves. Like he's been caught.

"Who was that?" I ask. Is he a secret lover?

Locke isn't going to answer me. His head is hanging low, and he won't give me his attention.

"Like you care."

"Like *I* care? What the fuck is going on?" This gets his attention. "Was it all some fucking lie this morning? Are you hustling me? Oh my god. Of course you are. I don't even have two functioning legs! I have no money! I'm not an omega! What the fuck do you want for me?"

I don't stick around to hear his reply. I turn and "run" back to the apartment. He just strides behind me. Keeping a distance and pretending this isn't so damned pathetic.

If they needed a beta for anything, why me? Why me? Apparently, that ugly guy named Mickey with the leathery skin couldn't fill in for me.

Are you in love with him? Why would he ask that? Why is everything to do with alphas so fucking dramatic?

I try to shut the door behind me, but Locke just throws his weight into it. It nearly breaks, and I turn around fucking pissed. He's not going to break shit in my mother's apartment!

"Who was that?"

Locke shuts the door and storms up to me.

"The fucking devil, Mads."

"Get out of my house."

"Not likely. We have to bond you. I'm not playing anymore. Get it around your pretty little skull. You are bonding with my pack as soon as possible."

I wait. I wait for a goddamned explanation.

"That was Mickey," Locke finally confesses. "A muscle for Legs O'Bannon. He has this fucking delusional plan that includes me bonding his omega daughter on her 19th birthday. Which is, unfortunately, next fucking Friday."

He sighs, realizing I'm still waiting for an explanation. And then he launches into a very long insane story about scent matches, Institute preferences, deals with gangsters and mob bosses...

Essentially, they need me to be eligible to speak to an omega. They need the omega to prevent Locke from an unwanted marriage (or whatever alphas and omegas get involved in). And he's not actually dark bonded like Mickey accused, he tells me.

I crash down onto the broken couch.

I rub my face over and over.

"I shouldn't have asked..."

Locke laughs darkly.

"I don't want to be involved in any of this."

Locke sits on the armchair near the couch.

"Can I ask you something?"

I make a noise like *sure*.

"Do you not feel what we feel? A connection. A pull. A familiarity?"

I shake my head back and forth. My hands are still on my face. It's a lie. I do feel something. And I don't want to give it a name. Then it would be real.

"Can you do me a favor and not tell Oscar or Kol about Mickey? I've been doing favors for Mickey so he doesn't tell his boss everything we've been up to. I've been protecting my pack, and I'd like to keep my shame."

And shame is what I see on his face. It feels like a privilege to be shown this. I'm not sure I've ever trusted someone the way he trusts me in this moment.

Until the incident, I always kept people at arm's length with jokes and good humor. I didn't think it was a mask at the time, but seeing how close all three of these men are and what they are willing to do for each other, makes me realize I've never seen such love and devotion. I've never shown it and I've never felt it.

I don't say yes, but he gets that I will keep his secret.

He stands up and heads for the door. He turns the handle on the door but before he opens it he says, "Your hair looks great. Thanks for letting me do that. If you choose to stay with us, after knowing this, I promise to take care of you. I've been dying to do it all day. I probably won't be able to stop myself next time. I have to go calm Mickey down. Take care."

I pop my head up to see the look on his face. Genuine. He's being genuine.

He leaves, shutting the door gently behind him.

There's no way. There's no way on this green earth I can go through with this.

I pull my phone out. I have a text from Oscar checking in. I have an email from Kol asking my opinion on a project for one of his properties.

Which I desperately want to review and give him my opinion. But instead I call Cadi.

"Hello?"

"Hey, Cadi. How's your night?"

I can hear her breathy smile. "Good. I saw you today."

"I saw *you* today."

"You were having brunch with alphas."

I smile. I love hearing her voice. It's so calming. It's slowly erasing all the intensity of the day.

"Yeah, I think I'm being courted."

"Oh goodness. I'm an omega and I'm not even being courted. I have to admit that's got me a little jealous, Mads."

She's halfway serious, I can tell.

So I decide to tease her.

"Maybe I'll put in a good word."

"Oh will you? Make sure to tell them how pretty I am. Alphas love that."

"Is that why they like me?"

"Probably. You are very good looking, Mads."

This girl.

"Stop. Things like that will make my head big."

"Will it make other things big too?"

A smile I haven't felt all day spread across my face. "You are in a saucy mood, Cadi."

She laughs and I ask about her day. It sounded really nice and normal and nothing like my day. I don't want to tell her about my shit so I keep her talking about her stuff. Her gossip. Her worries. Her friends. This event she's doing on Tuesday at the Omega Women's Shelter. And soon we've been talking for an hour.

She is like a breath of fresh air.

"Where are you now?" I ask, lying back on the couch.

"My nest."

Fuck me, the way she says that goes right to my cock. Omegas. Absolutely infuriating how sexy I find them. She has her own special little space she gets horny in. "I bet it's so comfortable in there. Do you have the best nest out of all your omega friends?"

"How would you know? You've probably never been in a nest before."

"You do, don't you. It's probably so soft and nice. Anyone would be lucky to get invited into your nest."

She's preening. "Shut up, Mads," she says with no heat. I bet she's blushing. "You know," she says with a low husky voice, "I've never invited anyone into my nest before."

"Does phone sex count?" I ask, jumping the gun. My hand is already rubbing my cock over my pants.

"I've never done that either. You're my first, Mads."

All the blood in my brain is now gone.

"I love how you say my name. You are so sexy. What would you do with me if I was in your nest?"

She sighs, but it hitches. She's turned on. Oh my god. What is happening?

"Clothes aren't allowed in here, so you'd have leave those behind."

"Do you have clothes on, Cadi? Or are you ready for me?" She makes another pretty, little sound. "Are you touching yourself?"

"Yes," she whispers.

"If I was there that would be my hand on your pussy. My mouth would be on your neck. Do you like your hair pulled, Cadi?"

"Yes, I like it a bit rough."

"I can do rough, duchess. My fingers deep in your pussy and sucking hard on your nipples."

I can hear her moving around and shuffling sounds through the receiver.

"What else do you like?"

"Threesomes," she answers quickly. Oh goddamn.

I find myself describing a threesome for her. Her and another omega, a female, wake up to me fucking her and fingering her friend. This imaginary friend sucks and pinches her nipples while I fuck her slow and rough.

I take her through the fantasy until we are both coming through the receiver. She's panting and whispering things like, "Oh my god, Mads. My skin is on fire. What the fuck. Oh my god, I feel so good."

And I whisper back, "You are so fucking hot. You take my cock so well. Like a good omega."

We stay on the phone for a while after we finish, just listening to each other breathe. I could fall asleep like this. I feel so close to her, even though we are a city apart.

23

Romancing

Kol

I get an email from Mads around midnight giving me his thoughts on the project. He shared some articles about similar projects that didn't do so well. He gave some feedback on if we did it anyway, how we could improve, and then presented his own ideas. God, reading through his email is like porn.

Well, not like *porn*, porn. But it was sexy as hell.

Locke is still out looking for our omega. I miss him. I don't like it when the pack is separated.

Mads is a long shot. I could tell he was trying really hard to be around us. Apparently, eating half the restaurant is what is needed to tolerate me.

In the morning, I take my Wrangler out to his place.

I text him that I'm here before walking up to his apartment. It's pretty early, and I don't want to scare him.

I'm kind of nervous.

Oscar asked me if I felt like I needed the muzzle today. I told him that if I went nuts and bit the beta, it might save us a step. He didn't think it was funny.

I bit Locke. With a permanent, sealing bonding mark.

I knew he was ours. And I was not in the right headspace. The alpha took over. Back then my blood wasn't pumping a hardened cocktail of suppressants 24/7.

Oscar wanted him too, which is what made it especially hard to resist. I was the one who bridged the gap and made it happen.

And, may I add, he was not dark bonded, so that means the little shit wanted it. I just made it happen a little faster than everyone was comfortable with.

I gently knock on the door and I hear him make his way to it. Slowly. Everything with the beta teaches me patience. Something I'm not well equipped for. The moment I make up my mind, I want to act. It's unnerving to wait for the rest of the world to catch up.

He opens up the door and he's not dressed.

Granted, the sky is still pink with the sunrise. The birds are singing their morning songs. The air is wet and cool.

He's in black underwear and a thin white undershirt. And I see his leg. Fuck. It is absolutely fucked. Shiny, healed skin. Oddly shaped. Coloring is all off. I don't worry about offending him with my assessment of him. I need to know everything about him. But when my eyes finally meet his, I see how unhappy he is about my actions.

"Kol," he says tightly.

And then I notice his hair. He's got white hair. Oh my god it's amazing. It makes his whole face stand out, no longer washed out. Did I know he had honey brown eyes? They are so intense they look like amber stone. What the fuck am I looking at?

He doesn't look amused.

I snap my jaw closed.

"Good morning, Mads. Can I come in?"

His eyebrow quirks up, but then he lets the door go and turns around, letting me into the apartment.

And it's a terrible little place.

But he won't be here for long.

"I have a few ideas for us for today," I say as I follow him to the kitchen table. It's a little thing. Oak. Probably his mom's. There's a pile of seashells as decoration in the middle.

He sits down with a hiss.

"You live with your mom?" I ask.

"Yeah, she's not here though. Yesterday was her day off and she spent the night with a friend. She'll probably stop by here soon to get ready for work."

"What does she do?"

"She sells shoes. She works at two different shoe stores since she needs more hours. The one that doesn't give her a lot of hours gives her health insurance. The other one gives her hours. Plus I think she likes the discount from both stores."

I want to jump the gun and tell him to give us her banking info so we can start her monthly transfers. It's part of his demands for being pack. But he looks tired and not in the mood for that conversation.

He also smells.

"Want to take a shower and we can get out of here?"

He sighs and leans back in his chair.

"Alphas," he mutters under his breath. And then to me he asks, "Where are you taking me?"

"I have a few ideas. We can work. I can rent out an office for the day and we can go through my portfolio, my fiscal year goals, and take care of some projects I'm behind on. But you'd need to agree to be employed by me by this point. You've already worked too many hours for free."

He makes no indication that he wants to do that today. His usually scalloped mouth is all straight.

"If you let me really be myself with you, I'd like to take you to buy a car. Locke told me about your walk around this city which sounded like hell."

"Did Locke also tell you I know he's being threatened? And you two as well?"

I purse my lips. "Yes."

"What happens if I agree to this and that gangster comes around and kills you all?"

"You can keep the car, and then move on with your life, I guess," I answer truthfully.

He thinks I'm joking. At least I got a little laugh out of him.

"If you are pack, you'll inherit everything we have. Honestly, it's a win."

He shakes his head, again, like I'm being silly. But it's true. If Legs comes around and takes us out, everything will go to him.

"What does your portfolio look like?"

"Eight million dollars in assets. I have one million short-term. And so much in cash right now. I had to sell everything in Salt Port. I'm flushed. Which is why I was trying to hire you. I need help getting it out of cash and into something. Everyday I'm losing value."

"A car is a terrible investment," he says.

And now I smile. It's true. They lose all their value until it's worth nothing. Which is why we aren't big car people. We each have a vehicle and that's it. The Soto Pack doesn't care for the idea of wealth. Only actual wealth.

I'm also not talking about the money my pack has. Only my business.

"What did you mean," he starts and then stops. I tip my head to the side, confused and wanting him to continue. He clicks his tongue and says, "What did you mean, 'if I was myself with you.' Locke said the same thing last night. If he was allowed to be himself he'd *take care of me.*"

I can't help but chuckle at imagining how difficult it was for Locke to not get to fuss over someone.

"Well, we are trying not to scare you with our alpha tendencies."

"Your alpha tendencies want to buy me a car?"

I stare him straight in the eyes. "Yes."

He sighs like he's lived a thousand lives and then stands up. "I'm going to shower. And then maybe I'll let you buy me a cup of coffee."

The alpha in me preens. I would love to buy him a coffee. It's a total win. While he's in the shower, I rummage around the place. It looks like most things are his mother's. Older furniture. Cute decorations, mostly "goose" themed.

The fridge is full of containers. Looks like they save a lot of leftovers.

Before he comes back out I've make him a butter sandwich.

Yes, I did ask for all the details from Locke. So did Oscar.

He stares at it for a while before he moves over to the counter and pulls out his medication, counting out his pills. He takes it with water. Then eats the sandwich.

"Ok, let's go. There's a coffeehouse on the water I like. We can drive to it."

He sighs, acquiescing to my plans. And then follows me out, locking up behind himself. I walk in front of him, ensuring the path is clear and no one is around to bother him. No one pays him any attention, which is good. I'm not sure I could keep my protective instincts subdued.

Courting is serious business for an alpha. It affects every part of him.

The object of my desire is in its most precarious position—not yet mine. I have to show Mads that I am strong enough to protect him. Clever enough to lead him. Discernible and stalwart. I want to show him my fucking muscles. Make him aware how tall I am. Taller than others around us. I want to gift him his true heart's desire. I have so much nervous energy building inside of me I'm afraid I may burst.

So after he gets into the car, I take a few deep breaths and try to fucking relax.

If I give into this instinct, I'll end up scenting him, neck to neck. Licking his face. Rubbing my body on his. So every alpha will know he's mine.

But I don't think Mads would appreciate that.

I slide into the driver's seat and smile at him. I wish he'd smile back, but he just kind of scowls at me.

"Your hair," I start to give him a compliment, but he stops me right away with, "Can we just get going?"

I shut my mouth and turn over the engine.

Fair enough.

24

Working Lunch

Kol

We park at the river walk, and I gesture towards the coffeehouse. It's strangely crowded. I guess Saturday morning is a busy time for a place like this. We can order coffees at the counter, or wait 45 minutes for a table. Mads won't look me in the face. His jaw is tight, and he's not interested in giving me his opinion on our situation. I put our names in for a table, and we stand outside with the other waiting patrons.

I've got my backpack with me, with my laptop and things I need for work. I was hoping he'd relax a little if we got to do some work together, but I'm doubting that. No wonder Locke went dark last night after he left his place. I'd also need to decompress after this. This being, feeling so out of sorts. I want to charm him, help him, or just relax him, and yet nothing I do is getting me the reactions I want.

"Have you been here before?" I ask.

"Yeah."

I suck in a breath through my teeth. This is going to be a long day.

The table really does take 45 minutes. And we stand there out front the entire time hardly saying a word. He got his phone and was texting someone for a while and that seemed to relax him so I didn't say anything.

We sit down, and he does his ordering thing where he tries to piss me off, or something. He orders an iced mocha and a double espresso. He orders several pastries and a bagel with cream cheese. Also, a tall glass of orange juice mixed with pomegranate juice. I don't know if I should pretend this is egregious behavior to encourage it or not. Because I absolutely love it. I want him to be spoiled.

I keep my face neutral while I order a drip coffee and my own bagel.

"Who have you been texting?" My jealousy gets the best of me.

He sighs and adjusts his leg. I wonder if it hurt standing all that time.

"I'm just confirming my date tonight."

"With the omega?"

He nods.

Instead of telling him he needs to break things off with her, I say, "What are you going to do on your date?"

"There's an art house in her neighborhood playing an old vampire movie she likes. And then there's an ice cream place nearby I'll probably take her to after."

I can't help finding so much joy in what he's saying, watching him light up talking about the woman. "That sounds very nice. You like her?"

"Yeah, Kol. I know you all want me to stop dating her, and while I will take that under consideration, it's ultimately my choice."

"And hers," I point out.

"What?"

"Well, maybe she wouldn't want to date you if your pack has a scent match. Have you asked her? Omegas are very sensitive."

It clearly hadn't occurred to him.

"I told her I was being courted."

"But you didn't tell her the whole truth."

He's a thousand miles away in thought when his items start to arrive. Omegas are demanding, selfish, and greedy little things. It's what makes alphas crawl all over themselves to serve. When Mads shows any of those behaviors, I come close to salivating. But does he like those qualities in someone? Maybe this omega is hiding her true nature from him. Maybe she's putting herself in a little box that a beta can safely digest. Would he run the moment she's herself?

I pull out my laptop and while we eat I force him to do work with me. It only takes him a single problem before he's in it. We go back and forth about each endeavor. He's well fed and we are flowing. We take up the table for two hours, but I tell the first server we can close out and start up with a new server, so she can go home. We order another round of drinks. Mads needs to get up for the restroom and I hover around him like a bodyguard. He hates it but I have to do it. I have to stand by the bathroom door and make sure he isn't bothered if he takes a while. My theory was correct, if he's well fed he's less inclined to be grumpy about my alpha tendencies.

I saw his house and his fridge. I doubt he's been well fed for a while.

Seeing how badly he's limping when he comes out of the bathroom gives me an idea.

We pack up our things and go stand by the car.

"Are we not getting in?"

I'm typing on my phone. "No, there's not great parking at the gym. We will order a car."

"The gym?"

"Yeah, we have memberships at an alpha gym. There's one nearby. They have hot tubs and saunas. I'm registering you as my guest for the day. Hold on."

Betas can enter the gym as a guest if accompanied by alpha. I've seen them all the time. It shouldn't be a problem.

"Hot tub?"

"Yeah, it's more like a hot pool, I'd say. They have an accessibility machine, if you want to use it to get in. Or I can just punch anyone in the face who gives you a weird look. I'd prefer the second one, honestly..." my voice trails off as I confirm the car. I got the upgraded one. It arrives shortly after I approve it, and Mads and I get in the back.

"I don't have a swimsuit."

"They have them there."

He makes a little irritated noise, but doesn't ask any more questions.

They are expecting us when we arrive so Mads doesn't get any shit. I scheduled us a spot and filled everything out prior. They get him his branded swim trunks, and we go to the locker room. Locke, Oscar, and I have lockers here. I take a second to smell their locked doors. I get tiny images of the two of them. Oscar smells of rich Colombian coffee brewing on a cool morning. Locke has a salty-sea smell.

"What're you doing?" Mads asks me.

I open my eyes and see him staring at me curiously.

"These are Oscar and Locke's. I can kind of smell them. We don't like being apart for long, and I haven't seen Locke since yesterday morning."

"He didn't go home last night?"

"Oscar has him out looking for our scent match omega. It's a low probability he'll run into her again, but we are running out of time."

Mads looks very confused. And conflicted. I'm waiting for another question but it doesn't come.

I open my locker and start undressing. I can feel Mads behind me. Watching but not watching. He's not breathing. I would turn around to see if he's dying, but I'm afraid that may speed up the process. His rented locker is across from mine, but I don't hear him opening it or undressing. As soon as my underwear is gone and my ass is out I hear fumbling with the locker door.

I keep my laughing to myself as I put on my swim trunks. I turn around to see only his shirt off.

"Do you need help?" I ask.

"Fuck off," he says with performative heat.

He sets his cane on the bench and fiddles with his belt. His eyes meet mine and his eyebrows raise. "Are you just going to stare at me while I get my dick out?"

I shrug.

He mumbles something like *Oh my fucking god, this fucking alpha*.

He turns around and drops his pants. I am having too much fun to give up now. Finally, he gets naked and I take a second to enjoy the view. But then I see the scars all down his lower back and his thigh. The skin is shiny and marred with both jagged, violent lines, as well as straight, exact scars from surgeries. His muscle on his thigh looks like chunks of it were removed. He slides on his swim trunks. I didn't even get a chance to appreciate how hung he was.

His face turns to mine, and we share a look.

"My scars are visible right now. I'd appreciate not being a spectacle or gawked at." He doesn't mean by me. He means by strangers here at the club. I nod in understanding.

We walk to the pool and I take a protective position around him. My eyes constantly scan to make sure no one is paying us attention. I don't get so lucky when we get to the steps leading down into the water. He needs to put away his cane. And he'll need to hold onto me. We don't say it out loud. I just take his cane and set it on a bench with our towels, and then I return and hold out my arm. He grips me tight. He needs my support. It's not for show. The men in the hot water watch us. I note their emotionless faces. They are just curious, but it doesn't stop me from baring my teeth at them silently. Most get the message and look away. Each step is precarious. Eventually we get down into the water and he's able to let go. His face is bright red. I find us a private spot on the edge of the pool where we settle in.

"This feels good," he whispers.

I bet. I bet his leg always has some weight on it, but under this heated water, he's able to actually relax.

The place is pretty crowded so it would be hard to have a private conversation, so I don't push for it. Mads lets his leg soak. I continue to give the other alphas in the water my death glare. After an hour and half he indicates he wants to get out. We get some water bottles and then go into the sauna for a while.

After leaving, he seems so loopy, I wish I could convince him at this moment to let me bite him. My teeth ache for it. My jaw is loose. What I wouldn't give just to scrape the sharp ends of my fangs across his bare skin...

We both take cold showers to close our pores and wake ourselves up. And to calm myself down.

25

The Faircastle House

Kol

It's well into the afternoon at this point. I think my day with the beta is going well. I am hopeful showing Mads that we can be normal guys who can spend a normal, no nonsense day together is possible. I'm an alpha, but I can also be a friend. He's got to know at the end of the day we are all humans, designations be damned.

"Hungry?" I ask. It would be an early dinner. He nods his head, still a bit tired.

We get dressed and head out. There's lot of good food spots nearby so I let him pick. He lands on a pizza-by-the-slice place. He eats nearly a whole pie, and I enjoy the show.

Next, I take him to an Irish pub for a drink. I answer emails and he texts that omega. I enjoy being near him. I could do this all the time. He orders a basket of fries along with his beer.

"So there's a historic building, the Faircastle House, I'd like to check out. It's up for sale for a fraction of what I think it's worth. It can go either commercial or stay a single-family home. After this do you want to check it out?"

"Yeah, and then I'll need to take off. Where is it at?"

I tell him the neighborhood.

"Oh, that's right where my date will be. Maybe I'll have her meet us there. She's in omega housing and she says her handler is very nosey, and she would prefer we meet somewhere. So, this is perfect."

I don't point out that Mads is freely giving me information I didn't explicitly ask for. That he's comfortable enough with me, he can just say what he wants to say. I think my day with him was a success. I didn't dye his hair a sexy white or get him his meds. But I think I did good.

I call Oscar who is at home working on some project for the pack. He's taking inventory of all our things and seeing what he needs to make sure Mads and the omega will feel like we have enough for them. Cups and plates. Forks and spoons. Throw blankets. Toothbrushes.

"I think we need to have a place ready to go. I know there's a lot up in the air, but Locke seems to think we need a house. Which made me start to look into it."

"I agree. I'm not sure we can even convince Mads to live with us for a while in the apartment. He needs quite a bit of space. You, me, and Locke can share a bed and be fine. I think Mads would be terrified," I say right in front of Mads who doesn't refute my conclusions. "I'll be home later and we can start looking at some listings. Something with a nest."

Even just saying that gets me so excited I have to adjust my legs. I just fucked that omega. I shouldn't be this horny again. That reminds me.

"Oscar, my teeth were aching earlier."

He makes a thoughtful sound and then asks me, "Muzzle?"

"I've got it."

"Would Mads put it on you?" I need someone to help me into it. It has a lock and the combination is only visible from the back and randomized, so they need to be able to see it to ensure it's locked. I wouldn't want it slipping off at the wrong time.

I tell him I don't know, and he doesn't push it.

Oscar runs a few more things by me, and then we hang up. I've got the check paid and we leave. The house is in another neighborhood, but Mads insists on walking. We are slow, but he doesn't seem in pain.

"So, today wasn't so bad, right?"

His face is soft. No scowl. No tight jaw.

"Not so bad. I've been dreaming about a hot tub, actually. My bathtub at the apartment doesn't fit my whole body."

I preen. I made the beta feel good. I gave the beta his dream.

We come upon the historical house, and both of us pause in awe. It's this chateauesque, medieval mansion with turrets, red stone, and leaded windows.

"I've never seen a Queen Anne Victorian home like this," Mads says.

"It's quite striking," I agree.

The listing agent greets us and lets us in. She says she has to leave, and to lock up when we go. We both wander the halls. She left us with a leaflet that talked about how the family was from Scotland. They had a pack of seven alphas. One omega. Twelve children. It was restored by an arts council in the 1970s but has sat unused for the last fifteen years. I guess it's just a lot of upkeep. And the city has shut off utilities to it until it can get back to code. But it is gorgeous. Original oak floors and staircases. Adobo walls. Stained glass. The tiling in all the bathrooms is a work of art.

"You can't buy this," Mads tells me from the piano room up front. There's a fireplace with a window above it. From the outside, you can see the flue splits in two to go around the window.

"No," I agree.

"A large organization would need to take this on."

"Yeah," I say. Still in awe.

"But damn."

"But damn."

I look over at the beta. He looks fresh and younger. He has a slight glow about him. I did that. My eyes catch on his pulse at his neck. Thumping lazily. I don't notice the ache in my canines until I close my mouth from salivating.

"Mads," I say to get his attention. He's busy looking at the details in the wood trim. Beehives and wildflowers carved into it.

"Hm," he replies.

"I need you to do a quick favor for me," I say. My voice is steady. He makes another "hm" sound.

"In my bag, that I left by the front door, there's a pocket in the front. The bigger pocket. Please retrieve the item in there." I have to say each word deliberately, otherwise I may start growling.

This gets his attention. Mads looks me over, and something innate triggers in him. His eyes blow wide and his pulse thumps harder. He slowly backs away from me and towards the front door.

Instead of running away, a possibility, he gets my muzzle from the bag.

"Kol," he calls out to me, "What is this?"

"Please," I beg. I'm hunched over, gripping the edge of a covered wingback chair, when he returns.

"It's a muzzle. Can you assist in putting it on?" I have to keep my language formal to counterbalance the absolute hell my body is going through. The alpha in me is pacing. Snapping his teeth. Snarling. Growling. Salivating. It wants me to bite the beta. *Bite the beta*.

"Yeah, sure," he says. He comes up to me and I kneel in front of him.

"Go behind me. There's a locking mechanism. It's not hard to figure out."

Mads walks around me, hesitates, then places the muzzle over my face. It sits over my nose and just above my chin. The leather wraps up to the ears. His cold fingers carefully, and respectfully, I notice, twist the lock into place. He tightens it well.

I breathe easy.

"Kol, why do you need that?"

I sit back on my ankles. Mads walks around back to my front, to meet my eyes.

"I have a biting problem. It's fairly well managed."

"You've bitten someone?"

I lower my eyes so he knows my shame.

"Who?"

"Locke."

He barks out a laugh.

"I'm sure he didn't mind."

"Maybe you don't understand. I gave him a bonding bite. It didn't turn into a dark bond, so there was enough of him who maybe didn't mind. But it was not approved by Oscar, my alpha. And I didn't ask Locke's permission. The whole thing was...chaos."

I hear a little "oh" from Mads.

After a long pause, he asks, "Am I in danger?"

I meet his eyes again. Not answering.

Eventually, I say, "Don't worry, you're safe now." I stand up. "I'll get my things and leave you to meet your omega for your date.

"Wait, Kol, are you ok?" He takes a step away from me.

"I'll be fine. I'm going right home. Oscar knows what to do."

"Should I," he pauses. He's conflicted. Should he help me or leave me like this? "Should I call him?"

"No, I'm leaving."

But Mads is in the doorway. So, I can't leave.

He's conflicted. My mask bothers him. A lot.

"I'm sorry, but you're going to have to explain the muzzle thing to me again. I'm just not understanding."

"Mads, it's fine. Ok? I bite. And this prevents that from happening. For the last couple of hours my teeth have been aching. And I've been feeling...bitey. Like with Locke, I could go a little rogue, and I know you'd never forgive me."

"What happened with Locke?"

"Oscar and I were at the O'Bannon pack house negotiating terms with Legs about dissolving my little business I had going with him. I noticed Locke. Oscar did too. We propositioned him privately, but he declined. He was Legs's ward. Additionally, Legs promised him to his own daughter. It was some power move to keep growing his pack in Salt Port. But he was ours. And the alpha in me knew he was ours. We'd finished negotiations, and I'd gone to the pack house to say goodbye, I swear. I was just planning on saying goodbye. But when I saw him, I attacked. I sank my teeth so far into his arm they couldn't pull me off of him.

"I'm trying to be honest here. But I don't regret it. That move, while absolutely crazy, saved him. Oscar was only worried I'd dark-bonded him. But when the bite mark came out silver, I'd known my alpha knew all along Locke wanted the bond."

"You gambled, and you won."

Of course, I gambled, but I'd do it again. My alpha is never wrong. The only reason I hold back is for my pack lead. I'm a loyal dog, even if I bite.

"And was he the only one you wanted to bite?"

"No, when I get into a rut, there's a possibility my alpha could take over and bite someone. I wear a muzzle when the urge kicks up."

"You're afraid you'll bite me?" He is so brave.

"Stop asking me questions you know the answer to."

"Answer the question, Kol."

I huff in frustration.

"Yes, I will bite you if I don't take precautions."

"Will it hurt?"

My head tips so far to the side that my ear meets my shoulder. What did he just ask me?

Will it hurt? Not, *would it hurt.*

My mouth prepares itself for a bite I won't allow it to have. Saliva edges out of my mouth. The pain in my teeth travels up my skull. I remember how good it felt to bite Locke. Sometimes he lets me put my mouth back on the bite. It eases me. Maybe I should seek him out rather than Oscar.

A feminine voice calls out from the front of the house, "Hello? Mads?"

Mads and I twist our heads towards the voice and then back to each other. Oh my god, his omega is here.

"Mads?" She calls again, this time closer. He's not saying anything. I'm not saying anything.

She calls out a third time and then steps right behind him. Mads is still staring at me. Wide-eyed. What would he have me do? I can't bull him over and run away.

He turns to face her, slowly.

"Hey, we were just finishing up."

He steps to the side, and I finally get a good look at her. And my heart skips a beat.

At the club, I never even got a good look at her face, and yet I recognize her instantly.

My hand shoots up my chest, and I take a step back, gasping. Her eyes widen, and her mouth parts.

"Oh my god," she says.

"It's you," I reply.

Mads whips his head back and forth between us.

"What's going on?"

26

It's Happening

Acadia

It's him. The man from the club. The man who fucked me within an inch of my life. Who gave me the first and second best orgasms I've ever experienced. God, he's tall. He's what you imagine when you imagine an alpha.

He's every omega's wet dream. I can't stop staring at all the parts of him. His broad shoulders. His trim waist. His formidable thighs. The way he stands like I could leap into his arms and he wouldn't even sway. And that's exactly what I want to do—leap into his arms. Mads stands between us, very confused.

He has no idea what this alpha and I are to each other. Just a few days ago, Mads was very surprised I was an omega. He's about to get a severe wake up call on what that means, because there's no way Kol is going to not smell me. And I'm very turned on. Mads, who I have been drooling over all week, stands next to my dream man. The omega in me is purring. I'm purring too.

The alpha is wearing a muzzle, just like that night. I thought it was some kinky, sex thing. But here he is, holding a computer bag, wearing slacks and a button-up, with a muzzle.

"Hello?" I ask again. "I'm sorry to interrupt. Mads, I decided to walk in. I hope that's ok."

"Yes, of course. I'm so sorry." Mads walks over to me and gives me a hug. A very awkward hug. Like it's the first time meeting. He turns around and gestures to the alpha in the room beyond, "This is...He's...um. He's..."

"Your friend?" I offer.

"Omega. My name is Kol," the alpha says. Oh, his voice causes me to slick immediately. He bows his head generously. I walk toward him without thought. I'm pulled to him by some unseen force. I can't stop myself. Mads stays at my side. I love the way Mads walks with his cane. His side to side motion. He's like the ocean waves next to me. Calming and sure.

Kol still has his head bowed when I stand before him. I can tell the moment he smells me because his eyes blow wide.

And then he falls to his knees, bowing before me.

"Please forgive me," he says.

"Kol, what're you doing?" Mads asks in shock.

I place my hand on his head, slightly moving my fingers to feel his lush brown hair.

"What am I forgiving you for?"

"I'm going to take him from you. He's mine, omega."

"Her name is Cadi, and I'm not yours," Mads says from my side. His defense is nice, but not needed.

I sink my fingers further into his hair.

He can't take my new beta from me. I'm just starting to like play-acting as beta lovers. He can't take him from me. That's silly.

Kol reaches out and places his hand around my ankle, steadying himself. I close my eyes and huff out a breath at the contact. His thumb strokes the inside of my ankle.

"Mads, I know this alpha," I decide he needs to know this small piece of information before anything more happens. I feel like I'm on a path and it would be very difficult at this point to turn around.

"You two know each other? Do most...alphas and omegas know each other?"

I laugh at his question. I can't help it. "No. Mads. Come on."

"Sorry."

"We hooked up at a dance club."

"Oh," he says with an elongated "o" sound.

"He wore a muzzle that night, too. What's this for, alpha?" I bring my hand down and stroke the leather strap. He leans into my hand.

He isn't answering right away, so Mads answers for him, "He said he was feeling bitey. His pack wants to bond me. We spent the day together, and when we got to this house, he was worried he'd take matters into his own...teeth."

I follow the strap with the blade of my finger, over the slope of his ear and into his hair.

"I would have bitten you that night," Kol admits to me with a low, broken tone. "I wanted to. But my pack has a scent match. We cannot court you. But we need Mads."

"An omega scent match?" I pull my hand away.

"Please forgive me," he says and holds onto my ankle tighter. "Your scent. Your cunt. You are so damned beautiful." He looks up at me. His stunning, vulnerable brown eyes hold me in place. "The alpha in me is roaring to lay you onto this floor and show Mads how well you take my cock into your perfect, wet pussy."

I whine. It's one of those insane omega whines. It affects the alpha subjugated before me.

"Fucking hell," Kol says at the same time Mads goes, "You can't say things like that."

"She wants me. I can smell her arousal. She's thinking about how I knotted her at the club. How I made her body submit to me and all my darkest desires. She doesn't know how often I've thought about her. How many times I stopped myself from hunting her down, tying her up, and making her my plaything."

His voice, muffled by this muzzle, will be the death of me. I've never even seen this man's face, and yet I'm ready to bare my neck to him.

I realize I'm panting. I have to break eye contact, and soon. I shut my eyes with a will I didn't know I possessed. I turn my head towards Mads, and when I open my eyes I see fear.

He's scared of us.

No.

"Mads, talk to me. Tell me what's going on in your head."

He turns away. But he does answer. "I'm not going to lie, you both are freaking me out. I'm afraid Kol is going to lose it at any moment. And I'll be the one to take the heat." His voice shakes a little.

I know alphas can be violent and outrageous. The way my beta grips his cane, I can only surmise he knows first hand.

I'm way too horny to think beyond this room and any consequences that could befall us. Kol just told me he can't have me. Mads is his object of desire, and if I know alphas, when he promises to make him part of their pack, it will happen. Kol already apologized for this outcome.

But I am not the kind of omega to roll over and take it. And I'm hardly the omega who feels this much lust for someone. I want him. I want them.

And omegas are never denied. We're spoiled little things.

"Kol, how confident do you feel right now that you would never hurt the beta that you are courting?"

"I would never hurt him." The conviction in his voice cannot be denied.

"Can you restrain yourself?" I take a step away from him, and his hand falls away from my ankle. "Can you show your beta that he's safe around you?"

He nods and says to him, "You're safe with me. With us. Is that what you've been needing me to prove to you?"

Before Mads can answer, I ask, "Mads, have you ever been taken care of by an omega? Do you know what we do?"

"I don't think I know what you mean."

"We take alphas and make them into better people. Better men. Because they will do anything for us. They will do *anything* we say."

"Is that true?"

I finally look at the alpha kneeling on the carpet. He sets his hands in his lap. An understanding passes between us. Kol will do anything I say.

"Kol will not move from that spot. No matter what. He won't move until I tell him."

I really hope Mads is into what is about to happen. And if he's not, I hope he speaks up. Because I plan on taking this far.

Kol growls at his beta, which is a bold choice because it makes Mads visibly quake. "*Mads, kiss Cadi. Kiss her and watch me keep you both safe.*"

He uses his alpha voice, but it has no effect on a beta, like it would me or an alpha—betas don't fall victim to alpha bark commands.

But that doesn't mean he doesn't know it's a command.

He looks so vulnerable and handsome. I know he wants me. He looks at me like he does, and I'm not stupid. His eyes dart to the alpha sitting politely on his knees. And then back to me.

I see the moment Mads decides he won't flee through those French style doors and out of this grand old house. I let him take his time. His hand reaches around my back, still holding his cane in his loose grip. He pulls our bodies together. I let him guide me. Just like the kiss from our first date. He's all in charge here.

He gets close to my lips but doesn't kiss me yet.

I see a glint in his eyes. His usual blank eyes actually glint, like there is life in there. For a second, I see the man from his dating profile. The lit-from-within, sunshine guy. His other hand moves over my body, up my neck, and into my hair. Oh. Oh, I see. What was it he said last night on the phone, *do you like your hair pulled?*

His fingers grip my hair at my scalp, and he gives a little tug.

I moan.

Yep. I like my hair pulled.

He pulls again, but this time his mouth eats up my next moan. His kiss is soft but unforgiving. I'm now mush. My bones aren't doing a damned thing. But he's got me. He's holding me up, encouraging me to lean on him. His tongue demands entrance, and I am eager to comply.

"God, you're amazing," Mads says with breathy desperation between our lips.

The sensation is out of this world, and all he's doing is kissing me. I rub my body into him so I can feel if he's hard yet. And fuck yes, there it is. I need him. I want him to take me with his hard cock.

The sound of his cane hitting the floor distracts me enough I don't notice he's pushed my shirt up, and his warm palm cups my ribs and part of my breast.

I'd say something, but his tongue is still in my mouth, churning me into a filthy, desperate omega. He's completely taken me over. His thumb and finger pinch my nipple over my bralette.

Mads pushes my shirt all the way up over my breasts and up my chest. He's decided this is going further than just a kiss, and I'm not upset about it.

He pulls away from me while I'm still spiraling in my lust. His hands are still on me, but there is space everywhere else.

"Do you want to do this with me? Like this?"

I can't even begin to answer. The pause is interpreted correctly. I need a second. He pulls my head down to his shoulder and I rest there. Catching my breath.

He strokes my hair and guides my breathing to a more normal rhythm.

"Little omega is overwhelmed," he muses.

I huff out a laugh.

"You're incredible," I whisper.

Kol is sitting still, but his whole countenance is buzzing.

"Is Kol going to just sit there?" he asks.

"You decide," I say.

He makes a little "hm" sound.

"Do you think he could hold himself back if I took off some of your clothes?"

I lift off of his shoulder and see his eyes. There's a shine there.

I lift up my arms, and he doesn't need any more clues. He pulls my shirt up, coasting his knuckles across my bare skin on the way up. He feels the back of my bra and then twists the clasp. I lower my arms, and my bra drops.

Mads holds my ribs and bends me back, then his mouth is on one of my nipples. I'm distracted, so I don't realize he's pushing my shorts over my ass. They drop to the floor, and I step out of them, and I'm naked except for my pink panties.

The sun has almost set, and the room is nearly dark now. We could go find a light, but the orange and pink sky is enough.

His hands are like magic. I feel like there are many more than just two of them roaming my body. His mouth leaves my nipple, and he nibbles up my throat and across my jaw. I'm leaning so far back it doesn't take much for Mads to lay me down on the plush carpet. I wrap my legs around his waist.

He presses his hard-on against my pussy and I moan.

"Have you ever been with two men at the same time?" Mads asks me.

I shake my head.

"Do you want to?"

I bend my head to see Kol absolutely hungry. His cock is fighting for its life in his pants.

"Kol is in pain watching us make out."

Mads looks over and sees what I see. It's a joy to see a little lift of Mads's mouth in amusement.

"Kol, show us. Let's see it."

I hear the zipper, and then suddenly Mads is pulling my panties over my knees, and I'm naked. He lies down, wrapping my thighs over his shoulders, then licks my bare cunt.

Fucking. Fuck. Fuck. Oh my god.

I turn back to Kol, who has his delicious cock in his hand, pumping it up and down. My mouth waters.

"Come here," I whisper, and Kol does what I say. He crawls closer to me and then sets his knees near my shoulders.

I lick the underside of his cock, and he lets out a muffled groan from underneath his muzzle. As I lick Kol, Mads devours me. My thighs press onto either side of his head, but that doesn't stop him.

We seem to escape into the fringes of time and space. I'm no longer worried that I am laid out naked in this ancient, empty mansion being serviced by two men. The beta I'm dating and the alpha who's been at the forefront of my fantasies. My primal nature is singing. She loves this.

I pull Kol down and suck his cock deep into my throat. He's so large, I'm finding trouble breathing. Kol puts his hand on my cheek and says, "Slow breaths, through your nose, little momma. Look at me. Slow, deep breaths, through your nose. This cock is all yours."

His hips guide his cock in and out of my mouth. Mads does not let up on my pussy. He gives it everything he's got.

I make eye contact with Kol, and suddenly I am coming.

I squeeze Mads's head too tight, but he continues to coax me through it. Kol speeds up his hips, and drool drips down my cheeks.

I pop off of Kol to say, "Mads, fuck me. I want you to fuck me."

He kisses me up my stomach and between my breasts until he is totally between my legs and his pants are shucked off.

His shirt is off too, and the feel of his skin on mine is everything. He notches the head of his cock against my pussy.

"I have a condom in my wallet. Give me a second."

"You can't get pregnant, and if you're clean, we can fuck bare."

I realize I haven't got checked since I was with Kol.

"I'm clean. I've only been with you since I was last tested," Kol says.

"Then I'm clean, too," I add.

"Bare it is, then," Mads says, and again, there's a beautiful gleam in his eyes. I suck Kol back into my mouth. His hands grip my hair at the scalp. Between his hips rocking into me and his hands holding my head still, I let him set the pace.

Mads pushes into me, inch by delicious inch.

I can't see him, I can only see Kol. And Kol is watching Mads. His eyes are filled with lust.

Threesomes are my ultimate favorite sexual experiences. I always thought I'd end up having two alphas, because of how much I love having two people worship my body at once. I'm not ashamed of it. I'm an omega, but I am also a woman.

27

Pack Life

Oscar

Both of my pack mates spent their evening fucking someone. I wait until they are ready to tell me what mystery person they've partnered with. They will always tell me the truth eventually.

Some lies are still waiting for the truth.

Like, who Locke goes and fucks sometimes when he leaves. I know all about his upbringing in the Legs O'Bannon pack house. How they treated him, reduced him to an animal. A background like that deserves time to heal. And that's what he'll always get from me. A safe, patient healing.

I'm curious mostly about Kol.

Is he fucking the beta? I'm not sure if that's a solid move at this time.

I clean the house so when Kol arrives home, he can feel good. His sheets are cleaned and put back on his bed. His bathroom smells of bleach and glass cleaner. The kitchen table is cleared, and his chair he likes to work from is turned out, so he can slip right in.

I then sit on an armchair facing the door and wait for him to return.

My day with the beta is tomorrow. And then he'll need to decide if he's in or not.

I hear the sounds of someone outside fumbling with their keys. Clinging. Jamming. Clinging. Jiggling. Is he drunk?

He manages to get the door open and takes a slow, tentative step inside. His bag slips off of his shoulder and he discards it by the door that he ensures to lock. He turns around and I smell him.

My face scrunches up to try to block the smell.

"Kol, did you take a swim in the river?"

He's soaking wet and his feet squelch as he takes a few steps towards me, head bowed, and turns away so as not to look at me.

"Yes, alpha. I had to get her scent off of me before I returned home."

"Her?"

He nods slowly. "The beta and I, Mads and I…" his shame is palpable between us.

"You and Mads shared a woman?"

A nod. He stands before me like a man standing in front of a judge for his crimes. His body is trembling.

"You're wearing your muzzle." The thought of him in that wild river with his muzzle on upsets me. Putting himself in danger to try to wash away his shame…

"I had to put it on earlier. My teeth were aching, and my mouth was salivating. I swear it was worse than before I bit Locke."

I nod.

I thought as much. He's under too much pressure. They both are.

"Kol, I'd like to help you. Will you allow me that?"

He blows out a laugh. "Oscar, I'm not going to take your virginity just to appease my rutting problem."

I realize now what that sounded like. I join him in the laugh. I have been saving myself for an omega. I have no compulsion to fuck men or alphas, and Kol knows this.

"No, something else. Come sit at my feet," I tell him soberly, my pack lead command in my voice. He does as he's told and sits between my legs with his back to the chair. I direct him closer so he can rest his arms on my thighs. His body is sopping wet. It's fine. I'll clean him up in a bit when we are done.

I lay my arm out in front of him, my elbow resting on my knee. He instinctively holds onto my forearm in front of him.

"It's not your rutting that I was referring to."

With my free hand, I unclasp his muzzle and it falls into his lap. "It's your biting. I realized that I can help with that. You bear my mark," I say, and stroke the two half moons on his shoulder, over his shirt. He shivers at the touch. "I can afford to bear some of yours."

His whole body goes still. I let him process my offer. It's non-conventional, that's for sure. Laying claiming marks on your pack lead. I'm sure they'll hurt, because a real claiming mark doesn't hurt—well, at first. There's a rush of endorphins after a claiming mark that erases any pain. I won't get that here. But Kol will be able to sink his teeth into flesh. He'll be able to quell his desire for it. This is a safe place for him to do it.

"If you're sure, Alpha."

He strokes my forearm and brings it up to his lips, rubbing my skin against his. He's already decided he wants to do it. I'm glad I didn't have to convince him.

"For all your shame you carry, Locke nor I have ever felt ashamed of you. Your actions have never hurt us so much we wouldn't claim you as ours all over again. You are mine. Do you hear me, Alpha Soto? You are mine."

We share a name. And a future. We share a home. Everything that is mine, is also his.

"Don't hold back. I'm ready when you are," I say.

His teeth sink into my flesh only a breath later. My arm is latched into his mouth. Warm blood drips down my wrist and onto the floor.

Absolutely pleasure, satiation, joy, and peace flood the bond. It's so powerful, I feel Locke awake from whatever he is. His side of the bond was closed off from us, but it's blown open with Kol's feelings.

And my pain.

It does hurt. A lot. But I bite down on a rubber pellet that I'd slid between my teeth as quickly as I could. My arm shakes in Kol's hold. He groans in pleasure, and I yell in pain. It's all involuntary. I wish I could hide my reaction from him so he can enjoy this fully.

As it is, he eases up his pressure and I feel a tinge of guilt. No. No, sweet Kol, don't feel guilty.

The pellet drops out of my mouth, and I wince as I stroke the back of his head. "It's ok. It's ok," I manage to say. He leans back into me as I lean into him, for support. I'm draped over him as my body rests. His jaw releases my flesh, and he takes to licking my wound. His saliva eases the pain.

We lay like that for a long while. Kol purrs and tends to my wound. Happy. Content. And I'm the same, for having been able to give him this.

28

A Look Within

Locke

I'm still gripping my chest at the feelings Kol had exploded through the bond. I order a car to take me home. I don't have it in me to be apart from them any longer. As I drive to the house, away from Mickey in the hotel, I realize I'm only driving home to Kol and Oscar, and not the beta and the mysterious omega. In my mind, they are already part of us. I get to the house and unlock the door. I find Kol's computer bag crumpled on the floor. It smells like river water. None of the lights are on. But I hear the shower, so I make my way to the one bathroom in this place.

Inside, I find Oscar and Kol, naked, showering. It's not sexual. Kol is tending to Oscar. He switches the shower off and directs the injured Oscar to the toilet to sit on its closed lid. Before he does that, I wrap a towel around Oscar's middle.

"What happened?" I ask, softly. Curiously. There's a strong intimacy here between them I don't want to rupture.

Oscar answers me with a strained voice. "I directed Kol to bite me. To help with his impulses."

He holds up his arm to show the deep wound. Kol did not hold back, it seems. Oscar gives me a little smile to show that he wanted this.

I find myself shaking my head, even though I'm not even sure what to think. I hand Kol another towel so he can wrap himself in it. He then kneels in front of Oscar and opens a med kit he's retrieved from under the sink.

I stay with them, basking in their closeness. Our bond sings between us. Kol disinfects the wound and then wraps his arm gently. He opens up some painkillers, and I get him a glass of water.

Kol says, "Thank you, Oscar. Thank you. That was a once in a lifetime gift. I don't deserve you. Truly. All the noise in my head is gone."

Oscar is about to reply, but I cut him off, "Did you find it hard not to bite the beta?"

"I had to make him put a muzzle on me. He was...freaked out."

"I bet. But he's not skittish about alphas biting him, right? Just jumping him?"

"I don't think his hindbrain cares to be that granular on what alpha threats are scary. But it's not an issue anymore, I don't think. We shared his girlfriend tonight. And when I left him, he was no longer nervous with me."

"You fucked the beta?"

"No, we fucked his omega girlfriend. Together."

Leave it to Kol to turn his day with the beta into a sexual adventure. Oh, to be a fly on the wall...

Oscar interrupts my fantasy—"I take it, he's not going to break up with her, then?"

Kol drops his head. "She's not someone easily discarded, alpha. I myself am not sure I could give her up."

"That good, huh?" I ask. A little curtly.

"She's spectacular. She is so sure of herself. She knows herself so well. She knows exactly what she wants and will tell you. She seemed to know exactly what I could offer her, too. I was her slave."

There's a long pause as the three of us all hum in one note. We all think that's nice.

"Would she..." Oscar asks, then pauses, clears his throat, "Would she like to be chased, do you think?"

All the air is suddenly sucked out of the room, and Kol and I sit there with our mouths open. Our resident virgin just asked us if Mads's girlfriend would be into him chasing her down and fucking her.

His face goes a little pink.

"Chased?" I manage to ask.

He nods.

I guess Oscar's thought about what he likes.

"Let's not get ahead of ourselves. Maybe our scent match omega is a bunny in the moonlight, Oscar. Or maybe it's this omega, what's her name?" I ask.

"Cadi," Kol answers.

"Either way, let's find the girl from the soirée first. Then we will go from there." I'm not usually the most practical person in this pack. The bite must have screwed with their brains.

I decide they need me.

I get them out of the bathroom and tell them to get dressed.

I don't want to ruin the moment by telling them they probably can never have Cadi. Our omega most likely wouldn't be comfortable with that. Two female omegas in the same pack?

Unheard of.

Kol insists on Oscar wearing his clothes. He brings over a pair of sweatpants and a shirt to Oscar's room and tells him he must wear it.

Oscar is bigger than Kol, so the clothes are a tight fit. I stand in the doorway, enjoying watching him tug at the bottom of the shirt that does not cover his belly button. Kol looks pleased.

"Did the bite affect your bond to each other?" I ask.

Oscar shakes his head. "No, but I feel really good. Like I've had a good day or talked with a pretty girl."

"I feel grand!" Kol says, hands on his hips.

Well, that's good. We haven't had too many good days since our timeline has been coming to a quick end, so this is good.

"I hope it makes a mark," Kol says quietly. Oscar looks down at his arm. I hope it does, too. I'm worried if it fades, it'll make Kol sad. And then he says, "I'm sleeping in here tonight."

That makes sense. I leave them to it.

I crash on the couch, and the waft of blood on the air comes from the chair nearby. River water and blood, along with the scent of their pheromones—joy, pain, connectiveness, love, and peace. It's a strange cocktail.

I want to know more about what happened tonight, so I text Mads.

> Locke: Hey, Kol is home.

> Mads: I just got home myself.

> Locke: That seems late.

> Mads: I took Cadi home first. I walked home from there.

I look at my watch. That fucker.

> Locke: It was far, wasn't it?

> Mads: It's fine.

> Locke: Kol said he was going to buy you a car. I'm guessing you rejected him?

He doesn't reply. And no ellipses pop up.

> Locke: I heard that you and he were with your girlfriend. And that things progressed.

Still no reply.

Maybe I'm being nosey.

> Locke: I hope you have a good day with Oscar tomorrow. He's the best person I know. Be nice to him.

I'm about to toss my phone away from me when a ping chimes.

> Mads: I will. Goodnight, Locke.

29

Slinging Pies

Oscar

I didn't get much sleep because Kol kept trying to spoon me all night. I'm not one for having sleepovers. I've slept in a bed by myself since I was a child. I'm not used to their heat, sounds, or movement. I got a few hours of sleep, and when I woke up, for good, Kol was snuggling with my arm. He growled as I removed it from him.

I've been thinking for two days about what I'll do with the beta on my day. I don't like going in blind to any situation. So I spent my time researching Mads.

He had a roommate named Arnold Bererra, Arnold Meier now—he's been bonded into a high-profile pack here in Cash City. But while they were roommates, they had a lot of fish tanks. They are in the background of every photo.

Arnold posts now from a large house out in the plains. No fish tanks. I've made the assumption they were Mads's fish before his accident, and Arnold decided to care for them.

On this wild assumption, I've scheduled an early morning, private opening of the aquarium.

I drive to his place and knock on his door.

His mother opens the door.

"Hello, I'm here for Mads," I say. I'm wearing sunglasses, since I've already got a headache from my lack of sleep.

She looks exactly like Mads, but 30 years older and a woman. But if he were to grow his hair out and don a dress, then they could be sisters.

She scrutinizes me, head to toe. I come out wanting, it seems, as she doesn't say a word.

"Which one are you?" she finally asks.

"I'm Dr. Oscar Soto."

One of her eyebrows kicks up.

"I'm Mads's mother, Tilde. He told me that you dyed his hair."

I shake my head. "No, that was another pack member of mine. His name is Locke."

She makes a "hm" sound.

Finally, Mads comes to the door. He smiles at his stern-faced mother, kisses her on the cheek, and says goodbye.

I stay at his side as we make our way to the car.

"My mother doesn't like alphas. And she doesn't quite understand why a group of three men are taking me on dates. And you are a lot older than me."

I nod in agreement. I can see how that would bode well for me.

"I think I just look a lot older. Seven years is not much. I greyed early."

He laughs, but I don't know where the joke was.

We stop at the car. He looks like he wants to say something. His eyes dart to the wrapping around my forearm, but he doesn't look at it again.

"Did Kol tell you about last night? With Cadi."

"He said you two had sex with her."

His face goes pink, all the way to his ears.

Yeah, he does not want to talk about it. I clasp my hand on his shoulder and give it a squeeze. His head hangs low.

"Mads, my focus right now is bonding you. It's the only next step. I'm warning you that keeping your girlfriend will pose problems, but if you want to face those problems, I'll let you."

He lifts his eyes to me. So that's it then. He's going to keep her. For now. I'd fight this harder, but the way Kol talked about her last night made me second guess this tactic. Let them keep their omega for now. There's no contract. Or courting intention. Mads is simply dating her. As betas do.

We get into the car, and as Mads is falling in, he grabs the handle on the glove box to steady himself, and it flies open. My holstered SIG P220 falls into his lap. It's not a delicate gun, and his eyes prove he sees that.

"Fucking hell," Mads says at the pistol. "What the fuck is this?"

"It's for protection."

"So you can lay a man down with 20 bullet holes in his chest?" Not everyone has a firearm for protection, so I don't judge him too harshly for his reaction. I take it from him and put it back into the glove box.

"It only has 8-rounds. So, eight holes."

He sits in silence as I get the car started and check the map.

Finally, he asks, "Are you a gangster? I know that Locke is involved in something..."

"I've tried to distance myself from that life. But my upbringing was very similar to Locke's. I was a child in a pack of gunrunners and drug dealers. I was slinging product at a very young age. I came to the US to study medicine and to remove myself from that lifestyle. But it never really escapes you."

I turn onto the road when I find myself telling him more. "I was in residency when I met Kol. He was running a scheme to get hormones.

He was a realtor selling houses to folks, and then claiming the new owners were omegas, using their information and address, to request hormones from my clinic. It was pretty sophisticated. Like now, he was having issues with rutting. If he went to the clinic himself they would have put him on a government list and forced him into programs he didn't want to be a part of. They often detain rutting alphas in Salt Port. I confronted him one day, out of curiosity mostly, not to expose his scheme. We knew immediately we were pack. I helped him get his hormones and then clean up his rap sheet. He had customers relying on him. Big clients. Like Legs O'Bannon.

"Being a supply source for Legs O'Bannon put him in a really bad spot. I was able to buy him out, but he had to give the details of his scheme to Legs. We spent a lot of time with his people during the negotiations. Kol had a fascination with Locke. I would have separated them, but I had the same one. We'd finished negotiations, and Kol was out. But then Kol bit Locke, even though he knew he was Legs's favorite plaything. It was a blowout. As pack lead, I am to protect my own. So, you can see why I have the gun."

Mads is quiet. I pull into the parking lot of the aquarium and shut off the car.

"Do you regret bonding with Kol? Knowing it led to all this trouble?"

"No. Not for a second. Kol is mine. His trouble is my trouble. And while I would have liked to have had a plan to take Locke from O'Bannon first, I'd never shame Kol for his impulses."

I sigh and rest my head.

I tell him more. "When it's just the three of us, I feel powerful. I feel calm and confident. They both satisfy so many of my needs. They are good alphas. It's my life's joy to care for them, lead them, and protect them. I would never regret them. I wouldn't even know how."

"You feel the same way about me?" he asks slowly. Choosing each word with care.

"In time. For now, I know that I want you. It's very clear you will work well with my pack mates. Kol has always tried to get Locke to work with him. But it's never been Locke's thing. Kol is very excited about the prospect of having a work partner. Locke is a lot like me. He likes to take care of people. And things. He's salivating at the mouth to be able to care for you. I like how analytical you are. It appeals to me. Both Kol and Locke make decisions based on their feelings. Sometimes it feels like I'm the only one thinking things through."

His breathing has sped up. I'm overwhelming him.

"Come on," I say, and unbuckle my seat belt.

He follows me out. I don't think he realized we were even at the aquarium until a worker met us at the door.

"Alpha Soto. Nice to meet you. I'll be your guide today. The entire place is open for you to explore for the next hour. Did you have questions?"

I smile and shake their hand. "No questions. We will just wander if that's alright."

He leaves us to it.

"What are we doing here?" Mads finally asks.

"Do you like fish?" I ask.

He nods slowly.

"I used to have some fish," he confirms, and the alpha in me purrs. I knew. I fucking knew it.

We spend the next hour observing the glowing jellyfish, watching the penguins get put out, waiting for the sharks to swim over us in the tube, and just being together.

He reads the placards along with me. He tells me the facts he already knows. We both opt out of touching the stingrays. He gets slower and slower, but I swear he's not as bad as he's been in the past. Yesterday, he went to the spa room with Kol. I think it did a lot of good.

We are still enjoying everything when the aquarium officially opens, and school buses full of children come swarming in along with moms with carriages. We decide it's over for us and leave to get something to eat.

"I really enjoyed that. Thank you. I can't remember the last time I just went to the aquarium. Or a museum. Or a garden. It's been a tough year."

I tell him it's not a problem.

There's a café inside a nice grocery store nearby, so we stop in for sandwiches. Also so Mads can take some pills.

"I didn't used to be this grumpy. Or combative," Mads says after he necks a handful of pills. "I used to be silly, actually. Always had a smile. My goal was to make everyone around me laugh or feel good. I don't even know how to reconcile that person with who I am today. I feel like I got the rug pulled out from underneath me. Everything that used to be important to me is gone. I feel like I lost Mads somewhere. Or got abducted by aliens. And there is just this shell now, with all my insides missing."

I set my espresso down and give him all my attention.

He looks at me with earnest. "What if it happens again? What if you bring me into your pack, and I change again, suddenly? Become unrecognizable. If it happened once, it can happen again."

That was not what I thought he'd say, so I am silent as I consider his question. It's easy for me to tell him that it wouldn't happen. Or that I'd be there for him. As I look into his watery eyes, I wonder what kind of response he's looking for.

"What kind of person do you want to be?"

His mouth parts. He's a bit shocked. "I don't know. Not this. I hate this."

"Well, if you decide to change into someone different, maybe someone you don't hate, I'll be glad to witness it. But I don't want any other Mads than this one. I like you. Just as you are."

His face breaks, but he catches it. Then wipes his hand down his mouth.

"You're kind of hard to resist, Oscar," he laughs. "Fuck it. I'm in. Let's do this. I have no idea if I'll regret it."

A weight lifts off my chest. I can breathe for the first time in months. My appointment at the Institute is Wednesday. It's Monday, and I'll have Mads bonded tonight.

"Thank you. Thank you. I will take good care of you." I pull out my phone and start drafting a text to my pack about the details. We will need to gather tonight at the apartment. I'll have Kol get our paperwork started in order to add Mads to all our accounts.

"Yeah, my only hesitation is still with Locke and that weird Mickey guy." He stops short. His teeth click shut. I stop typing.

"What? How do you know about Mickey?" I wonder why Locke would tell Mads about Mickey. Seems kind of odd. Mads holds his hands under the table.

"Oh, nothing. Just Mickey was at my place."

"Why?"

"He was upset at Locke. They got in a fight."

I'm torn between being shocked and angry—one emotion wants to win out. I didn't know anything about this fight.

"Mickey told me he was spending the weekend in Salt Port. He wasn't in town this weekend. When was he at your place?"

Thankfully, Mads answers quickly.

"Saturday evening."

"What did they fight about?" I don't hide my alpha voice from him. "Do not lie to me."

Mads grits his teeth before saying, "Locke told me not to tell you. I'll be betraying his trust."

"Betray it. Now."

I know I'm scaring him, but he needs to tell me what he knows.

Between his heavy breathing, he answers:

"I didn't hear the whole fight. Mickey was upset about me. I think he'd followed us. I heard Locke yelling that if he wanted to court a beta, he would. I thought they might be in a lovers' fight. The way they yelled. Mickey asked if he was in love with me. That's why I thought that. Later, Locke admitted that whatever is going on with Mickey and him is because he's protecting you guys. They have an agreement. Mickey promised to keep things from his boss in exchange for...I don't know."

In exchange for sex.

I know exactly what the arrangement is.

Locke has been fucking Mickey to protect us. They have him collared again. Absolutely the fuck not. Locke will not sacrifice himself like that. Not again. I leave the café and storm to the car.

Mads tries to keep up, but he can't.

I check Locke's location, and it's off.

Fuck!

How long has it been turned off? I get into the car, and then I pull up Locke's credit card transactions. I never, ever look at this shit. But he's in trouble.

There are several charges to the hotel.

Mads is in the passenger seat before I can stop him.

"I'll take you home, Mads," I say tightly.

"And then where are you going?"

I pop open the glove box and take out my P75. I toss off the holster. I check the magazine by slightly pulling the slide back to see the round in the chamber. Clear.

"Oh, I see." Mads realizes I'm going to go shoot Mickey in the side of his head. Well, he might not know where I'm planning on putting this bullet, but he knows it's going into Mickey. "I'm coming with you."

I stop.

Mads can't see me like this. He can't know who I'm capable of being.

But.

If he is going to bond, he will need to know.

"Tell me when it's too much. I'll point you to the nearest bus stop."

I turn over the engine and drive with purpose to the hotel. Once I'm parked on the street out front, I call Locke.

It goes to voicemail.

I call again.

And again.

And again.

Finally, he answers.

"Oscar?"

"Where are you? Your location is off."

I hear a door shut.

"What's going on?"

"I need you to meet me. Where are you?"

"Anchorage and Lake Ave." A block away from the hotel.

He's lying to me.

He's fucking lying to me.

"Five minutes," I tell him, and then hang up the phone. I check the gun again. I went to the shooting range just a few weeks ago. It's been cleaned. It's ready. I wish I had a jacket to hide it under, but it's too hot for that. I'm in linen pants and a short sleeve button up shirt.

I make sure my sunglasses are clean before putting them back on.

Mads is silent in the passenger seat next to me.

No one turns Locke back into a whore. I never wanted it to happen again. We got him out of Legs's house of horrors. I made a promise he'd never have to do that again. It's only been months. Months!

It makes me think that I failed to take him away in the first place. Like he never truly left.

In two minutes, Locke comes out of the building heading towards the cross street. A few minutes later, Mickey comes out and heads in the opposite direction. I slide out of the car and follow him, twenty steps behind.

30

Hard Read

Mads

I seem to be experiencing some sort of time shift, alternative reality. Everything feels hyper-colored and amped up. Mickey has been blackmailing Locke for sex, so it's not exactly a situation that would call for calm.

I'm struggling to keep up with Oscar. His strides are long and sure. Mine are clunky. But I have to keep up. I observed every emotion known to me and mankind flit through Oscar's face as it dawned on him his pack mate was being taken advantage of.

Suddenly, he's gone and so is Mickey.

I rush up to where I last saw them, far up ahead of me. There's a small passageway between buildings, barely wide enough for a person to fit through, but I have a feeling this is where they went into. I push in and find myself in a small court, shadowed by the buildings. Oscar has his gun drawn on Mickey, who's on the ground with a bloody lip.

"Oscar!" I call out so he knows it's me. He turns for a brief second, and I see only my reflection in his sunglasses. He's going to kill Mickey. I just know it.

Mickey's hands are up in front of him, protecting his face. "Oscar, calm down! Come on man. You don't have any idea what's going on!"

"Don't fuck with me! I know exactly what's going on. You didn't get to fuck him when he was at the O'Bannon pack house, so you found a way to do it here. Did you not think I was as powerful an alpha as Legs? That I wouldn't *delete you* if you so much as batted your eyes at my alpha!"

Unfuckwithable.

That's the word to describe Oscar.

If I thought he was a powerful alpha before, I know it now. He's the scariest thing I've ever seen.

Mickey doesn't seem to get it, because he says, "He's been drooling over me for years! Ok? He approached me with his little crush. It's not my fault I indulge him every once in a while."

I shake my head, and even though I'm silent, it gets both their attention.

"What?" Oscar asks me.

"It's bullshit. Mickey is obsessed with Locke. He came at him the other day like a jealous lover. Locke is disgusted by him."

Oscar turns to Mickey.

"The beta doesn't know what he's talking about."

"You are taking advantage of Locke, and you know it! You're a fucking creep," I say back.

Oscar realigns the barrel of his gun, deciding between his head or his heart.

"Are you really going to kill him?" I ask.

"Yes," he answers soberly.

"No. No. No. You can't kill me! Legs will come after you!"

"He's already after us! You stupid fucker. If you just sat in your car and did your job, we wouldn't have a problem. But you decided to throw your weight around."

"Fuck you! Locke came to me! He was a blubbering little mess, as always. That emotional fucker. No wonder they'd call him a puppy and kept him in a kennel, he whined like one. *Oh, don't tell Alpha O'Bannon that my pack is going to the Institute. Please, Mickey, I'll do anything. I'll suck your cock if you'll just keep this between us.* It's not my fault I never got a turn on the community bicycle before coming to Cash City..."

Wrong thing to say, Oscar aims between his eyes. But I do something even more insane, I push Oscar to the side and swing my fist into Mickey's smug, stupid, ugly face.

A rush of endorphins so great I suddenly feel two feet taller and stronger than an ox rushes through me. My injury is forgotten. The sting of the hit on my knuckles feels incredible. So I grab him by the front of his shirt and hit him again.

And again.

And again.

I ram my knee into the soft tissue of his belly. Over and over until I lose my footing and have to back up and stand to regain it.

Mickey is curled over himself against the brick building, the dripping of his blood splashes on the cement under our feet.

A fire burns through me.

I haven't felt this alive in so long.

I go to kick him with my bad leg, but Oscar stops me.

"You'll feel it later. Best to stop now."

I meet his eyes and they see right into me. He sees what this is doing to me.

He accepts it, too. No judgement.

His eyes dart to both my fists, where the skin has been torn open. I shake my arms. I don't feel any pain.

Oscar turns back to Mickey, who is doing his best to sit back up. His face is covered in blood. Mine and his. Oscar aims his gun for a third time and this time shoots him right between the eyes in two quick shots.

The wall behind his head explodes with red, and a chunk of the brick comes flying off. The bullets fall somewhere on the ground with a soft clink, like they weren't just careening straight through Mickey's skull.

The body crumples lifelessly on the ground.

Without taking a second to assess what he's done, Oscar simply holsters his gun in his pants behind his back, scoops up the bullet casings and my cane from the ground, takes my hand, and we walk out of there.

He pulls me along at a brisk pace. I can hear everything. Like I had cotton removed from my ears. Doves, robins, and chickadees sing and flit around the treelined street. The sun shines through the leaves of the silver leaf lindens, dancing their triangular green leaves all over. I can feel the texture of the cement under my shoes. And I can smell everything: good or bad. The garbage piled up on the street. The fumes from the sewer grates. The flowers in the plants on the windows near-by. Car exhaust. Chicken frying inside the restaurants. And I can smell Oscar. He smells like brewing coffee on a cool morning. Goddamn.

I'm taking deeper breaths than I've ever taken before. I'm drunk off the oxygen.

We aren't going back to the car. We've been weaving through streets and find ourselves at an apartment complex. Oscar pulls me into their unit. A small two bedroom apartment. It doesn't remind me of them in any way. Why would they live here?

Oscar makes me sit at the kitchen table. Kol's laptop is open, and my packet I gave him the other day is next to it, along with two mugs of coffee and a Diet Dr. Pepper.

Oscar leaves the room and returns with a first aid kit. He pulls a chair next to me.

"Give me your hands—" he barks. It's probably an alpha bark. Those don't work on betas.

I still give him my hands. He makes a very disappointed and irritated sound.

"It's fine, Oscar. It doesn't even hurt," I say with a smile on my face. The muscles are untrained, and it stretches my skin past the point of comfort. I'm smiling! I'm really smiling!

Kol comes in from what was probably the bathroom. He stops short at my smile. His head tilts to the side.

"Mads? What's going on?"

"Nothing," I answer, a smile still plastered on my face.

"Come here, Kol, I need your help. He needs ice. Bag some up and bring it over."

Kol just stands there.

Oscar hops up and fills a bowl with water, and then he comes back, holding the bowl and a rag. He starts to clean my hands up.

"What happened?"

Instead of answering, Oscar says, "Actually, take all the ice we have and fill the bathtub. Run down to the corner store and get more. We're going to put him in it."

Kol does as he says. A dutiful alpha. I sit and enjoy the feeling of being this fucking happy. God. Everything is ok. I can't remember the last time everything felt so damned *ok*.

This concept that I never needed hope at all, that things would be ok whether or not I believed in it, hits me.

Were things always going to be ok, and I just needed to wait? People always say that things get better, but I thought it was empty words, but now I wonder if people are right.

"Oscar, that was amazing. The way you…"

"Let's talk about it later, *cielito*."

I nod excitedly.

"Should we go get some food? I know a place that sells those really tall beers. They are so clear they taste like champagne. Or! There's a food truck that sells fry bread. It's close by. They put seasoned beef on it and iceberg lettuce. Which, I know, iceberg lettuce? That can't be good. But I swear it's the only way."

Kol comes back holding two bags of ice. Oscar and he dump them into the bath and fill the rest with water. Oscar directs me to stand up and takes me into the bathroom.

"I'm going to need you to get naked."

"No problem!" I take off my shirt and pants. God, I feel so tight and strong. I feel taller than I've ever been. Did I get taller?

I take off my briefs and stand in the small bathroom with Oscar. Kol is at the doorway, and he looks right at my dick. They are both fully clothed. I kind of want to show off my body to them. Show them how strong I am. Nothing hurts! I could probably go for a run right now. Climb a mountain. Ride down it on my old bike.

"Into the tub," Oscar says to me.

"I should call Cadi. She'd love to see me like this. We could probably take her to the place with the tall beers."

Kol pushes into the bathroom and holds my shoulders for some reason. I push back on him.

"Ok, come on, my sweet prince, into the tub," Kol says. I preen under his nickname.

I don't move. I have more I need to say. Kol's face is close to mine, but not close enough, so I touch our noses together.

"Kol, it was crazy! That ugly motherfucker first called Locke a puppy, which pissed me off to no end. It seemed so derogatory."

"What?" Kol says and then turns to Oscar.

"And then when he called him a community bicycle..."

For a second, I think Kol is going to shake me, but he lets me go to grab onto Oscar.

"What the fuck is he talking about? His pupils are huge! Is he on drugs!?"

I scoff. I've never been more fucking sober in my life.

"He's high on adrenaline and possibly having a nervous break-down. Mads, into the tub!" Oscar raises his voice at me. I frown. Fine. God. He didn't have to yell.

I put one foot into the freezing water, and instantly my body gives something up. Something vital. Oscar practically pushes me the rest of the way in.

"Now, your arms."

I sink my arms into the water.

My whole body relaxes. Everything normalizes.

Oh my god. I saw a man get killed today.

I look up at Oscar and Kol, a question on my lips, I don't know how to ask.

Oscar nods in understanding.

"We discovered that Locke has been exchanging sexual favors to Mickey to keep our secrets from getting back to Legs. I approached Mickey on the subject. Mads decided to beat the pulp out of him. And then I shot Mickey between the eyes. I left his body there. The bullet casings are in my pocket."

My leg awakens at that moment, and the most horrendous pain registers. I turn my head out of the tub and vomit on the floor.

Oscar rubs the back of my neck. I'm staring at his shoes, covered in the mess.

"Kol, can you get Mads's pain meds? And a glass or two of water?"

"'Course. Goddamn. You guys had a day."

Oscar continues to rub my neck and shoulders. "Sorry, I had to kick you out of it. It's called a dive response. I was worried you'd continue to hurt yourself. You were putting your weight on your bad leg. I know it sucks to feel pain, but it's our body's way of keeping us safe."

I don't realize I'm crying until the taste of salt bleeds over my lips.

"The water will help with the swelling."

Kol comes back with meds. He also asks where Locke is. Oscar has to tell him he sent him to a random street corner. But there's no way to know where he is because he turned off his location.

Reality comes to me like it never left.

I've never been violent. I've never hit someone like that in my life. Just the way he was talking about Locke was so upsetting. Locke has been nothing but kind to me. I couldn't help but see his face when he asked me not to tell Oscar.

I knew even then, his secret wasn't going to be a secret for long.

I debated keeping it from Oscar. But I knew that Locke was in danger, and that was more important. If Locke hates me forever for telling his secret, so be it.

My whole body is shaking. My teeth chatter.

"Here, take your meds and then I'll help you out," Oscar hands me a glass of water and five pills. I neck them without a thought. I reject the water.

He and Kol both help me out of the bath, and my shame still hasn't quite returned, so it's quick and no-nonsense. Oscar wraps me in a towel, and they take me to his bedroom.

I'm just trying to think one thought at a time as they dress me in their clothes.

"Whose clothes am I wearing?"

"My underwear. Locke's shorts. Oscar's shirt. Now lie down." I lay down on Oscar's bed.

"Why?"

"Your leg looks really shitty. Oscar wants to look at it."

"Hm," I say.

They fuss over me and chatter about whatever. They prop my leg up over some pillows. It's so relaxing I fall asleep almost immediately.

31

Face the Music

Locke

I return to the hotel, and Mickey is no longer there. He said he was just stepping out for a moment.

Oscar never met up with me. He didn't pick up his phone when I called, and his side of the bond was shut down.

I clean up the room and pace around for a while, waiting for Mickey. If he doesn't come back, it could mean he finally went to talk to Legs about everything he fucking shouldn't be telling him about.

He wanted to mess around again this morning, and I turned him down. Should I not have done that? Fuck! I can only give so goddamned much! This shit was easier when I was Legs's plaything. He always set the terms. He said when to start and when to stop. I could just turn off my brain and be at his mercy. I'd just escape into my head and not have to be present.

But with Mickey, it's like I'm always one bad choice away from everything being meaningless. My betrayal of my pack. My dignity, that Kol and Oscar fought for. It's all a waste. I'm a waste.

Why is it I was the one with a scent match? I'm not worthy of such a thing. It should be brave Kol. Or trustworthy Oscar. Not me. Who's barely one step above a dog.

I say, fuck it and leave the room to get a drink at the hotel bar. One drink turns into many drinks. And before I know it, it's dark outside and I'm walking back to the cross streets, drunk off my ass. I call Oscar again.

"Locke?"

"You asshole. You stood me up! Oh god. I didn't mean to call you an asshole. You know I love you, Oscar. I'm so sorry. I'm just...I'm just not doing so well right now. And you hurt my feelings."

"Come home," he says so simply. "Come home, *mijo*."

I nod even though he can't see me.

"Ok," I say and then hang up.

I manage to get my keys into the door and get myself inside. My head is swimming, and all my emotions are on the surface. It's dark inside. Just some lamps on. And it smells like...

"Oscar?" Kol sits at the kitchen table under the low light of a floor lamp, and Oscar is doing the dishes. "Why does it smell like Mads in here?"

It's this subtle croissant smell. All buttery and tender. I noticed it while I did his hair. I've been wanting to get my nose into his neck and really understand it.

"He's sleeping in my room."

He says it so simply, I have nothing to say back.

Mads is in the apartment. Sleeping.

"Why?"

Kol looks up from his computer.

"Why don't you come sit down. Eat something. We have to talk."

Suddenly, it's half a year ago, and I'm so very small again. So very powerless. And these two alphas are looking at me like they will try everything they can to rescue me.

I hate that I need rescuing.

Eventually, my feet take me to the table where Oscar lays out some cookies and a glass of milk. They don't say anything as I eat the snack.

I am small, aren't I? I am powerless.

"Locke, I saw Mickey today," Oscar says as he sits next to me.

My eyes bulge out of my head, and I nearly bolt.

"Where is he?"

"He's dead."

I can't breathe.

"Breathe. It's ok. Mads and I disposed of him quickly and quietly. Kol took care of the body. I doubt they'll find it for a long time."

"Mads?"

"He wants to be pack. And as any good pack mate does, he told me your secret because he felt you were not being safe. I hunted Mickey down to delete him, but Mads got angry about the things he said about you, and he tried to kill him with his fists. I nearly let him. But it was me who finished him off."

A wave of flattery rushes through me. Mads defended me? Oscar killed him for me?

But it's replaced quickly with guilt. My choices led to Mads and Oscar doing something horrible.

"You told me you didn't want to be violent anymore. You told me you would never be dragged back into this world," I say.

"You're more important than that promise."

I hang my head and a heady cloud of shame fills the space. "What punishment can I expect for what I did? I betrayed my scent match. I lied to you. I was having sex with..."

Oscar cut me off. "It is not my job to be the deliverer of shame and guilt. I am not your master. If you want to feel shame, you feel it. If you want absolution, I will assist you in finding it. But I do not hold the other end of your leash. It is firmly in your own hand."

And then, he adds, "Even Mads has your back. His knuckles are torn and bloody in your honor. Don't forget his gift to you."

Well, that does it. I curl in on myself and wail a cry. God, it hurts. Everything hurts. Kol drapes himself over me. He holds me as I come apart.

He rubs my back and shushes me. Oscar manages to hold our hands together, despite mine being held in a fist.

Eventually, they lead me to my bed to lie down. Kol lies on his bed next to mine. I appreciate the company. And then I eventually fall asleep.

32

The Phone Call

Acadia

"Hello, is this Doctor Oscar Soto?" I ask when a man with a thick Hispanic accent answers the phone.

"Yes, this is him. Who am I speaking with?"

"Hello! Hey! I volunteer at the Omega Women's Shelter in lower Cash City. We have an event today. We are offering free exams and prescriptions to hormone supplements to our clients, but our regular omega physician is sick. She gave me your number. She said that you were in Cash City and that you are one of the premier omega specialists in the country. I understand you are a very busy man, but if you are available today, I'd love to talk to you about volunteering."

It's been such a shit show organizing this event. First, we had too many omegas sign up. Most of them have children, so I had to organize childcare. Our caterer backed out, so I've been calling restaurants all morning asking for donations. A local grocery store is donating food from their bakery. I got a Greek restaurant to donate a food truck, happily. I also got an inflatable slide for the kids. Half the volunteers are unaccounted for, so I've been phone tree-ing everyone. And now my doctor, who is usually very reliable, is suddenly ill. The omegas need the exams.

They can't participate in the orgy later that evening without one.

"I could assist. What exactly do you need?"

I breathe a sigh of relief.

The alphas and betas who we've secured for the orgy are already vetted and tested, and most are professional omega companions.

But my omegas, they need the exams. For some of them this is their only chance to not only get tested, get hormones, but also seek relief.

"Thank you. Thank you. It starts in an hour, so the sooner you can come, the better. I'll text you the address. The shelter has an exam room you'll be working out of. There were twenty omegas who signed the sheet who need to see a physician, but I'd expect more since not everyone likes to sign their name. Our omegas come from various backgrounds. Struggling with economic instability. Dealing with domestic abuse. Our mission is to treat everyone with respect and provide them with as much support and care as we can. We will be working with a therapy group as well. And there's a local government group that will be filling our prescriptions for the day. How does all that sound?"

"That sounds great. I've never been a part of anything like this before, so you'll have to help me out."

"Of course, Dr. Soto. I appreciate it so much. The omegas will too. I know most of them, so I can help you with individualized care as well."

"I'm sorry, I don't know if I caught your name."

"Oh! I'm Acadia. I'm an omega. I'm the Director of Volunteers at the shelter. When you get here, I'll be sure to give you everything you need."

The line goes silent. I'm in the middle of setting out one of the folding tables in the parking lot with the other volunteers, so I don't quite know if the call dropped. I look at the screen. It's still connected.

"Dr. Soto?"

"Acadia?" He asks like he knows me.

"Yes?"

"Sorry, I..." he goes quiet again.

"Is everything ok?"

"Yes, it's fine. Please send me the address." And then he adds, "I'm an alpha. I'd like to bring my pack with me, if it's possible."

"No, no, no," I say quickly. Some of these omegas are going to experience a heat. They will ask Dr. Soto to give them hormone shots to trigger a heat. I can't have alphas here that I don't know. "I really don't want to offend, but many of our omegas have trauma surrounding alphas and packs. Unless they knew you, like you've volunteered before, or were part of the volunteer staff, I would caution against it. Dr. Zheng is a beta, and she's done very well with the women. She did tell me about you being an alpha. That's already a lot to ask. If you brought your pack..."

Honestly, this whole thing may be a disaster just because of Dr. Soto's designation. But I didn't want to cancel, not with so many omegas signing up already.

Some of our women are bonded to alphas their inner omega won't allow in their nests, due to abuse, and events like this are their only chance to have a heat on their own terms. Others are single mothers who don't have the connections or funds to seek sex. We have coeds from Fair Castle who come here because they don't have any other choice.

This is important.

"I understand. I did my fellowship at an omega clinic. I'm not offended. Could they come and volunteer in other areas?"

"How many?"

"Two alphas. One beta. All male."

Four men. I guess I could put them in charge of the trash cans. Or moving large things around. I'm not sure the omegas want them doing childcare. The Greek restaurant is bringing their own staff.

The more I think about this, the less I like it.

Can you imagine if they made their way into the sex room? It's on the main level of the shelter. There are double doors leading to the comfortable space. There are a dozen alcoves curtained off. Several private rooms. I usually just let the omegas roam. They all end up with partners and have a great time.

The kids will have a movie, snacks, and sleep on cots in the multi-purpose room. We even have a taekwondo instructor coming later for them.

"Dr. Soto, I really do need your assistance here. But I'm thinking of the omegas first. I'm going to say no for now. If I change my mind, I'll let you know. Is that fair?"

"I understand. You still have me. I'll be there as soon as I can."

"Beautiful. Thank you."

I hang up the phone and send him the address. He replies right away: *On my way*.

I just stop as the volunteers continue to put up the canopy and rope off the parking lot. The way he said my name...like he knew me. Like I'd surprised him.

That was strange. It's got me checking my outfit. A tight fitted vest and jean shorts. No undershirt. It's too hot.

I threaded a brightly colored scarf through the belt loops of my shorts. I give it a little adjustment and tug. And then I pat my hair, if there are any flyaways. My hand sits on my chest as I take some deep breaths.

Damn. I'm horny. Over some man's accent over the phone.

Maybe I should ask him for some suppressants. I couldn't imagine accidentally participating in the orgy. That would be so unprofessional.

I swear I went many years of my life able to speak to men and not be this affected. But it all started with Mads. Then Kol. And now Dr. Soto.

If only I could just collect them all and form my own little pack. I'd package them all up and never let them out of my sight.

Wait.

That doesn't feel right. There's someone missing.

Mads. Kol. Dr. Soto. Mystery other man.

And...

Maybe a mystery woman, too.

I am, after all, pansexual.

That feels right.

Around the clinic there's a tall wall made of bushes. It's to make the omegas feel safer and keep the parking lot cool in the summer. There's one entrance, and I have the gate open to allow the volunteers to get in. Alpha Meier with Meier Protections Group meets me by the gate.

He's a tall, dark, and handsome alpha with a face that would make any girl swoon. But he doesn't do it for me, and that makes me feel better about the harem of men I've been drooling over lately.

"Acadia, nice to see you again," Sebastian says.

He was there with his omega, Bianca and Cornell's daughter, when I first met her.

"Nice to see you, too. Thank you for coming today. I have a big list of omegas that will be stopping by. It may be fine, but you never know."

I hand the list to both Sebastian and one of his agents.

"No, this is exactly what you'd hire security for. Well, even if we weren't going to invoice you." He watches the street like at any time someone horrible is going to pop right out. I'm so grateful they offered to do this today for free. "You said some of the omegas are escaping abusive situations?"

His agent walks away from us.

"Yes, and a few live at the omega housing. Just keep any alpha out that isn't on the volunteer sheet. Oh! Let me update that list," I say as I pull out my phone. "Dr. Soto is coming."

"Dr. Soto? The omega specialist?"

My mouth drops. This is such a small world.

"You know him?"

"He gave a second opinion on my omega. For her chronic bond sickness. It's managed now."

All the blood in my body seems to run away from me.

"Wait, the Whitehorse's omega daughter has chronic bond sickness?"

He looks like he regrets sharing that information. He adjusts the holster of his gun that wraps around his shoulders.

"I thought you knew. That's why you left them. I didn't realize you didn't know."

"Alpha Meier, I knew they sucked. I didn't realize they were evil."

"Jake, my pack lead, has a case against them. He wants to make sure it's on their record in case they ever want to bond with anyone, they'll know."

That's good. I cannot believe I let myself get wrapped up with them. What if I hadn't met her before I bonded with them? I shudder to think.

He tells me he has a couple of his agents out on the perimeter, making sure people feel safe. I thank him and leave him to his work.

The morning goes by so fast with preparations. I feel this weird feeling and need to step away for some air. That's when I see Dr. Soto at the gate talking with Alpha Meier. The doctor is pointing across the street, where I can't see. I wonder if he's asking if his pack can join him?

I don't know why, but that kind of pisses me off. I told him not to bring them. It's clear that's what they are saying because Alpha Meier is shaking his head no.

I go to stand in the middle of the parking lot, with my hands on my hips, and wait for him to come over. Oh fuck me, he's handsome. In that older, daddy way that kills me. His beard and mustache are peppered with white hair. Absolutely gorgeous. The way he walks, no marches like a prince, towards me is enough for me to start slicking.

God, calm down, pussy.

He comes up to me, staying about five feet away, which is an appropriate distance between an unbonded omega and alpha. His politeness doesn't go unnoticed by my primal omega side. She loves it.

"Omega Acadia," he says with a tilt to his head, like a bow.

"Dr. Soto. Did you just try to get your pack into this event even though I told you that wouldn't be possible?"

His teeth click shut.

"What made you think that alpha over there had more authority on that decision than I did? Tell me what I should be more offended by. Is it my designation? My gender? Which part of me telling you no made you think our volunteer security agents could overrule? I'd like to know how to frame my dressing down."

His eyes are huge. I don't think this big, tall alpha is used to being berated. Good. I'm glad I could be the one to do it.

"I owe you an apology."

"Yes, Dr. Soto, but we aren't there yet. You owe me an explanation first."

He swallows.

"I would never rob you of the opportunity to give me a dressing down. Which would you prefer, and I'll confirm? Would you rather me have insulted your designation, gender, authority, or ability?"

My teeth click shut this time.

He's teasing me.

I scowl at him.

"Don't be fresh."

He turns his head so I don't see him smile.

"My pack is nearby, yes," the doctor admits as he turns back to me, serious and polite. "I was pointing them out to your security in case they looked suspicious and garnered too much attention."

"Nearby? Doing what?" That sounds suspicious as hell.

"We have a new bond, and we are staying close in proximity to assist with the connection. He's a beta, so it may not matter to him, or physiologically, but to my other pack mates, it's important. They are sensitive."

I watch his face as he tells me his explanation. Love eeks out of him. His lips stretch into a soft smile. His eyes, sparkly. All signs that he did just bond with someone.

"You're close?"

I don't know why I ask. I have a million things to do. I shouldn't be wondering anything at all. I should just move on.

"Yes. They are my world."

My cheeks heat and I look away. He's probably with them, with them. Not just bonded, but together. If I ever find my pack I want us all to be together. All of them at the same time during my heat. All of them in my same bed. Fucking me as much as possible. I want it to be one of those things where we sit in a parked car across the street because we would miss each other so...no, that's silly.

But I've got things to do.

I shake my head and meet his eyes.

How would it be to be someone's world?

I know it's a weird thought for me to have, but I wonder if I'll find a love like that.

I clear my throat and say, "Let me show you the clinic."

I take him to the little diagnostic room we have in the basement of the Omega Shelter.

There's no hired staff doctor, so we try to keep it as neutral as possible for the volunteers. Dr. Soto takes a look around at what we have for him.

"Each omega has their time slot. While they see you for their exam, we watch their kids at the event in the parking lot. When they are done, they can join them, get their meds, sign up for other programs, and spend the day here until tonight. Some omegas may just need the clearance, but others may need more."

I show Dr. Soto everything he needs along with the schedule. And it's an ordeal. He smells like fresh coffee. Morning coffee. With the cold, dewy air. The cream and sugar. The whole lot.

I'm drooling.

33

Fate Calls, Alphas Answer

Oscar

The omega's pheromones are driving me wild. The entire exam room is filled with her sweet lilac scent. She is what I've been waiting for all these years. I've never even kissed a girl. My inner alpha wouldn't allow it. He's been as particular as me when it came to our first relationship.

One day I will tell her about the fence of lilac I used to pass every day on my way to school. How I'd rub my body along it because I loved the smell so much. I once went to a park with a tunnel of lilacs hanging down, and I spent all day there bathing in the sensory experience. I should have known it would be the scent of my future omega.

And she's so beautiful with her long tan legs with thick thighs, narrow waist, and fucking gorgeous breasts. Her green, cat eyes that want none of my bullshit. I've never seen an omega this beautiful. Sexy. Charming. Commanding. Unapologetic. With her by my side we'd be unstoppable.

I can't let her walk away from me.

Her phone call this morning tilted my world off its axis.

Kol, Locke, Mads, and myself were not even fully awake after our long night when I got the call. I thought I might be going insane. How is it the omega we've been looking for this whole time just simply calls me? And asks *me* to see her? After our call, I just stood there in my room processing the coincidence of it. Unable to fully comprehend.

Acadia called me.

Acadia wanted to see me.

Acadia said my name and knew my reputation.

What a small world.

Cash City is a magical place.

She wouldn't let my pack come, but they would not be deterred. Too bad Meier Protections Group is here otherwise, my pack might be scaling the stone wall and bushes that surround the shelter. Instead, they are dutifully sitting in Kol's SUV. Waiting.

I don't have a plan. My brain is muddled.

All I knew was I needed to confirm it was her before I told the rest of them. I'll tell them soon enough she's here.

"Well, you should be all set. I'll leave you to it."

Something in my head switches.

She's walking away, walking backwards, out the door. She's hesitating. She doesn't want to leave me anymore than I want her to go.

There's no one around.

"Do you want to be my first?" I ask. A second meaning undeniable to me, maybe even perceptible to her. *Do you want to be my first?*

"Patient," I add.

"Oh," she says. Her green cat eyes don't stray from my face.

"I'm here to see omegas. You're an omega. Here." I gesture to the soft pink exam table with the paper overtop. "Come sit. You can tell the other omegas about it. Maybe it'll calm them if they have worries."

She thinks about it, and I wait. A calm settles in the air. She takes a few steady steps towards me and then turns to the exam table. She sits up on it, her feet dangle over the side.

I pull out the paperwork from the folder she showed me. I take the first few sheets and clip them to a board.

"Will the patients want me to walk them through this form, or would they prefer to fill it out on their own?" I ask.

She looks at me like I'm up to something, but then says, "I guess it depends."

"Should we walk through it together?"

She gestures for me to hand it over.

"Well, it's pretty standard. Name. Age. Height and weight. Would you really need to know my weight, Dr. Soto? That seems kind of invasive and unnecessary."

"It's not a courting profile, Acadia. I'd need to know it to calculate medication dosage," I say, and she sits up and looks at me wide eyed. Surprised, I challenged her.

"I guess that's fair." She hands it back to me. "I'm 24 years old, if you want to fill it out. Acadia. And I'm 5'5" and weigh 115 pounds, last I checked."

I smile at her as I fill in the form.

"And I'm a Virgo."

"Of course you are."

"Hey!"

I wait until she doesn't look as fake mad at me before I ask, "So what brings you in today, Omega Acadia?"

"I'm about to be railed by any number of volunteer alphas and betas upstairs in the sex room later," she teases, batting her eyes.

"Wait, are these exams to prepare for a group sex event?"

I don't know how I missed this detail.

Her hand goes to her mouth. "Oh my god, did I not say that part?"

I wait as she realizes she left that part out.

When she gets over her initial embarrassment, she shrugs.

"It starts at seven," is all she says as way of explanation. When I did my residency at an omega clinic, I did exams for the group sex events they'd host. So, I'm familiar. I never felt the desire to participate until this moment.

I clear my throat, trying to make the fantasy of participating with Acadia go away.

"Ok, so, you'll need a shot and some hormone supplements. When was your last heat?" I slip into my professional role easily.

"I was just teasing. I won't be participating. I'm here as an organizer. But we can still do the exam. I actually have a concern. My heat is coming up. I'm unmedicated."

My face drops.

"Why are you unmedicated?"

"I haven't had a chance to go to my regular doctor to let them know plans have changed. I'd been preparing for an unmedicated heat with a couple of alphas who were courting me. We'd gone into a contract. But I broke the contract, and I just haven't had a chance to figure out what I'll actually be doing for my heat."

I want to ask what happened, but my medical training takes over.

"Well, you have a few options. You can continue down this path and secure some new alphas to help you through your heat. Or we can talk about suppressing or minimizing your heat. How do you want to proceed?"

She sighs and leans back on her hands. The little vest she's wearing pulls tight across her chest, and I don't look at all like I want to stare at her breasts.

"I don't know. I haven't had a heat in a long time. I was looking forward to it. Just not with them."

Why not with them? Are they the reason you are at the Institute? Are they the reason you have your beta preference?

"Acadia," I say, with the wrong voice. So I clear my throat and start again, "Listen, I understand that things don't always go our way. That we are dealing with an unstoppable force and trying to live in a world that no longer functions for our primal selves. We find ourselves wanting to chase down and claim. Bite and fuck. Possess and consume. All while trying to maintain a good credit score and pay our phone bill."

Her green eyes lock to mine.

"But I can assure you it's going to be ok. You can have your heat. It'll work out."

I'd say the same thing to any omega in her situation sitting in my exam room, but with her, I want her to know that she's my priority. Always.

34

Marked

Kol

The three of us, Locke, Mads, and myself, sit in an SUV across the street from the omega shelter. It's an older street filled with tall leafy trees, so we are sitting in cool shade, that's nice at least.

Locke cannot stop staring at Mads's bite mark. He got it prominently on his neck. It would be difficult to hide. He chose the spot, and Oscar didn't give him a chance to reconsider. We all felt the same emotion at that time—desperate glee.

I'm staring at it, too.

It's just so beautiful.

Mads levels me a look.

"You are actually drooling, Kol," he says. I wipe my mouth. "What is up with you two, it's just a mark."

How could he know how it feels to see Oscar's mark upon his lily white skin? It's like sex. Or pleasure. Its ownership as well as belonging. Bites are everything to a chronically hungry alpha.

"Why did you want it there?" Locke asks the question that I've been too nervous to ask.

"On my neck? Isn't that where it is supposed to be?"

Locke and I share a look—he didn't know. Mads didn't know what it would mean to have a mark on display like that. He's so sweet. All three of us grew up in the culture of alphas and omegas. He's not flippant about these things, he just doesn't know.

I lower my voice and ask, "Did you point to that spot because you thought that's where marks go?"

He doesn't respond.

Yes.

The answer is yes.

I pull down the collar of my shirt and show my mark near my shoulder and top of my chest. "Here's mine. I can hide it with a shirt."

Locke's mark is on the back of his arm. He takes off his shirt to show it to Mads.

There's a pregnant pause in the air.

"Oh."

"Usually, if you pick a spot not easily covered, it's a message," I continue to explain.

"What kind of message is this sending?" He points to his mark.

"That you want everyone to know you belong to Oscar. To not talk to you. Not bother you. That you aren't to be fucked with, honestly. And you being a beta...the message hits even harder. Imagine an alpha tries to sit next to you in a bar, with a mark so obvious like that, Oscar would have every right to knock him on his ass."

Mads goes silent.

If I'm staring right at him, and we are close like in this car, I can feel what he's feeling. Betas don't have the same connection we alphas have. But it's still there.

I can tell he likes this idea. He likes that it sends a message.

And I guess, if I think about it, it's not a bad thing. Mads is still nervous around alphas. His mark may be the ticket to make sure they keep their distance from him. He's thinking this, too, because I can feel his acceptance.

How nice.

Maybe that's why Oscar didn't ask him if he meant it when he chose his neck. Maybe Oscar knew that would be the best spot.

I just thought he wanted his claim to be obvious because it feeds into our alpha egos.

It's a win all around.

Speaking of wins.

"Did you take a look at that listing I sent you?" I ask Mads.

He makes a listening noise, but he's not really listening.

"Yeah, what about it?"

"What did you think?"

"It's a two-bedroom ground floor condo. It's clean, well construct-ed, in an established neighborhood with a doorman. Not sure it's a great investment for your portfolio, but it's not bad."

I make a listening noise, too.

He stares across the street at the security guard near the fence. He greets an omega holding two little kids' hands as they pass through the gate.

"Why do you want it?" he eventually asks.

"Oh, I already bought it."

"Why?" His face is all screwed up like he's judging me.

Oh, silly beta.

"For your mom."

His head swings to me, and his eyes bug out.

"What?"

"It's part of your bonding gift from us. I bought it with cash. Set up the utilities for her. She gets a monthly allowance from Pack Soto. Wasn't that part of your requirements?"

I finished the sale of our last place in Salt Port and got a huge deposit in our account yesterday. So absolutely flushed with cash, I closed on the condo. A property was the easiest thing to buy.

His mouth slowly falls open like he's lost control of it.

"What?" he asks, a loss for other words.

"She'll like it, right? It's between her work and her boyfriend's place. I thought it would be an easy move for her."

"Her boyfriend?"

I laugh at his silly face.

"You didn't know?"

"How did *you* know?"

"Social media? Come on Mads. He's all over her page."

Locke laughs from the back seat.

I think Mads might be a little slow because of our big day yesterday, and then the intensity from the bonding.

I give him some slack. There's a lot going on.

"Well, thank you. It sounds like a good investment."

I chuckle to myself as I continue to stare at his neck. Would he let me lick it? Would Oscar? Oscar might be possessive of his mark.

The time continues to pass as we camp out in the car. I schedule a moving truck for later this week and send the confirmation to Mads's email. Locke and I fight about the price of the new Nintendo console. Mads has to shut it down with an Internet search.

The whole time we wait no one gets bored or anxious. We know why we are here. Locke and I need to be near Mads. He doesn't have our mark on him. Oscar is the bridge. Both of us need his presence to fully accept him into our pack.

Eventually, Locke passed out in the back seat.

Mads adjusts his leg with a small hiss. I completely focus my attention on him, and I feel it through the bond. The pain. Holy fuck. The pain. It's throbbing and everywhere.

"Mads, where are your meds?" I ask in a tight breath.

"I got them. But they'll tear my stomach up if I don't take them with food," he says.

I reach back and shake Locke awake.

"Oh goddamn," Locke says with a hiss as he wakes up. "Mads, that pain is unbearable."

His jaw clenches.

"It's fine. I can go a bit longer."

I turn the engine over and start driving. I think there's something around here. I saw a Chinese market when I was driving down here the other day. The pain is indescribable. It's not a throbbing or a sharp pain. It's like the font of pain.

"I can't sit back here and do nothing," Locke says with a strained voice. I look at him through the rear view mirror. I can't do anything either.

"I'm sorry," Mads says, and I hate that he just apologized for that. I pull over at the first spot I see near a large park.

Locke hops out and opens Mads's door.

"Let me do something. Anything."

Mads doesn't reply. He *is* in a lot of pain.

I come around, too, and we help him out of the car. I push his hair off of his forehead and hold his shoulder with my other hand. Locke, incapable of having boundaries, is crouched down, rubbing his leg.

"Guys, it's fine," he mumbles. I pull Mads into a hug, and Locke continues to massage his leg. He doesn't stop us and we don't intend to stop.

35
Tea Break

Locke

"He's hurting so much," Kol says with the beta leaning against his chest.

"Where are your meds?" I ask Mads gently as I continue to massage his knees and thigh over his jeans.

He looks guilty.

"You can't let the pain get this bad, buddy. It doesn't make you stronger to endure this all the time. It just hurts."

"You can feel it?"

"Yes."

I didn't think we'd be able to feel it, or maybe I didn't think it was this intense. It's made it impossible for me to sit idly by anymore, though. He's going to let us take care of him now. I refuse to stand down.

"The Crimson Lion is a block away from here," Mads remarks.

"What's that?"

"We're in Chinatown. That's the town center, run by Alpha Man-ho. It's nice. There's food."

Cash City has a large Chinese population, but I haven't been to Chinatown yet. I look up and notice the street signs are in Hanzi. The gardens beyond this gate are stunning. We will have to come back. When things settle down. And if we are still alive.

"Let's go eat there, and you can take your meds," I say.

We hold Mads between us, and by the time we make it to the shopping and food center known as The Crimson Lion, we got a good rhythm going. I set them up on one of the picnic tables and then patronize some vendors in the food stalls they have. I get as much as I can and then some.

I place all the food in front of my pack and then go back out for some drinks. I get us three bobas.

I remember how much Mads had to eat at the café, and assume that will help.

We have sesame balls, dumplings, little burger buns, fried dough, and handmade noodles. The market is starting to get busier for lunch, but it's pretty sparse.

The streets all felt empty too.

I pull out my phone and sure enough—it's a full moon tonight. Cash City is a heavily populated city of Alphas and Omegas. Higher than most cities. The full moon means people will start acting crazy. It can even make a beta act funny. An alpha like myself? I can get into a lot of trouble. Most omegas go into heat on a full moon. Alphas can go into a rut. Most babies are born on a full moon. More crime. More deaths. It's wild time out there.

Things may be empty now, but it's like a calm before the storm. This evening and into the night, the streets will be crowded.

"It's a full moon," I tell Kol, whose mouth is full of noodles. Mads finally takes his meds with a full pull of his boba.

Mads realizes he swallowed boba pearls and his meds at the same time. I chuckle at the expression on his face. Both shocked and confused.

I hear Kol mumble *fuck* and then look to the sky. He's most likely to go into a rut.

Gosh, we are fucked. We still don't have our omega. My scent match. I bite into a candied strawberry on a stick. It's delicious. It kind of helps.

We sit in silence, enjoying our food. I see the alphas nearby notice the mark on Mads's throat. They look at us. Look at Mads. See the mark, and then find somewhere else to be.

Kol's panic eases with Mads's pain reduction. We will have to be better beta keepers, knowing how closely tied their emotions are together.

36

Full Moon

Acadia

I can't stay away from the clinic. All day, I go back and forth between the event and the clinic. I hover around under the guise of helping the omegas. Not one of them is deterred by Dr. Soto.

Not one.

Maybe it's the fact that they are gearing up for an omega sex party, or the fact it's a full moon tonight. But they are fawning over my doctor.

Not my doctor.

No, fuck that.

He's my doctor.

The omega in me has decided. Dr. Soto is hers. He's ours.

I like how he teases me. I'm so turned on by the fact he's an omega physician specialist. Well known. He's so handsome.

I go back upstairs when it's obvious his last omega patient is not coming out anytime soon. Plus, I don't want to look like I've been waiting for them.

We've moved the kids into the multipurpose room and started up the movie. There's a volunteer for every two or three kids, so they are well taken care of. There's a buffet table for them to take from. Hot chocolate bar. A reading nook. They are good to go.

I go to the other end of the building. The omegas have started mingling with the partners. Getting to know each other.

Dr. Soto gave a few omegas suppressants and other stimulants to ensure they have a good time tonight. We've done these events before. By morning, most of the omegas will be coming out of it. Dr. Soto seems to know what he's doing.

I avoid the sex room. The smells are starting to get to my head. Or my...other head. Do women have "other heads"? Maybe just omegas have other heads...

I find myself back at the exam room.

The last omega is not leaving the room. The exam seems to be going on way too long. This is ridiculous. I raise my hand to knock and then decide to give them another...no, fuck that. I knock like I'm the police.

The door opens before I can decide if I'm gonna knock a second time. It's just Dr. Soto on the other side. I push past him and look around the empty room. Where is that omega hiding?

When my search turns up no hidden omega I turn to face the doctor. His eyebrow is raised, and his mouth is quirked in a smile.

"Omega Acadia, is everything ok?"

I narrow my eyes at him.

"I thought Giselle was still in here."

He suppresses a smile. "No, she left a while ago. Eager to go meet the males."

I frown and nod.

"I'm all done here if you'd like to join them upstairs."

I don't need to join them. Why would I join them? He must think that's what my plans are for the night. I am dating a beta. I've messed around with Kol, my beta boyfriend's alpha—twice. I don't need a sex party.

But he doesn't know that.

"No, I'm not participating tonight."

"It might help with your impending heat to participate. Maybe you'll meet an alpha who will help you through your heat."

I startle backwards. Like I'd been hit.

"What?"

The omega in me does not adhere to logic or understanding. She's offended he would suggest another alpha take care of her. She's pissed, actually. And so am I.

"Go to hell," I say before I can stop myself. Stupid fucking full moon.

I try to run past him out of the room, but he grabs my arms.

"As your doctor..."

"We were just playing make-believe earlier, Dr. Soto. I'm not your patient. And I didn't come in here to talk to you as a patient. So, don't talk to me like you have authority over me, like you're my handler."

He yanks me even closer to his body. I want our bodies to touch, but there is space between us. I bare my teeth at him. He's so much taller than me, so I have to tip my head back severely to look him in the eye, and he curls over to do the same. The overhead lights flicker. Like there's so much electricity between us, it's blowing out the building's fuse.

"How do you want me to talk to you then, Acadia?"

His nose flares. He can smell how aroused I am.

His fingers press harder on my arms. My breaths deepen. He smells like brewing coffee on early mornings when the dew is just settling on the ground. The birds are just starting to wake.

"Dr. Soto," I start, but he interrupts me.

"Call me Oscar. Please."

"Oscar."

His whole body shivers.

God, I'd like him to do that again. I'd like him to shake all over while I suck his cock dry. I'd like his body out of control while he fucks me from behind, and I'm biting a pillow so hard I rip it open.

"Do you have an omega?" I feel like I know the answer. He said his pack, the one waiting for him, was two alphas and a beta. And it's a silly question for so many other reasons. He could be committed to his pack. The way it is. Stepping out to be with me could be cheating. They could be uninterested in an omega. He could be gay. He could be uninterested in me specifically. He could be in a bad place to be pursuing someone like me...

His hands ease off my arms. I close my eyes. I'm not ready for him to step away from me. But he doesn't. One hand comes up to my face, cupping my cheek.

"*Mi amore,*" he breathes out, barely even speaking.

"Oscar," I say in response. My hands reach out and touch his stomach, and then I wrap my arms around him until we are hugging. And while I'd like it to be a sexy hug, it's just a hug. Like any two people would give. But it's so nice. It resets my brain. He eases my head to rest on his chest, and his thumb strokes my cheekbone. "Is this ok?"

"Of course this is ok."

The omega in me purrs.

He says it like he's already mine.

"Who are you?" I ask because I don't know how else to put my question into words.

He moves us so we can see into each other's faces. This time I'm not baring my teeth at him. But looking up at him with curiosity. He looks like he's in awe.

The lights flicker again.

So odd.

"I'm Oscar Soto. Pack lead of the Soto Pack. I'm from Colombia. My mother was Irish, and my father was Colombian. I wasn't raised by my parents. I emigrated to Salt Port when I was a young man, where I got my undergrad and doctorate in medicine. My pack moved to Cash City a few months back to find an omega. I've waited my whole life for you. I hope I'm worthy."

Oscar's alpha influence floods the space around us.

"And I apologize for overstepping earlier when I suggested you find an alpha for your heat. It was out of line."

God damned. My knees give out, and he holds me up. I've forgotten how sure and powerful an alpha can be. The Whitehorses hardly used their influence. They never made sweeping statements like this. I figured they would grow into it. That we would gain more trust and intimacy, and then they'd reveal their hearts to me. But they were shallow and weak.

Oscar is sweeping me away into his depths. His amber eyes have me in a trance. He strokes my spine with his thumb. It's so soothing.

I want this. I've wanted someone like him. Someone who helps people. Like he did today. Who loves his packmates. And who holds me both lovingly and dominantly. My fingers do the same on his spine. It's an invitation. It's me consenting to whatever he wants to do with me.

"Thank you for your apology. I accept it." I lick my lips. "Is this a formal offer, Alpha Soto?"

I like things to be clear.

"Yes. Acadia, I would like to court you. My pack would like to court you…"

He's about to say so much more, but the lights go out, and we are completely drenched in darkness. We both gasp, and I grapple on to him tighter.

At first, I think about us, and what we will do, but that thought goes away quickly. The kids. The omegas. I let go of Oscar and stretch out my hands to find the cabinet with the flashlights in it. We keep some here in the exam room. It's one of the lower ones.

"The power's gone out. There are flashlights...here," I say as I pull out the box. I try the first one and it doesn't work, but the second one does. I look back in the cabinet for the battery and pull out the big pack, throwing it in the box. "We have to get upstairs."

"Yes, of course, give me the box, and you lead the way," Oscar says to me, and I hand him the box.

We get halfway up the stairs when I get a call from Sebastian Meier.

"Acadia?"

"Yes, Alpha Meier, did you see we lost power?"

"We just found the electrical box–" Just then, the lights come back on.

"What happened?"

"Just a breaker flipped."

"Thank you for looking into it."

"No problem. It's been quiet out here. It was a little bit of excitement for our night."

I smile. He's such a nice guy. I'm happy for Ondine to have an alpha like him.

I check on the kids first, who are fine. A little rowdy, but fine. Apparently, they all started screaming when the lights went out, and that was the worst part. We leave the flashlights with them.

I make my way to the sex room. Oscar stays just behind me. Like a protective force. There's a hall before the doors to the sex room, and some people are taking a break. They are wearing robes or are huddled under blankets. I walk up to a volunteer, my friend Jamie.

"Is everyone ok?" I ask. Oscar stands beside me. His presence is such a comfort.

Jamie sighs. "Cadi, I'm glad you're here. Everyone is fine. I'm not sure most of them even noticed. It was scarier for us volunteers."

"Oh, I'm so sorry, Jamie. Are you ok?" I pat his arm. I'm paying attention to Oscar's reaction to me touching my beta friend. His reaction could make or break my interest in him. If he's one of those dick-ish alphas who gets bent out of shape for me having friends or being close with my colleagues, I won't be happy. But Oscar doesn't react at all.

"I've just had a bad day. My wife is gone for the week for a work trip, and I've just been eating slices of cheese from this huge block of cheddar I bought on the first day. And the block is nearly gone, but she's not back yet."

I stroke his arm as he tells me his woes. Oscar does react slightly at this, but I have a feeling he's trying not to chuckle.

"You can't just eat cheese. Why don't you go to the multi-purpose room and get yourself some real food from the buffet we have there? I think that'll make you feel better. They have hot chocolate, too."

He perks up a little. "Yeah, I'll do that. Everyone in there is doing really well, by the way. You always put together such good events, Cadi. Everyone has been partnering up without drama. All the work you put into this shelter really shows."

My cheeks flush pink.

"Thanks, Jamie."

Jamie nods towards Oscar.

"And thanks, Dr. Soto, for stepping in. We almost needed to cancel if we couldn't find someone to replace Dr. Zheng." Oscar nods his head in thanks. I almost expected him to boast about his reputation or that he is so great for volunteering. But he's humble. I'm inclined to think Oscar is the perfect man at this point. Jamie then adds, "I would be careful about going into the room. I'm no omega expert, but it's a good thing most of the volunteers are betas. We lost Emma to the frenzy. She's in there with Ping. The full moon mixed with your careful vetting has resulted in quite an intoxicating orgy."

He smiles at us both and then leaves to eat something other than cheese.

I take a deep breath, knowing I'll need enough oxygen in order to tell Oscar this.

"I have to go in there to check to make sure everyone is ok. I'll be back."

"I'll go with you," Oscar volunteers.

Hm. Is that a good idea? I'm not sure if this man I'm definitely attracted to, who just made me a courting offer, and I should walk into an orgy together.

I look at him skeptically.

"As a doctor. Unless you want me to go in there as your alpha. I can do that."

Oh, I love a plain speaking alpha.

"I'm going in there as someone running this event, making sure everyone is doing well. Since they are my responsibility. You can go in there however you want."

As I'm talking, I'm removing my shoes and putting them against the wall. There are duffel bags, each person brought lining the hallway. But most of the shoes are against this wall.

I'm trying to get funding for a nice locker room. That'll come in time.

Oscar takes his shoes off as well. I nod at some of the volunteers as I walk toward the double doors. We've kept the lighting in this hall low, so the transition from here into the room isn't so intense. I open the door, and Oscar takes it from me so I can let go and walk in first. I step in and the first I notice is the smells.

It's intoxicating. It speaks to that primal part of myself. It's begging for me to join in.

Then the sounds. A chorus of fucking.

My eyes are still adjusting. Oscar closes the door behind us. I haven't moved an inch, so Oscar reaches down and holds my hand. Our fingers interlace. We wait together until things start becoming clearer. I'm so surprised he can keep himself together in the melee.

I can barely keep it together. And I've done this before.

I know we have eleven omegas, and I guess Emma, too now. I take a deep breath to calm my nerves and head in. The middle of the room has different couch shapes and options, and I find four omegas with their partners splayed across the forms. They are getting fucked from behind. Getting eaten out. Riding their partners from on top.

I try to make eye contact with the more coherent ones, asking with no sound if they are ok. I get nods all around. I'm still holding fast to Oscar's hand. We walk to each private alcove as I count in my head. Oscar looks, too, but with an impassive, professional gaze. Ensuring they are ok.

Eleven omegas and one Emma later, we find an empty alcove. It feels serendipitous.

Oscar looks at me, and in the hazy dark room, I can see the look of lust fill his eyes. Would it be so bad, I think, to use this room? None of the volunteers would judge me. I'm not needed anywhere in particular. If I am needed, any of the other volunteers can cover for me for a bit. We have a whole team of security outside this building, ensuring we are safe. And I'd like to get to know Oscar.

Ok, and I am horny as a freight train.

Oscar takes the first step into the alcove, and I follow him inside. There are noise dampening materials on the walls, so it's quiet within here. There are little orange lights on the wall, so I can see him a little better. He sits me on a half-moon couch. He goes down on one knee in front of me. We are so close. I lean in even closer to him.

"Acadia, I have to tell you some things."

"Ok," I say, and then he takes my hands. I also have things I need to tell him.

I need to tell him about Mads. And Kol. I don't know if I can give them up. I need to tell him how the Whitehorse pack affected me so much. I need to tell him I am technically still enrolled in the Institute, and I need to close that loop with them.

He needs to know that I am a headstrong omega, who talks a lot, likes to be in charge, and I have to have fun, or I will die. And suddenly, realizing we need to talk for days, I decide I don't want to talk.

"Wait, no. We can talk tomorrow. It's the full moon tonight, Oscar. Can you kiss me and make me feel good tonight? Everything else can wait for tomorrow. We can tell each other where we are at. What promises we've made to others. The terms of your courting, and my terms, too. You aren't going anywhere, right? We can talk about it tomorrow?"

He doesn't rush to agree or disagree. He thinks about it. He looks me in the eyes as he thinks about it. I feel so safe with a man who hasn't already made up his mind, who can think in the moment.

"Tomorrow, *mi encantadora omega*. Tomorrow we will talk." I can tell he would prefer to talk tonight, but is letting me get my way. "My pack will want to meet you. We will talk about the terms together. But

I have to warn you, there are things at play here, which require fast courting."

I tip my head to the side. "You want to be bonded for my next heat?" Alphas sometimes won't participate in a heat unless they are bonded with the omega. It's a preference made for many reasons.

"That's not why. We came to Cash City to find an omega, and we are almost out of time. I am so sorry it took us so long to find you."

Curiosity almost wins over my desire to kiss now and ask questions later.

"I understand that you want to talk now, so I am going to assume it's important. I won't hold that against you when I learn about it tomorrow."

And then I lean in for a kiss, and he meets me halfway. It's such a tender kiss. Apprehensive even. I press into him further, and he makes a startled gasp, then presses back. But his lips are closed, and he isn't moving. I take the lead. I guide him through the kiss by licking the seam of his lips until he opens up. He's still letting me lead, so I run my tongue into his mouth. I hold his head steady, tipping him to one side, so we can deepen the kiss.

He moans.

I sigh.

His hands grab my waist. They are big and sure. He rubs my body in little up and down motions.

He breaks from the kiss with a huge smile.

"That was everything I dreamed about."

Something about that doesn't make sense. Is he being cheesy? He just met me today.

"Wait." It hits me. "Was that your first kiss?"

Oscar is much older than me. There is gray in little tracks above his ears. That can't be right.

"Yes, I told you. I waited."

My hand flies to my mouth.

He waits to see how I am going to react. So far, it's just shock. I check in with my primal side, and she approves. She loves the idea that there isn't another woman on this planet that gets to have this handsome alpha other than her. For me? I am a confident woman, but it does shake my own confidence a little, because it's a lot of pressure.

Fuck it. We will talk about it tomorrow.

I throw myself at him.

37

Courting Gift

Mads

We eventually leave The Crimson Lion. We haven't heard from Oscar. It's like he disappeared into that Omega Shelter. Kol and Locke don't seem worried.

Speaking of emotions.

Being bonded to alphas is weird as all hell.

There are some perks already. No one came anywhere near me at the Crimson Lion. I haven't been there since before my accident. Lee Man-ho, the man who owns the mall, keeps a lot of alphas nearby. The place is always crawling with them. And they have a reputation for being kind of wild. But one look at the mark on my neck, suddenly there was a ten foot bubble around me, no alpha was willing to breach.

An unexpected downside is how much my pain affects them. Anyone who lives with daily pain would never wish their worst enemy to be emotionally connected to them. Suddenly, enduring my pain is not a private matter. I'm not sure if we knew this would happen.

The whole time we head back to the shelter, I try to wonder if I need to change how I take care of myself. I have to stop walking so much. I have to elevate my leg. Take my meds on time. Rest. Constantly.

I am not sure I'm ready, though. I'm not ready to limit myself because of my disability.

But I have to. For Kol.

And the rest of them. Right? Otherwise, I'm hurting them.

"Hey," I say as we park. Kol and Locke give me their attention. "When you bond with the omega, will she feel my pain, too?"

They look at each other.

I wince.

"I would imagine," Kol says.

Fuck.

"Why did we do this?" I ask, but not really looking for an answer. Locke puts a hand on my shoulder and squeezes.

"It's ok, man. You'll just have to let us take care of you. I can be in charge. You don't have to do it. I can do it for you."

"No."

He takes his hand back.

"You're not going to get some sort of prize for enduring the most pain, Mads," Kol says.

"But it's all I have..."

"What?" They both ask.

"It's the last thing I have left. Those alphas took everything from me. All they left me with was this pain. If that's gone, I have nothing left."

I don't want to hear what they think of that. I can't even believe I said it out loud. I turn on the radio and start switching through stations.

I decided yesterday to bond with these guys to help them out with their omega. I knew they wanted it to be forever, but I can't wrap my head around that. How are we going to deal with my pain, when my best way so far is to ignore it as long as possible? What a shit show. Kol and Locke just stare at each other. Having a silent conversation.

"Can we go to my apartment? I'd like to tell my mom about the new place."

Kol looks at his phone and then to shelter.

"I'll text Oscar. But yeah, let's go do that."

"Can we make a stop first?"

I guide them to the animal shelter. I tell them about Mr. Snoots, my mom's companion animal. She has mentioned getting a new dog nearly every day; well, until I didn't get the settlement money. Then she stopped.

We spend about an hour with the dogs, even though I found one right away. I fill out all the forms for Benny, a Cocker Spaniel and Shitzu mix. It's evening by the time we get to the apartment. The three of us and Benny go into the apartment, finding my mom on the couch watching tv. I like to see her relaxing. She hardly ever does.

"Mom," I say as I hold Benny. She pops up off the couch, looking very confused.

"Who's this?" she asks, and then repeats the question in Dutch.

Kol and Locke go sit at the kitchen table, since the living room doesn't have enough seats. I hand Benny to my mom and she loves all over him.

"This is Benny. He's yours."

"No, that's silly. Mads, I can't take care of a dog. We can't. And this apartment doesn't allow dogs. They'll kick us out."

"Good, because I have a new apartment for you."

She sets Benny down and puts her hands on her hips, asking for an explanation.

"Mom, let's sit," I say, mostly because I'm starting to feel the familiar ache in my leg. We sit down next to each other. Benny is already glued to my mom like he knows who is his.

"I've bonded with the Soto pack. As part of my bonding package, they've bought you an apartment. They also have an account set up with a monthly allowance. It's more than you make now."

She shakes her head. She's just like me. Not used to others providing for her. But we can't really turn this down at this point. I need her to be worry free. I have to have her be ok.

I ask if she wants to see it, and she needs me to explain this all three or four more times. Which I do.

"Why?" she asks, wondering why I bonded.

"The offer was too good," I say instead of any real or honest answer.

She knows I'm barely giving her a reason. But she pats me on the cheek anyway.

"You're a good man, Mads. I hope they know how lucky they are to have you."

"We know," Kol says. "He's in good hands."

"I don't like this. You come in here with a puppy and a new house, and a bite mark like an angry bear dug his claws into your neck. But I guess this is the world we live in. Your father was courted by a pack once."

She says that last thing so flippantly, I barely catch. I didn't know this about my dad. I knew he died when I was three. I have no memories of him.

He had a heart attack while driving and sped into a lake. My whole life, he's been this missing person. No one came to take over for him.

I look at my mom. I really look at her. My mom has seen a lot of grief. She's raised me all on her own. She deserves a nice place and a cute puppy. She deserves so much more.

Kol gives her the keys to the new place and explains when the truck and movers will be by. He leaves information on where her mailbox is and the parking stall. She kisses me on the cheeks and forehead, and we say our goodbyes.

"Goodbye, mom."

"Goodbye, sweetheart. I'll see you tomorrow."

38

Virgin Alpha

Acadia

We've been making out in this alcove for so long, time has lost all meaning. We lay horizontally next to each other. He's so gentle with me. His hands explore my body like he's memorizing every dip and curve. In return, he is so sensitive to my touch. It's all so new to him. I didn't think having a virgin alpha would be this exhilarating.

I stroke his cock over his slacks. He's a big guy. My god. His head tilts back, and he moans. And then he grabs my wrist to stop me.

"Stop, or I'll..."

"That's kind of the point," I say.

"No, show me how to make you...have a point." His deep growl reverberates through me. His hand finds my inner thigh, and he moves it up towards my center. I lift my leg to give him more access.

"Just pay attention. Do what makes me feel good," I say.

He does just that. He looks me in the eyes and watches as he strokes my pussy over my shorts with his hand. His movements are slow and effective. He's working me real good.

His hand goes even higher, allowing his thumb to coast under my panties. I whimper at the sensation, so he does it again and again.

I'm stoked. So, I stop him and undo the button of my shorts and panties, then slide them down my thighs. He takes over and takes them off completely. Suddenly, with nothing down there in the way, I'm a little nervous. I'm never nervous when it comes to sex. But this is different. Oscar is different. It feels brand new to me, too.

He starts again at my thigh and runs his fingers up. He takes his two middle fingers and swipes them gently over my pussy lips. I moan and drop my head to the side.

"Wow."

He sets his two fingers there until the pressure eases him in. Then he spreads his fingers as he continues pushing into my cunt.

I'm panting. I'm grabbing onto him.

"Oscar," I plead. I need him to fuck me with those fingers. "Don't tease me."

He adjusts himself and then, before I can take another breath, he starts pumping his fingers in and out of my very wet cunt.

I'm gripping onto his shirt. I'm kissing his mouth. And I start fucking his fingers back. I want to come. I want to come like this with him.

Like he can hear my thoughts, his thumb pressed down on my clit.

"Fuck yes!" I cry over his mouth. "More! Harder!"

He pushing harder and starts circling my clit aggressively as he continues pumping his fingers inside of me.

I'm squirming and moving, and everything is climbing higher and higher. He adds a third finger, and I explode. I cry out in ecstasy as my climax greets me fully. It takes over my entire body. Oscar kisses my jaw, neck, and shoulder. Leaving little bites and sucking marks. His hand leads me through my climax completely.

"Fuck, Oscar," I pant.

He gives me the biggest smile.

I wrap my arms around him and pull him closer. I throw my legs over his and pull him tight against me.

"Wow," I say.

"You're so beautiful."

"Do you want to do more? Is it your turn?" I touch him again, and he's hard as all hell.

"Let's just lay here a while. Is that ok?"

"'Course."

And we lay there while he massages my thighs and runs his fingers over my scalp. It's all so relaxing and peaceful. He kisses my cheeks and tells me how beautiful I am.

This is the kind of alpha you want courting you. A man focused solely on you. Amazed by you. I can only imagine the kind of lover he will be. He's going to be great during my heat.

We stare each other in the eyes, just basking in this feeling. It's going to be the start of something great.

I sigh and make my way out of our bundle.

"I need to get back to my pack. They've been waiting all day for me. You'll meet me tomorrow? To discuss the terms of our courting? Yes?" Oscar asks, hesitant to let me go.

"Yes. Where?"

He twists to get his phone that had fallen onto the floor at one point. "I'll text you the details."

"I have an appointment in the morning. I can meet any time after that."

"Good. Good."

He pockets his phone, and we stand up. He helps me into my panties and shorts, using it as an excuse to touch my thighs again.

He kisses my knees and then rises to kiss my neck and jaw, and then finally the lips.

We interlace our fingers again and leave the alcove.

The orgy is still going, and I check on the omegas again on our way out. I feel like I'm floating.

39

The Scent of Her

Oscar

My pack is sitting in the dark in the parked car. I knock on the driver's side window, and Kol lowers it to look at me.

"Whatever you're selling, I'm buying, handsome."

I roll my eyes.

"Sorry to have you wait here all day," I say.

"We went out for lunch. Then went to Mads's apartment for a bit to talk to his mom. It's fine."

My chest relaxes being closer to them again, but there's a pinch of dissatisfaction from leaving Acadia. My lips are swollen from our kisses. I just want to return to her as soon as possible.

"I have something important to tell you all. I'd like to wait until we get to the apartment. So, try not to lose your minds when I get into the car."

Kol looks confused. I get into the back seat with Locke. As soon as I shut the door Locke and Kol stiffen up.

"Oh my god," they both say, their voices strained and cracking. Loud and accusatory.

"What?" Mads asks.

"What the fuck is happening right now?" Locke asks with deep, heavy breaths, like he's about to lose it. He's pushed against the door as far away from me as possible. His eyes are the size of moons.

"Why is everyone freaking out?" Mads asks again.

I put my hand on his shoulder to calm him, even though it's my other two pack mates who need it the most.

"I met Acadia. She was running the event."

"Did you fuck her?" Locke asks.

"No. But we were intimate."

"I don't smell Acadia," Kol says. He turns around as much as he can in the front seat. "You don't smell like Acadia. You smell like Mads's omega girlfriend, Cadi."

A heavy silence falls in the car.

"Yes, I sorted that out as well when the staff called her Cadi. I suspected she was the same omega. And your reaction to her scent confirms it. Mads, you've been dating the omega we've been seeking. Locke's scent match. And my soulmate."

Kol opens his mouth to speak, but nothing comes out. Locke unpeels himself from the car door and inches his way closer to me, to get a better sniff.

"When I went to the club last week, Locke, to find relief, I was with an omega. She was so perfect. I wanted her more than anyone. Mads and I were together when Cadi, his girlfriend, came to see him. She was the same girl from the night at the club."

The omega from the soirée at the Institute. The girl from the club. Mads's omega girlfriend. And the woman who needed me at her event at the Omega Shelter—all Acadia.

"Do we believe in god?" Mads asks. Using "we" like he's now part of something new.

"My clan believed in Fate," Locke says. He doesn't talk much about the clan who gave him up.

"Fate has her hands in the destiny of alphas and omegas," Kol says. "I don't know about betas. I was a kid when I left them. You'll have to Google it."

"So wait," Locke says, "Do we know why she had a preference for betas?"

We all try to think.

"She met me on a beta only dating app. She didn't bring up why she was on the app, and I didn't ask. I know she'd never dated or been with a beta before."

"She told me she'd been courted and under contract with a pack until recently," I add.

Locke growls. Aggressively.

"I made an offer to court her. She said she is willing. She kissed me. Held my hand. She said we will meet tomorrow. I didn't tell her about you three. She didn't want to talk. She said she wanted to kiss now, and talk tomorrow."

Kol and Locke both love that. They are impressed.

"How was your first kiss?"

Mads's shock gets through the bond.

"She's wonderful. Fiery, but kind. And so beautiful. I've never seen anyone as beautiful. She took the breath out of me. Locke, we found her."

Locke is feeling a lot of feelings.

I'll let him cycle through them for now.

"Kol, let's get home. It's been a long day."

We drive home. On the way, Kol keeps bringing up how insane this is. He uses words like serendipitous, chance, fate, and destiny. Locke is silent. Mads is making noises instead of words. He's too shocked.

I don't blame him.

He gets to keep his girlfriend.

Kol gets to keep his mystery omega.

Locke gets his scent match.

I get the girl of my dreams.

We just have to play this right. I need to write this out on the whiteboard when we get home. It's Tuesday now. Tomorrow, Acadia will go to the Institute in the morning and be presented with our file. She'll see that we are who we are. She'll be able to process it without us breathing down her neck. Then she will meet us after. We will explain our situation.

She needs to bond with us by Friday. Locke's birthday is Friday.

I'll go to Salt Port and tell Legs that we reached his deadline. Locke is ours.

He will have to find a new alpha to bed his spoiled daughter.

If he won't let us go, then I'll have to take matters into my own hands. I'll have to show them why I'm Pack Soto's lead alpha.

I want my pack together. Alive. Healthy. Happy. Unconnected with Legs and his people.

We arrive at the apartment, and Locke starts making us sandwiches. Kol pours us each a beer. We sit at the table, and I start writing the timeline on the board.

"Kol, while I'm in Salt Port, you'll be here with Acadia. I'm hoping she can help with your rutting. Locke, I'm not sure you can be away from your scent match after bonding. I know you. I think you should stay with them."

He doesn't react. He's deep in thought.

"Can I go with you?" Mads offers.

I consider it. It would make the most sense. Mads is clever. He can be violent. He wears my mark prominently on his neck, which will show the Salt Port alphas how much influence I have. It will only give evidence of my reputation. I got the omega I said I would get, and now also have a loyal beta.

"You know there will be lots of alphas there, yes?"

Mads sucks in his lips. He thinks about it. Finally, he says, "I'll manage."

"Ok, you should come. I would like you there with me."

I go over the timeline again. It's tight. Real tight.

"I need everyone together this whole week. Kol, no working. Locke, you're a house alpha this week. I want you glued to our sides. Mads, is that going to be a problem?"

He shakes his head.

We eat our sandwiches and drink our beers. I type up our letter to Acadia, and everyone reads through it and adds their own lines.

I take the couch. Mads sleeps in my bed. Locke and Kol go to their room. I can hear them whispering inside.

Everything is going to be ok.

40

Places, Everyone

Acadia

I put on my lilac colored dress today. My necklace feels warm against my chest. I do my hair in little twists and flower clips. My appointment at the Institute is soon and I decide to take a car service to it.

The rest of the event went great. My team is there now cleaning it up. They understand me not being there for that. The Meier Protection group left early this morning. I got about six hours of sleep, which I think is pretty good all things considered.

I cannot believe what happened with Oscar. It feels like a dream. I'm not even worried about Mads or Kol. For some reason, it feels like everything is going to work out. Like Fate.

I'm admiring my outfit in my mirror when my handler, Maria, comes into my room. She's eating a bowl of ice cream and wearing an orange and pink tropical floral dress.

"You look very pretty. What're your plans today?"

Maria has access to my calendar, and I know she checks it. But she probably noticed something different about me.

"I have my appointment at the Institute. But I've been given an initial offer to court by an alpha. I'm going to meet with him and his pack after to discuss the details."

"Oh my god, Acadia!" she exclaims. She sets the bowl down and comes over to me with open arms. I take her up on the hug. She has a pine needle scent. It irritates my nose a bit, and so I try not to breathe until we part.

"Tell me about him!"

I smile and go back to fixing my outfit in the mirror.

"His name is Oscar. He's older. Not as old as the Whitehorses. He's Latin with an accent. He's so kind. He's a doctor."

"Oh my god, that's enough to make any girl wet."

Oh, Maria. That's so much. I do not want to talk like that with you.

"Have you told them about your family?"

I knew she was going to ask that next.

That is the whole reason I am 24 and haven't found my pack. The reason I wanted things to work out with the Whitehorses. They didn't ask questions. They didn't care. They never brought it up again.

My family has a reputation and history in this city. And it's not pleasant. Growing up, I was a pariah. No one wanted to invite me over. No one came to my birthday parties. When I grew up and got a chance to only go by my first name—things got better. I made lots of omega friends here in the housing. I only ever had to bring up my family when courting. And usually, when an alpha heard who I was, they were out.

The Institute is a different story. They fawn over me there because of who my family is.

I sigh.

Yes, that's one of the things we will need to discuss today.

"Not yet."

"Ok, then we won't get excited until that's done." She picks up her ice cream and twirls out of the room.

I pat my necklace. I'll probably have to take it off before I meet the Soto pack. Is it gauche to wear someone else's courting gift?

I admire it on my neck. It's so beautiful.

Wait.

Didn't Angeline at the Institute tell me the alpha who gave this to me was a Latin man with a mustache? She said he had an accent.

No, that would be a huge coincidence.

She also said they were three alphas, but the Soto pack is three alphas and a beta. So that doesn't add up. I get a text that my car is here, so I grab my little purple purse and run out of the apartment.

"Goodbye, Maria!" I call out.

I get into the back of the car and we drive out. Something isn't right. My mind is whirling. The necklace came from a Latin man with a mustache.

Oh my god.

I remember. Angeline said, *I shouldn't be telling you this but they are courting a beta*. She said that. Oscar also told me they'd just bonded a beta.

My god.

I gasp, and my hand flies to my face. The driver looks back at me, and I signal I'm fine.

I think Oscar saw me at the soirée. Or someone from his pack did. But they must have missed me. He gave me this necklace. It's probably what he wanted to tell me last night.

When we pull up to the Institute, I race out. The steps never seemed so severe before. I fly up them to the glass doors and rush in. I go through security on bouncing feet and then rush up to the room I usually see Angeline in. The big glass conference room.

Thank god she's waiting for me.

I burst through the doors, calling out her name.

"Acadia! What's going on?" She stands up to match my energy. She's wearing a yellow dress and her hair is slicked back into a bun.

"Who gave you this necklace?"

There's a smile there on her lips she is suppressing.

"Angeline, tell me."

"Why don't you take a seat?"

I collect myself so I don't attack her and get arrested for assault. Plus, I like her. I wouldn't want to harm her.

I sit down. Angeline fires up the display on the large wall and then slides me over a file across the glass table.

"Acadia, I'm excited to show you a pack that meets all your requirements and preferences. Meet Pack Soto."

My hands coves my mouth.

Soto.

41

Preferences

Acadia

Angeline clicks a button on a small device, and there's a photo of four men. They are sitting in various poses on a couch, like they'd propped the phone up on a TV. I gasp and kick my chair back. It's not seeing Oscar smiling politely in the middle that gets me. It's seeing Mads and Kol flanking him.

What the fuck is happening right now?

And if that's not crazy enough, there's a new alpha in the photo that garners all my attention. He has long blonde hair. A strong oval face. Piercing clear eyes. He's wearing a zip up hoodie and black jeans, and a band t-shirt. A Delta 3 band t-shirt, with the logo of three delta symbols sprawled across the front like they were spray painted on. I have the same t-shirt in a babydoll cut at home, and I wear it all the time.

"Who is that?" I ask even though I have a hundred other important questions. I point at the unknown man, and I can't look away. I lean in, he's wearing my fucking shirt.

"Oh, that's Locke. Locke Soto. He's an alpha. He likes EDM, animals, and home repair shows."

I walk closer to the projection. I can't help but believe that I made this happen by my will alone. Am I a witch? I feel like I'm going to pass out. I need to sit down. I sit on the conference table, but I'm still staring at the photo.

He likes hiking and repair shows? I wonder if he watches the same ones I do.

"There are more photos, if you want to see," Angeline offers. I think I nod. I'm not even sure if I'm blinking.

"Ok, here's Dr. Oscar Soto. He's 34 years old. He went to Meribelle Marquis Salt Port Medical University. He's an omega specialist. He did his residency at the Omega Clinic in Dune Acres. He's published three articles in very well respected medical journals. He lectures and attends conferences. He's looking for a permanent position here in Cash City. He likes cooking shows, coffee, kayaking, and whiteboards. His scent profile is described as brewing coffee."

Oscar is shown in his lab coat at the Dune Acres Omega Clinic surrounded by happy omegas. He looks so handsome.

Angeline clicks to the next slide. Kol stands there in a very nice pinstriped suit, sitting on the concrete steps of the municipal building downtown.

His face.

I've never seen his whole face.

"Can you zoom in?" I ask, and she clicks around until she finally zooms into his handsome face. My imagination didn't do him justice. If I didn't know him, I'd think he was all good looks and nothing else. He has the kind of face that can get him anything, if he just asked. But I know Kol. I know how big his heart can be.

"This is Alpha Kol Soto. He is 29 years old. He's a real estate investor. He runs his own firm, KOL Investment Management." She pronounces it Kay-Oh-Elle. I note it's their initials: Kol, Oscar, and

Locke. It's also cute because it's Kol's name. "There, he manages a small property and real estate portfolio. This is where most of the pack's money comes from. He likes dancing, making cocktails, sailing, and fine dining. His scent profile is…" I say it silently at the same time Angeline says it, "earthy fall leaves."

She clicks to the next slide.

My eyes are drying out from not blinking.

"This is Alpha Locke Soto." Locke is smiling and looking off camera at someone who clearly made him laugh. He has a 100 watt smile. "He's 24 years old. He works for KOL Investment Management with Kol. But he describes his dream job as 'house alpha' since he prefers domestic work. As I mentioned, he loves animals, specifically dogs and cats, but said he could tolerate a bunny, and enjoys amateur DJing, like I said. His scent profile is the salty sea air."

Salty sea air. I take a deep breath and imagine what that would smell like on an alpha. All I can see are my memories of me and my family on the beach. Not this beach on the river, but during our summer on the Gulf of Mexico, where we would rent a house and do nothing but swim and eat food on the boardwalk.

Or is it more like the beaches in Oregon? Where you can hear the seals and the tumultuous ocean waves. The hard packed sandy beaches and large black rocks.

I'm desperate to know.

She clicks to the next slide.

Mads peers down at me. He is leaning on a brick wall with his cane carefully hidden near his leg. His white blonde hair is combed and in place. He looks like how I know him. A tight smile. Strain in his eyes. I just want to help him. I know I can help him find that spark again.

"This is Beta Mads Soto. Newest bonded member of the Soto pack. He's the personal assistant, PA, to Kol Soto at KOL. He has his

Master's of Business from Fair Castle University here in Cash City. He likes aquariums, hot springs, flying his drone, and tall beers. His scent profile is not available. But I heard Kol and Locke argue between a scone and a croissant."

I'm not sure if it's the not blinking thing or the emotional turmoil I'm in, but I have to wipe both my cheeks from the tears running down them. I take a shuddering breath.

I turn to Angeline, who is very shocked that I'm crying.

"Oh my god, Acadia. Are you ok? Do you need anything?"

She sets the remote down and rushes to a cabinet for a box of tissues. She comes up and hands it to me.

"Are you ok?" she asks again.

I nod.

I think.

"I know some of them." I dab my face and blot my eyes with the tissue to not ruin my makeup. Angeline sets her hand on my shoulder in comfort. Professional comfort.

"You know Pack Soto?" I don't answer her. I don't really want to. I want to go to them. I feel the distance between us, both physical and otherwise, and it aches. "Well, this is a good thing, no? I'll start up the paperwork for courting now. We can bring you in to work out the details. Call your handler and lawyer. Should we plan a meet and greet for tomorrow?"

"No, now. Right now. I'm not waiting."

"They seem motivated as well. I'll call them now. Get your lawyer here. Get your handler here."

She looks so concerned for me. I don't think she's ever seen me this much of an emotional wreck.

My hands are shaking.

I'm having trouble focusing.

I ease off the table and walk over to where my purse and phone are.

I am not even sure if I call the right people. But hopefully my lawyer and Maria are on their way.

This is happening. This is really happening.

Mads's picture still sits on the projector.

Why do I feel like it all started with him for us all? The keystone to our pack. Mads needs us, and we are desperate for him. I check my last messages with him. Yesterday I told him I had the event and would text him today. He said he had news to share with me. It was probably that he'd bonded with the alphas who were courting him. I smile at the little red hearts he'd sent me.

Angeline comes back into the room with a huge smile on her face.

"I just called them and they are on their way. This is so exciting! I love this part. Their lawyer sent over a preliminary contract for you to review, as well as a courting letter. I'll let you review those. I'll have everything set up. The meet-and-greet will happen first, and then the paperwork meeting. I've got the room almost ready. I suggest letting the men wait for you in there for a bit. So just sit tight here. Do you want a water?"

I nod, and she gives me a sparkling water from a mini fridge. It's the same flavor and brand Mads got me on our date to the movie on the waterfront. The lime seltzer.

I open it and drink half.

She slides the folder over with the Pack Soto name across the top of it. I glide my finger over the words, then I open it up.

"Here, I printed out their Intent to Court letter for the file."

I take it from her and set it on the open file.

It reads:

Dear Omega Acadia,

By now, you should be aware that you know some of Pack Soto, and that we have intended to court you for a while now. I will tell you the story so you know how it happened. Kol, Locke, and myself enrolled at the Institute because we need an omega. We attended many soirees and meet-and-greets, but it wasn't looking like we'd find you. At this last one, Locke took a walk to the pond where he saw a beautiful omega looking out over the water.

He was able to smell you, Acadia, and he believes he is your scent match. Overcome with emotions, he came to find us first, so we could approach you together, but by the time we went back out to the pond, you were gone.

We asked Angeline about you, and she gave us your name based on our description. Acadia. I think that's when Kol and I started to fall in love.

But Angeline said that you had a preference, keeping us from courting you. You only wanted to be presented with packs that have a beta in them. It was, or something like that, that brought us to Mads. He answered an ad for a personal assistant job at KOL and interviewed with Kol that next day. Kol was sure he was the man for the job.

We courted Mads, who was reluctant at first, and we all became closer than ever before. He agreed to the bond the day before last.

We knew Mads had an omega girlfriend. And we knew she was the same woman Kol was with at the club recently. We didn't know, until yesterday, she was also you.

You called me. You found my name, and you called me.

Acadia, I don't pretend to know the ways of the universe or the powerful forces that dictate our lives. But if something is urging things to happen, this is it. We are it.

We have much to discuss. But know this, we desire you. Every member of this pack has their reasons for choosing you. We'd love to share them with you.

I promise you our love and fealty. I promise my days will be to your satisfaction and benefit.

We only ask that you consider our timeline. We desire your bond this week.

Talk soon, mi amore—

Dr. Alpha O. Soto

I'm crying again. Angeline pushes the tissues towards me. My makeup has got to be insane right now. Whatever.

"A scent match is a wild claim normally. But based on your reactions to their photos and letter alone, I don't doubt it."

Angeline read my letter.

"Do you not have any privacy, Angeline?"

"Not at the Institute, Cadi."

I'd been avoiding the Institute for so many reasons, this was one of them.

I touch the pendant. It's warm from my skin.

"Where do they live?" I ask, imagining I'll yell at someone about my privacy soon enough, and can let it go now.

"They are renting an apartment in the Kestrel Burrow. They intend to buy a place that their omega chooses with them."

Oh wow, ok. I take another sip of the sparkling water, the bubbles bite at my nose.

She gets a message on her phone.

"They are here in the meet and greet room. Take your time. We will head over when you are ready."

This feels like it is all converging at this one moment, but I need to keep my head on straight. The whole reason I said I wanted a pack with a beta was because I wanted to be with a pack that didn't discriminate because of designation. I wanted to have babies and have those babies be loved, no matter how they come out. I'll have to find out if they truly want Mads or just did it because it was the path to me.

I also need to tell them about my family.

I stand up and fix my dress.

"Let's go."

42

The Last Meet-Cute

Locke

We arrive as soon as we can. Oscar had everything prepared. He spent this morning ironing our shirts. He made sure we wore our suits. Kol wore his emerald suit. I wore my black and gold paisley suit. And Oscar has his well tailored burgundy suit.

Mads is in a black suit and a white button up. We didn't have time to get him into a color. Oscar told me that Acadia is purple, so that only leaves blue or orange for Mads.

"Black and white is great," Mads insists.

"But you look like our staff. Maybe we can do all black or all white?" Kol unhelpfully says.

We are in the meet and greet room. It's an atrium. It is a glass building in the gardens, sunken low into the ground. There are tables and chairs. Along the wall, a table with a white cloth over it is covered in finger food. There are drinks and a bar cart.

Against the wall are some couches and upholstered chairs.

I check the labels on the wine. Good stuff.

I'm sure we will be billed for it all later.

Oscar says, "We will take him into the men's store and try out a few colors. I think blue would look nice. Or maybe silver, to be the opposite of Locke."

The two of them will talk about clothes all day if no one stops them.

I stuff some grapes into my mouth.

It's been 45 minutes. I thought she'd be here by now. I'm the last one to meet her. I keep going back to that night I saw her by the pond. It doesn't even feel real anymore. Like I made it up.

Kol's been with her twice. Oscar and she shared his first kiss. I don't even know what intimate things Mads and she have done. Movies, jokes, talking about their days.

And the whole time I've been screwing Mickey in a hotel room.

"Stop," Oscar says from across the room. He's looking at me. He can feel my anxiety and my shame. I meet his eyes. "Go for a walk. Clear your head."

Kol and Mads look over at me, too. They'd been talking about work together. But they stopped to look at the mess I am. I close my eyes and take a deep breath.

"I'll be back," I say, and take the stone steps up out of the atrium. I walk across the lawn and towards a path that leads me through some trees, and then suddenly this looks familiar.

This path leads to the pond. Trees and flower beds lead the way to that place that haunts my every waking thought. I can't close my eyes without seeing this pond. Fiery lines of energy coast up and down my skin, the closer I get. I've slowed down to a crawl.

The bend in front of me opens up to the expanse of the water. The midday sun glistens over the ripples, nearly blinding me.

And standing at the edge of the water is an omega with short black hair wearing a purple dress.

The closer I get to her, the more details I can see. There are little embroidered butterflies on her dress. Her hair is done up in twists. She faces the water, but I have a feeling I'm not sneaking up on her. She's been waiting for me.

My cock is responding to her like I just went through puberty.

I take in a deep breath, and her lilac and honey smell penetrates every part of me. I keep taking steps closer, letting the gravel under my shoes make as much noise as possible. She still doesn't turn around.

I stand next to her, looking over the water—side by side. I put my hands in my pocket and will my cock to chill the fuck out.

She takes a deep breath. My scent mate is taking me in. I wait to see how she reacts.

She hooks her arm with mine and leans into me. Touching her elicits a physical reaction unlike any other. We don't even know each other.

Yet our bodies sing the same song.

"Hello Acadia," I say.

"Locke, is it?"

"Yes. God, it feels good to be near you."

"Like you quieted a noise I didn't realize was always playing in my head?"

Yes. She quiets all the noise. The hunger. The fear. The anxiety. I lean against her and she lays her head on my shoulder.

If nothing else, I can always offer this solace for her. If she ever needs to feel this, I'll be there for her. If we have nothing in common, if she loves them more, at least I can offer this.

"Didn't try to find me?" she asks. I turn to see her face. I need to look at her. She stands up straight and turns as well.

"I did. I wandered the city like a fool. Little did I know, everyone else in my pack already had you."

Her eyes narrow. "No one has me."

I smile.

God, she's beautiful. She has freckles and green eyes. A little silver nose ring. I want to push her hair back to see more of her. I lift my hands.

"May I?"

She looks a bit confused but nods.

I lift her hair and look at her ears. One is covered in piercings. The other only has only one. All silver and pearly. I touch the little charms and gems, then tug on her earlobe. I trace my knuckle down her neck to her clavicle and shoulder. Goosebumps erupt under my touch.

"You're so special, aren't you?"

Her dark lips perk up in a smile.

"You're special, too, I'm guessing."

"Me? Nah. I'm no one. But I'll be good to you. You can always rely on me. I'll take good care of you, omega."

She tilts her head. Does she believe me? She should. I can already tell I will love her more than anyone. More than how I feel about Oscar. More than the kinship I feel with Kol. And more than the feelings I have for our new beta.

"Speaking of looking for you, I have a gift for you." I reach into my pocket and pull out a palm-sized flat stone. I lay it on my palm and present it to her.

"What is it?" She asks and takes it.

"It's just a rock. I picked it up on the night I scented you. The night of the soirée. I came looking for this pond to skip the stone across it, but instead I found you."

She smiles as she takes it from me. Her thumb rubs across the surface.

"How weird was that—finding your scent match?"

"It scared me half to death. I went to get Oscar and Kol, who will be much better alphas to you, and when we got back here you were gone."

She continues to look at the stone as she says, "I'm excited to get to know you, Locke. Oscar and Kol are wonderful alphas. They wouldn't have you in their pack if they didn't believe you were also wonderful. We have a lot to look forward to."

At this moment, I'm glad for my instincts to go get Oscar and Kol when I first recognized her. I love that she's here, already knowing and accepting them before me. It calms my anxious heart.

"Come on, let's go meet your pack," I say and smile away the last of my anxiety.

She turns and the sun hits her eyes, so I put up my hand to block it from her face. She smiles under the shade of my hand.

I was so scared to meet her, but she's like someone I've known my whole life. A missing part of me. Or I'm a missing part of her.

She steps away from the pond. "Ok, I'm ready."

She takes my hand and we walk together.

43

Pack Soto

Acadia

L ocke holds my hand, and it's like a puzzle piece locking into place. There are no thoughts in my head. I'm not thinking about how nuts it is that I don't know anything about this person, aside from the fact he apparently likes pets and DJing. It feels like I don't need to know those things right now. Those are future problems to face. It feels like, for now, things have at least started out on the right foot.

Things are going to be ok, now that I have Locke Soto next to me.

He's tall, like most alphas. His naturally blonde hair has grown out to his chin. He's got a pointy chin and oval face. The first thing that I noticed about him are his million year-old eyes. They look like he's seen it all. I wondered if he and Mads are friends. They both are weighed down by the world around them. Burdened. But there's a light hidden inside still burning. I can see it in fleeting moments.

He leads me to the atrium, and we open the glass doors and then stop at the top of the stairs, looking down at the space. It's nice. I've been here for cocktail hours. But it's no longer full of strangers. Three men look up at me.

Mads grins at me, and I grin back. It's the first time I've seen him in a suit. He looks really sharp.

Next is Oscar. I cannot wait to make out with him again. He's holding a present in his hands and a bouquet of lilac blossoms.

Then there's Kol, who doesn't have his muzzle. I take a sharp breath. My imagination did not do him justice. He's a genuine hottie. A face fit for Superman with a cut jaw and pillowy lips. He looks like every celebrity crush I've ever had.

I cannot stop staring.

Locke leads me down the steps and down the middle of the room to meet them. It feels like a wedding. Like I'm the bride.

Oscar meets me first.

"Acadia," he says.

"Cadi is fine," I correct for the first time. Now that we are doing this, I'd prefer Cadi.

He dips his chin. "Cadi."

"Are you doing ok?"

I laugh and hold onto Locke tighter.

"This is wild."

Kol laughs, too. He looks great in his suit.

"I told them last night, and I'm not sure we all thought it was real until we got the call from Angeline."

"I'm still not sure if I know this is real."

"I'm going to hug you, and then we'll talk."

I nod, and Oscar hands the gift to Mads, then pulls me into a hug. I bury my face in the crook of his neck. He smells so good. Smells like home.

When he lets go, Kol is there to take over. He's so tall. I take the opportunity to rub my face on his for the first time, and then he takes the opportunity to scent me. He rubs his neck and face against my neck and face. Our scents mingle, and it's euphoric. The omega in me loves it. She's so happy.

Oscar pulls him away from me and then gestures for Mads to hug me next, taking the gift from him. Mads. My beta. I feel like I know him the least. And that thought nearly knocks me off my feet. I kiss him on the cheek as he pulls away.

"Come sit," Oscar says, and we all take a seat at a round table. Oscar sets the gift in front of me.

It's a purple bag with purple tissue paper. I pull them out and take out a live pothos plant.

I mean, I love it, but what a strange gift. I look to Oscar, who defers to Mads.

"I picked it out. In your profile pictures, you had lots of plants on the window. I wanted you to have a new plant. For your new...adventure."

I finger the leaves and smile. I love the gifts.

"Thank you."

Oscar is across the table from me, next to Kol. Locke is next to me, and Mads is on my other side.

This is it, huh? All boys. And me.

"We need to talk."

"So you say."

Oscar shakes his head and smiles.

"We are highly motivated to bond with you this week. I understand that's soon. We intend to continue to court you for a long time, but this has to happen. Now. As soon as possible."

"Why?"

Kol speaks up, "We each have our reasons. So, Oscar will tell you his first. Then mine. Then Locke. It's a lot. So, we will be patient. React how you need to."

I see how serious they all are suddenly. I look to Mads, who definitely knows what they are all going to say. He heard them out and bonded them, so maybe it's not so bad?

Oscar unbuttons his suit jacket.

"I've been unable to secure a job here in Cash City, being an alpha with only male alphas in my pack. I know the omegas don't mind, but the administration in the hospital I'd like to work in does. I'll need to bond with an omega before I apply again."

Ok, that's fucking bullshit. I cannot believe they would openly discriminate against him like that! What am I thinking? I know firsthand how discriminatory businesses can be to alphas and omegas.

Kol leans forward on the table.

"I go into ruts. And they are getting worse. It used to be once or twice a year. Now it's monthly. Weekly...Oscar has me on medication and treatment, but it's not helping. I need an omega. Oscar is sure that if I don't bond with an omega soon, I'll become feral."

That's a huge concern. I look around to see if anyone from the Institute heard. They wouldn't let him even near the building if they heard that. But I've met feral alphas before. I've worked with them during volunteer events. People think they are so removed from them, but we are all so close to becoming feral, truly, no one wants to talk about it.

I'm three bad heats away from being feral, truly.

Kol dips his chin to Locke.

Oscar's reason was understandable. Kol's reason was serious and personal. What does Locke have to say?

"Cadi, I'm so sorry you're coming into my life now. When things are so...fucked up. After hearing my story, you can walk away. I'll do whatever I can to make that easy for you."

My face pinches in confusion.

"Wait, hold on." I put up my hand. "I have something to say first. Before Locke says his thing, if he thinks whatever he has to say is going to be a deal breaker, then I should say mine too."

Mads puts his hand out on the table towards me.

"What do you have to say?"

I take his hand.

I'm looking at his nice face, his bleach blonde hair, and his sad eyes, and ask, "What's your thing, Mads? Tell me yours first?"

"It's too sad."

"If they know…" I point to the alphas. "Then tell me."

"But this doesn't have to do with why they need to bond you so soon."

"But you bonded them soon. You must have had your reasons."

He sighs. "I did."

"Then tell me."

He takes his hand back and gently pats his cane.

"Ok, I'll tell you. A year ago, I met an omega. I'd never spent time with one or really ever talked with one before her. She came up to me at the park while I was flying my drone. Nancy was a small ball of light. We fed off each other's energy. We'd talk for hours: in person, over the phone, texting, sending photos. I don't think I slept more than a few hours during our entire quick relationship.

"It was a whirlwind. I took her on dates. She told me her alphas, two brothers, didn't care. That they were mean to her. They weren't fun. They were always so serious. But she said I was fun. I thought they knew she was dating. I could have sworn she told me they knew about me. But I didn't actually ask. I didn't check up.

"They had a big fight one night, and she told them about me. She called me crying, begging, and pleading to come pick her up. She gave me this crazy address in the old rundown part of the city, across a bridge. She kept changing her location. Eventually, I had to park my car to walk to try to find her.

"I was so scared that she was hurt. She kept screaming at me over the phone, like I wasn't doing all I could to find her. That's when I found myself on a bridge with a giant, stupid truck barreling towards me.

"They chased me to the other side until they hit me with the corner of the bumper. I flew and landed on the road, but managed to roll off the edge, behind a concrete barrier. So they couldn't hit me a second time. Instead of giving up and leaving, they got out and beat me. Kicked me. Hit me with a piece of rebar they found. Stomped on my leg. I think Nancy watched from the cab of the truck. I will never forget what they said to me while they did it. Their words were put into me, and I'm not sure they'll ever not be inside of me.

"I was in a medically induced coma for a while, so they could do all the surgeries. I sued them and settled, and I was supposed to get the money, a quarter of a million dollars, last week. I guess I did get the money...but first, my lawyer took his cut, and the insurance company took the rest. I didn't get a penny. I still owe medical bills. I lost my job. My apartment. I'm in pain all the time. I no longer have insurance. Cadi, I'm miserable."

Tears track down my face. I can't hear this story. Holy shit. Mads. My Mads. He's so closed off. His hands are in his lap. His shoulders curl in on himself. Oscar leans across the table to hand me a handkerchief to wipe my tears with.

But what about my beta? All three of his alphas are affected by his emotions. Before I can step in and do something, he continues.

"I am actually afraid of alphas." He laughs and wipes his hand over his mouth. "I can't be around them. I applied to work for Kol, and he wouldn't let me say no. Locke spent the day with me, convincing me to join them, be one of them. He showed me care and kindness. His focus on me was something I've never experienced. He trusted me with his secrets.

"Then Kol spent a day with me. He put up with my bad attitude all day, and not once lost his patience. And later, at the mansion, he was so good to you. He showed me that even a big, scary alpha can be tamed.

"Oscar gave me the best opportunity. He gave me the chance to stand up for someone who deserves it. Who would have thought revenge was what I needed?"

He sniffs and takes a deep breath. We are all so focused on him that we breathe in sync.

"I didn't know what purpose a pack served until I met the Soto Pack. They lean on each other. Accept one another, even flawed. They make each other better. They provide a safe space. If I could be part of that, for even a small amount of time, that would be worth more than a million dollars. I was happy to be able to give back to them."

My mouth hangs open. And I'm just weeping. Locke comes off his chair to kneel next to me. He takes my hands. But I don't need comfort, Mads does.

"I'm sorry. God, Mads. I didn't know."

"It's ok. I know. I didn't think it would be appropriate to tell the pretty omega who wanted to go on dates with all my trauma."

I gasp. "That's why you were so shocked when we met and I was an omega."

"Yeah, I hadn't planned on the first time I went out since the incident would be with an omega."

"I kept it from you because I didn't think it should matter. But it did. It does."

"Oh, Cadi, it's ok. You're not in charge of my boundaries. I am. I decided to stay. I decided I wanted to get to know you."

That's a nice thought, but I shouldn't have assumed why he was so shocked when he met me. It's a good reminder for me to be more patient. I want to do it over again. I want to be more kind. More honest.

"Mads, you've been through a lot."

He gives me a tight-lipped smile.

"It's ok."

I shake my head. It's not ok.

"What happened to the alphas? To Nancy?"

"I don't know. Nothing? The alphas served some jail time, but are already out. They were out before I even got out of the hospital the first time. As far as I know, they are still together. I like to imagine they don't exist on the same planet as me. Let alone, Cash City."

I turn to Oscar, and we seem to have the same thought, because he looks at Locke and Kol next. There will be retribution. One day.

44

Roundtable

Acadia

Hearing Mads's entire tale has shaken me to my core. It's rewritten parts of me. Each one of these men have etched their stories into my heart, earning their place.

"Locke, can I hear your story now? I need to know everything." I look down at him kneeling next to me. He looks so sorry already.

"I'll do it here. On my knees." I give him a reassuring smile. "Mads knows only part of this story, so it's good to say it all at once. I was sent to live with a very bad man named Legs O'Bannon when I was young, around ten years old. Later, I found out he gave my parents a lot of money in the exchange. Do with that what you will.

"You gotta understand why he took me—Legs can't bond. Years before, he'd stolen an omega from a pack and got her pregnant. When her pack found out what happened, they pulled all of Legs's teeth out as punishment. He wears veneers. Legs is obsessed with the idea of growing his pack. Since he can't do it with his teeth, he's found a creative way to make it work. And I am at the center of that plan. I share a last name with him. We aren't related. I don't know how he met my parents. But that's how I ended up with him.

"His fucked up plan is to force me to bond with his daughter, Aurora, creating a Pack O'Bannon, and making more O'Bannons at his discretion. He'd be pack lead by proxy because he'd control me. He started his grooming early. He subjugated me. He controlled everything I did. Who talked to me. What I ate. When I ate. Everything. I was his pet. His plaything. The things he made me do, Cadi, I would never repeat. They are only for my nightmares.

"I was waiting for Aurora to come of age and then for Legs to force us to bond. She thinks we are soulmates. She was kept in the dark about my treatment. Aurora is in love with me. I do not want anything to do with her or her father.

"How I met Oscar and Kol...well, they had business with Legs. Kol was a supplier who wanted to cut him off. Oscar was facilitating negotiations. They settled on an agreement. But instead of just leaving and enjoying his freedom, Kol bit me. Claimed me."

"Oh my god!" I exclaim.

"I thought we were dead. But Oscar came up with another agreement. If we find an omega before Aurora's 19th birthday, he'd let me go. If we didn't, I'd come back to him and bond with Aurora. Leave the Soto pack. Legs agreed because he thought he could blacklist us from any prospective omega in Salt Port. Which he did. But we came here. To find you. Aurora's birthday is Friday. It's mine as well..."

I need to stand up. But as soon as I stand up, my head spins and I need to sit down, but I just rest my hand on the table for a second.

"You share a last name and a birthday?"

I don't know why that's my only thought, but it is. I step away and pace around a little. I go up to the table of finger food and throw a baby carrot in my mouth so I have something to distract me with.

"Cadi?"

"That's a hell of a story, Locke. My god. My god! Are you ok? Oh my god, of course not. I can't believe the pain you've endured. All you've been through."

I find I'm still clutching Oscar's handkerchief, so I blot my face with it again. It's Kol who turns my shoulders and then pulls me into his chest. He hugs me tight, and I tuck my arms between us.

Oscar says, while very close to us, "Do you understand why we need to bond soon? I must keep my pack together. Kol, Locke, and now Mads are more important to me than anything. I will not let them be taken away from me. Not for anything. I will fight for them until my last breath."

The conviction in his words ring through me. I've never heard anyone talk about their pack the way he does. All my life, I had to stop myself from caring as much as I do about those around me. Even those I read about or see on the news. I care. But I've never cared like he does. I want to help him. I really do.

I look out from Kol's comforting chest and see Locke still by the table on his knees.

This pack has been through so much, and yet they are so strong. I can't imagine anyone breaking them.

"Acadia, if we had more time, I'd take it. I'd earn our bond by gifts, trips, fucking, orgasms, and food. I'll just have to do that stuff after, to prove you made the right choice."

Oscar saying *fucking* and *orgasms* absolutely gets to me. I'd get to fuck all of them, right?

At the same time.

All at once.

I'd wear them the fuck out.

"Would all of you want to be intimate with me? I know everyone has their preferences..." I look to Locke. I don't know the details of his abuse. And I don't need to know, necessarily.

He says immediately, "We all want to fuck you, Acadia. As much as possible. All the time."

From above my head, Kol says, "No one has private relationships right now. Oscar, Locke, and I aren't like that with each other. But we'd be altogether for your heat, focused on you. Giving you everything of ourselves."

Locke says, "I have to admit I am going to try to convince Mads to be with me sometimes. If that's ok? With both of you."

Mads laughs from where he's sitting at the table still.

"Fuck you, Locke," he says with no heat in his words. Locke winks at him.

"Hey, I don't want there to be any confusion when I seduce you at one point in the near future."

"Oh my god!" Mads buries his face in his hands.

"I'm pansexual," I say before we get off topic. "My last pack that I was in contract with was two alphas, a man and a woman, and I was with both of them."

"Why aren't you with them now?" Locke asks.

I unpeel myself from Kol, whose heat had done its job to relax my body.

"This is important, actually. I'd planned to bond with them on my next heat, and I've stopped taking all my heat suppressants. But I went to meet their daughter for the first time...

"I know there were red flags. Like, that I hadn't met her yet and they'd been courting me for two years. Or that she is only a year younger than me. We met her new pack, and it went very poorly. She was a late-presenting omega. So they'd thought she was a beta growing up. And after she stopped being a cute little girl and started growing up, they abandoned her. I didn't know. They left her at their summer house when she was twelve and only saw her once or twice a year until she left for college. Even when she said she perfumed as an omega, they had no attachment to her by then and didn't care.

"She has chronic bond sickness. Oscar, you helped diagnose her. She's Ondine with the Meier Pack."

"Yes, I did. I helped Dr. Chen with a second opinion."

"I was so horrified when I learned about it I left them. Dissolved the contract. I couldn't imagine having a beta child and doing that to her."

"I think I understand now," Oscar says as he walks toward me. "You wanted to make sure that your pack didn't discriminate against designations. That's why you told the Institute that the pack had to have a beta bonded."

"Yes."

"You did it after meeting Ondine?"

"Yes. My heart aches for her. I wanted to make sure that I would be with open-minded alphas. I could very well have a beta daughter. I would tear your hearts out if you ever made her feel any less loved than an alpha or omega child. Do you understand?"

Oscar nods his head, and I look at each of them. They each say yes.

"You are a wonderful person."

"Any decent person..."

"No, you're empathetic, Acadia. You love those you don't even know. Any child would be lucky to have you as their mother."

"Thank you. Do you want children?"

"Yes, and I believe Kol wants a child as well."

"Yes, if it is possible." He stumbles over his words. He doesn't mean if possible. He means he doesn't want to pressure me. He can be quite bashful, I realize. Suddenly, Oscar moves Kol away from me in a quick yank. Locke jumps up and runs toward me, grabbing me and spinning us so his back is toward Kol and Oscar.

"What is going on?!" I shout.

I hear growling and wrestling.

"Kol can get bitey," Locke says close to my ear. "Oscar felt the change in the bond. We don't want him to bite you like he did me."

While I'm very opposed to getting bitten without my permission, the omega in me feels permission has been granted and would have loved to have been bitten by Kol. But that's just not how things are done.

Plus, I like talking to them first. Telling our stories. Making sure we know each other. I hear more grunting and wrestling. I twist in Locke's arms so I can peek at Kol. He's on the ground, and his arms are pulled behind him. Oscar has a knee in his back.

"I'm fine! I'm not going to bite her!"

"And yet we all felt it. Remember how fast you were with Locke? I didn't even finish blinking, and your teeth were in his arm."

I shiver all over at the image.

"Here, I want to help," I say, and Locke lets me go. I walk up to Oscar and Kol in their little pile.

"Will you get him on a chair?" I ask.

Oscar tips his head at me. Maybe debating whether he is going to listen to me. Then pulls Kol up. Oscar is strong!

Oscar manhandles Kol into a chair, and I stand in front of him.

"Remember how well behaved you were when it was just me and Mads? Do you think you can do that again?" I ask with a smile. Kol is breathing hard and gritting his teeth.

"I won't bite you."

"You're drooling, Kol." And he is. It drips down his jaw and neck. I turn to Locke, who stands next to me.

"May I?" I ask, gesturing to his tie.

"Sure."

I carefully undo his black and gold paisley tie. Our faces are close, and he's staring wide-eyed at me. After I take off his tie, I pat his chest in thanks, then I walk around to Kol's back. I ask Oscar, "Can you tie a good knot?"

"I can."

"Will you tie his hands together?"

I hand him the tie. Oscar chuckles slightly and then ties Kol's hands behind his back.

"What're you going to do, little momma? Now that you got me tied up," Kol asks with a tilt to his lips and a deep, sexy fray to his voice.

"Whatever I want."

45

Sunday Candy

Mads

The atmosphere has shifted. If I look directly at each alpha, I can discern their emotions really easily. Especially now. Lust. Since all three share this emotion, it whips through the bond like a live wire.

I feel my dick get harder, and I shift in my seat. It's been three and a half hours since I took my meds, so to avoid feeling pain and ruining the moment for Cadi, I go to the table of food and eat three little cream puffs, then neck my meds. I wash it down with some lemonade.

While my back was turned, Cadi positioned herself between Kol's legs.

I'm still not even sure I've wrapped my head around the events that transpired here. I'm about to be bonded with the girl I've been dating. I truly don't know if bonding is like marriage, but I have a feeling it's so much more. She doesn't seem opposed to this idea of tying herself to me for the rest of her life. My feelings are confusing.

I have this strange excitement making waves through me. Every wave of excitement washes away one of my other feelings—fear, apprehension, and loneliness. It's actually hard to be lonely when three male alphas feel what you feel and then push their own emotions onto you.

Oh no, I think, as Cadi keeps glancing down at Kol's crotch, where an obvious hard-on is. Is she going to get on her knees and suck him off? She's looking at the hard stone ground, and I just know she's debating if it's going to hurt.

I have to intervene.

I grab my cane and walk closer to them, just as I make it to Acadia, she's lowering to her knees in front of the tied up alpha. I grab her arm, stopping her.

"Not a chance, Cadi," I growl at her. Her head snaps to me, and her face flushes pink.

"What?" she asks.

The other two alphas are wondering the same thing.

"You're not going to get on your knees to Kol. I may not know much about alphas and omegas, but the Soto pack is here to show you they are worthy. Don't get on your knees for them."

Some part of my old personality emerges from the recesses of my mind, and I feel it snap into the place where it used to be.

"If you want to take things there, then I have a better idea, babe." I wink at her, and her jaw comes unhinged. I look at Locke, who stands a few steps away, because his lust doubles.

I look back at Cadi, who says, "What do you have in mind?"

I check in with Oscar on how he feels about taking things in this direction, but the fact that he wasn't going to stop Cadi from sucking off Kol right here in this atrium doesn't make me think he's opposed.

It seems like I'm right. He nods at me. I check in with Kol and then Locke, who do the same, then I turn all my attention to Cadi. I loosen my grip on her arm and then stroke the spot I was holding.

I take a few steps and move Cadi with my body until she's between Kol's thighs as he sits on the chair, but she's facing me and not him.

"Can you sit in Kol's lap?" I ask. She swallows deep, her throat bobbing, and then turns to look behind her. I grab her face, stopping her. "Look at me. Not him. Can you sit down?"

She nods and then sits down. Her back is flush with his front. Oscar is still behind him, and he checks the knot tying Kol's hands.

"Kol, don't bite me," Cadi whispers.

"Kol will be a good boy and not bite you, right buddy?" I say, and Kol grits his teeth together. His mouth is right at her neck and shoulder. It's a gamble if this is a good idea for sure, but Kol went to a lot of work to convince me he can show restraint. Let's see if I can trust that.

"I won't bite you," he confirms.

Oscar steps closer. He's like a spotter behind him.

"Cadi, you look so pretty sitting there. Like a queen on her throne," I tell her, and she blushes. "Are you scared?"

"No."

"Are you turned on?"

"Yes."

"Can I see?" I ask and she lets out a little gasp, but doesn't respond, so I ask again, "Can I see how turned on you are?"

Her big emerald eyes look at me like I'm in charge here. Like she's giving up control, but just for me and just for now.

"Yes."

I let my cane drop to the ground, and the metal rings out in the space. Locke is suddenly next to me, and in a move that should not be as smooth or hot, he helps me kneel in front of Cadi. The move ends with both of us before her. Locke has one leg up and one knee down. I'm on both knees. The stone is fine for now. I'm sure I won't notice. All the blood is only in one place in my body right now anyway.

I wrap my hand around her ankle and then up her calf. I bend down and kiss the inside of her knee, and then I pull her leg up and over top of Kol's leg. She gasps as she's forced to open up. Her dress rides up higher on her legs, pooling in her lap.

"Do you like this?" I ask. "Exposed to me and your alphas?"

"Yes."

"I'm starting to think you love being on display, omega."

Locke and I each take a side as we push up the skirt of her dress until she is exposed. Now it's our turn to be surprised.

"You're not wearing panties."

She gives me a look that makes me think she's been in charge this entire time.

Her bare cunt is wet and gloriously open. Locke can smell her even more intensely now, and he adjusts his dick in his slacks. Kol is emitting a low-level growl.

"What are we going to do with you?" I tsk.

My hand rests on the inside of her creamy thigh. I push and open her up even more. Locke takes her other leg and pulls it up over Kol's leg. She lifts her arms and wraps her hands around Kol's neck to keep herself steady.

"Can I touch you?" I ask.

"Yes. Please. Now. Stop fucking teasing me."

I rake my knuckles over her pussy, and she moans and her head falls back. I use two fingers to open her lips so I can see how unbelievably wet she is for me. For us. I give her clit some attention. I press my thumb and circle her clit, and she squirms and moans.

"Hold her still, Locke."

And those are my last words before I lean in and devour her in front of everyone.

I'm diving headfirst, pun intended, into this whole group sex thing. Why I'm taking the lead may confuse my new pack, but until ten minutes ago, when Acadia was about to kneel in front of Kol and fucking suck him off, did I realize all three of these alphas are subs.

Kol not so much, but he's tied up. Oscar for sure. The guy has been waiting twenty years for an omega to come and plant one on him.

Locke, despite his words earlier, will wait for me to make the move until we are both dead.

They are perfect for Cadi, who is very dominant.

But this situation doesn't call for Cadi to be dominant.

Sensing an empty seat, I sat in it. Metaphorically.

I'll be in charge this time.

I push two fingers into her saturated pussy and suck on her clit. Hard. Locke holds her leg and hip still, but she's getting close and is moving her body to help herself to her release.

"Are you close, my scent match? I want to see you come. Kol is being so good for you. So, you need to be a good girl and come."

I moan into her pussy, working her faster and harder, until she screams. Suddenly, her hand is in my hair, pulling at the scalp. It feels incredible, and I want her to pull harder.

She screams and she comes while I eat her out. Her legs shake underneath my hands. Locke and I hold them steady. I lick her up and down a few times, even though she's so sensitive, she tries to move away from my tongue.

I look up and make eye contact with Kol. His eyes are bloodshot. Oscar's hand is over Kol's mouth.

Blood drips down the bottom of Oscar's hand. Shocked, I'm ready to apologize or something, but Oscar gives me a little shake of his head. No. Don't react. Don't ruin this for her. She's surrounded by us. Coming for us. Lying over Kol with Locke and I between her legs. She's smiling and catching her breath. She's relaxed.

Locke squeezes my arm once to show he understands too.

Oscar had to stop Kol from biting Cadi. He used the palm of his hand. That must have hurt like a bitch. I didn't feel it at the time, but Cadi was coming, and my whole body was tuned in to her. Not to my bond. I'm sure Locke felt it.

I notice Oscar's other hand is stroking Cadi's hair sweetly.

I lift Cadi's legs and put them back together. Locke steps in and helps me up, handing me my cane, and then takes Cadi in his arms. He walks them over to a couch and sits down with her in his lap. He cradles her close.

"How do you feel?" he asks.

"Like it's still happening."

I grin. Damn.

I walk behind Kol and watch Oscar try to hide his hand. Using Cadi's trick, I take off my tie and hand it over. He turns his back and wraps his hand with my tie. Should I untie Kol?

The veins in his neck are standing out.

Maybe not.

"You ok?" I whisper to Oscar. He nods just once. It's not a yes, it's a *don't ask me again.*

Guilt swarms around me.

Cadi wanted to relieve Kol so he'd feel less inclined to bite. But I'd riled him up and pushed him over the edge.

"I can feel that, you know. I am sick of feeling guilt from my alphas. I don't need it from my beta as well," Oscar says to me with a serious tone. "You were thinking of Cadi. Always think of your omega first. Put her first. Every time. You made the right call."

I bite my tongue from doubling down on my guilt.

I didn't think of Kol, and now he's worse than before. Except...he's not. His breaths are evening out. His body is relaxing. I untie his hands.

"Biting or fucking helps with his rutting problem," Oscar continues to tell me. "Like I said, you made the right call. My hand was there to get in the way when he got too wild. I knew what I was agreeing to, Mads."

Oscar knew the whole time it would end in Kol coming or Kol biting. My guilt does ease off. The way it happened was the best way. For Cadi.

I look over at Locke and her. He's whispering in her ear.

Kol stands up out of the chair and Oscar and he hug. They whisper in each other's ears. I hear them apologize and say thank you.

They let go, and Kol turns to me. His lips have blood on them, and before I can blink, he's grabbing my chin and kissing me.

My whole body goes stiff, and my arms shoot out. I drop my cane. But he's not really kissing me. He's licking Cadi's slick off my lips. I relax and open up a little so he can get better access. I grab onto his arms to hold us close.

"Goddamn," I hear Locke say from the couch.

I haven't told anyone this because I just haven't had the chance, but I am in fact bisexual. I date men and women. Beta men. Not alphas. So, Kol smacking on my face is both new and not.

I kiss him back, and he doesn't seem to mind. But I let him finish tasting Cadi on me while I taste Oscar's blood. And when he's satisfied, he pulls away.

"Did that make you feel better?" I ask.

He looks at Cadi and says with a devilish grin, "Yes. I looked down and saw Cadi had a tattoo on her thigh, and I just lost it entirely. A little omega symbol on her upper thigh."

He tastes like Halloween, I note. All sweet and cool with the fall leaves surrounding me.

He pats my cheek, retrieves my cane, and then walks away to get a drink. I hear the wine bottle open as I stumble into a nearby chair.

Goddamn, indeed.

46

Exit Interview

Mads

We take some time to drink a glass of wine each and decompress before we head off into the main building, and up to the conference room.

Kol still has some dried blood on the side of his mouth. A mouth I keep looking at. My tie is still wrapped around Oscar's hand. Locke and Cadi hold hands.

The Soto pack's lawyer is already in the room along with Angeline, her boss, and two more people I don't know. I'm guessing they are Cadi's lawyer and her handler.

Every single person looks at the mark on my neck and stiffens up. They look from my mark to Oscar and then lower their eyes in deference.

This thing is really sending a message.

The woman in the fuchsia matching set hugs Cadi, who doesn't let go of Locke's hand. She's introduced to us as Maria, Cadi's handler. She tries to hug Oscar, and Cadi steps between them.

"Maria, let's not," she says. Cadi is feeling possessive. The alphas love this behavior.

We sit down, and all three Soto alphas look over at me because I wince as I get into the chair. I need to elevate my leg. It's getting inflamed. Locke takes his hand from Cadi and wheels an extra chair over. He moves it to the tallest setting and carefully helps me put my foot up on the chair. Then he takes my cane and props it up against the table. Everyone is staring at me. The whole time.

Kol is already getting some sparkling water from the mini fridge. He puts one in front of Cadi first, me second, and then asks if anyone else wants one. He gets one for Maria, who was more than excited to accept.

I know this is some alpha behavior. The fact that the omega is served first makes sense to me. I'm not sure why I was second. As a beta, aren't I at the bottom of the hierarchy here?

Kol stands by the windows, and we begin.

"We always encourage a temporary contract first. That gives you all a chance to see if you are a good match physiologically. Or, more commonly, a temporary contract allows you all to settle your hormones and then part ways without the pressure of forever," the older boss lady explains. "We have one drawn up that we can start with."

I think the alphas are going to lose their shit. Their faces are impassive, but they are pissed. A fiery steam is sure to come out of Oscar's ears.

Cadi speaks up, "With all do respect, I will be bonding with the Soto Pack immediately. So draw up papers for that."

Oscar's head snaps to her. I don't think he knew she'd made up her mind. I mean, she let me go down on her until she came while she sat in Kol's lap and the other two watched, but I guess there was still a question. She reaches over and squeezes his hand.

I'd like to say it was as easy as that, but Cadi is an Institute omega. They have rules. Apparently, a lot of rules. We spend the next two and a half hours on the agreements. I need to take my meds again. Kol paces the giant glass windows. Angeline's boss, whose name I never caught, knows Spanish, so at one point she and Oscar argue in Spanish, and I catch a few colorful words.

Acadia is exhausted. She keeps yawning and sighing.

We sign the papers, and it's done. Cadi is going to bond.

The relief Oscar feels floods the bond, but you can also see it on his face and his unburdened shoulders.

The sun is setting outside, and it's casting a red light into the conference room.

Oscar goes to Kol, and I hear him say, "I know you're out of time."

Kol needs to bond an omega.

The lawyers, Institute workers, and Maria say goodbye and leave us alone.

Oscar turns to us.

"I've booked a nest at the Sky Nest hotel. Let's all go pack and then meet there. We will bond. We have all day tomorrow to enjoy the bond. Friday, Mads and I will head to Salt Port to finish out our business there. We will return and shop for houses. Yes?"

We wait for Cadi to say something. God, she looks tired. She rests her head on Locke's shoulder.

"You'll bite me, Oscar?" she asks.

"Yes."

"Then Kol and Locke?" Kol stops pacing.

"You want our bites, too?" Kol is so taken back. He sounds shocked.

My face scrunches up.

"Mads is confused," Kol says.

They all turn to me. I shake my head. "Sorry. It's just more stuff I don't understand. I thought alphas always all bite their omega. I mean, I was surprised that only Oscar bit me."

"You want my mark?" Kol asks with reverence, the same shocked reference he used with Cadi.

"And mine?" Locke asks with a matching tone.

I throw my hands up. "Sure, why not?"

There's a strange, excited tension in the air. What did I do?

Cadi says to me, "There's a lot of politics with a bite. A lot of community expectations. History, too. It sends a message."

"What kind of message?"

"For omegas, we get bitten by every member to strengthen our bond. Kol and Locke are honored. I want that kind of strong bond so quickly. But I believe it's the only way. Trying to dissolve a bond is never something I want. Plus, I think I *need* my scent match's bite."

"That makes sense."

"For a beta, your mark sends different but similar messages. Often they are ownership marks rather than...bonding marks."

"He's pack," Kol growls. "It's not ownership." He doesn't growl at Cadi, more at the idea I wouldn't be considered an equal.

"I thought that was a pack hierarchy. Cadi is the top. Then the alphas. Then me."

"No," all of them say at once.

"Oh, lord," I mumble under my breath. "It's fine. I get it. You are all ruled by your inner wolves or whatever. I get it."

"No," Oscar says first. "I'll just be candid with you, Mads, most alphas and omegas view betas just like you are saying. Like charms. Or pets. Or lesser members. It's archaic and barbaric to view betas that way. I don't like explaining to you how traditionalists will view you, but you should know. Betas are usually marked by an alpha in the pack, and not the pack lead. I'm pack lead, so my mark says you are pack, but having Kol's and Locke's mark as well will reaffirm this. They are also honored that you'd want their marks. They are not given out freely.

"Alphas are different. Any alpha or omega Kol bites will be bonded in the pack. Same with Locke. But doing it without my permission makes it a silver bond. It's not just a term. The mark will heal with a silver coloring. Have you heard of this?"

I shake my head.

"What about a dark bond?" he asks.

"Oh, I've heard of that. That's one where it was forced."

"Yes. A dark bond is given without the recipient's permission. It heals black in color. There are lots of problems with a dark bond. With a silver bond, like the one Kol gave Locke, there are no major problems. But his connection with other members is weak. Like his connection with you. He may not feel your emotions like Kol or I can."

It makes me wonder, what makes someone a pack lead? A pack of two has a pack lead? Is it just the more dominant alpha? I don't understand that part.

But Oscar keeps going, "When we get to the hotel, all the alphas will mark Cadi. Then I will mark Locke, if he'll have me."

Locke looks misty eyed, and he nods, saying, "I'd be honored."

Oscar continues, "And Kol and Locke will bite you. We will have a strong bond that no one can dissolve."

Cadi yawns.

"Tell him what his mark is telling alphas and omegas, Oscar. I don't think he knows," Cadi says.

Oscar waits until I make eye contact with him before he says, "I wondered if you'd noticed the strange behavior from people since I bonded you. Mads, they think you're an omega." I gestured to my neck. "It's a common mark placement for a male omega."

"What?"

"Do you know about Orrin Cash?" Cadi asks.

"The guy who founded Cash City a hundred and fifty years ago?" I say with the utmost confusion.

Why are we bringing up Cash City history? I thought the message my mark was giving people was to stay the fuck away from me.

I guess a marked omega is definitely someone you'd want to stay the fuck away from...

With a tired voice, Cadi explains, "Orrin Cash was an omega. He had a large pack of alphas he never bonded. Twelve of them. They called them 'the tribe.' All male. After they founded the city, built the roads, and erected the buildings, Orrin finally bonded with an alpha who was not part of his tribe. Porter Nightingale. Porter marked Orrin on his neck, just like yours."

I didn't know the mark was significant. The part of the story I know is that Orrin got pregnant with Porter's baby. Male omegas can get pregnant. It's obviously the most interesting part of our founder's history. It's hard to remember anything else.

Kol says, "It's probably where you thought marks go because you've seen his portrait. It's been in fashion ever since for male omegas to get a mark on their neck, just like that. Even outside of Cash City. All over the country. When people see your mark, they first think you're an omega, and then probably don't give you any more attention, especially since you are surrounded by several alphas. I doubt they even look long enough to notice you are actually a beta."

My mouth bobs open and shut like a fish. I don't even know what to say. I am not even sure this is a bad thing. It probably is a good thing, right? I don't really care what designation people think I am. I just don't want random alphas approaching me. My mark was doing that for me, I just didn't know why. Until now.

Cadi's eyes shut as she lays her head on Locke's shoulder again.

"I can ask more questions another time, you guys. Just know that I will have more."

Oscar nods.

"Understandably. Cadi, you want all three of us to mark you?"

She sighs and yawns again, "Yeah."

I'm guessing it's a big deal, and her "yeah" is understated.

"We would be honored."

The red light fades, and the room is too dark to see our faces, even though there's still light in the sky. It's time to leave.

Oscar wraps his arm around Cadi's shoulder, and we follow them out.

Maria is waiting for Cadi in the lobby. She agreed to drive her home to pack some bags, and then Oscar will have a car ordered to drive her to Sky Nest.

Oscar kisses her goodbye on the lips. I turn my face, wanting them to have a private moment. Kol hits me on the arm. I laugh at him.

Locke kisses her next.

Then Kol. They look so good together.

Then she steps up to me. I kiss her, and goddamnit, I want to do it again as soon as it's over.

We help her into Maria's car and watch her drive away. The street is pretty busy. It's in a populated part of the city.

"Let me order us a car, too."

"It's not that far," I say, and Locke groans.

"Please do me a favor and let's drive," he begs, and I shake my head at him.

"Don't be a baby. We could all use the fresh air."

I'm staring at his smiling face. He's only a few feet from me. It's dusk, so it's not quite dark yet, but it's like the sun suddenly winks out.

Two men in black clothes throw a bag over Locke's head. And it's all I see before a bag is thrown over my head, and I'm dragged away. It's so fast I'm not even sure my heart beats more than once before I'm thrown in the back of a van, on top of Locke. My leg lands funny, and pain shoots through me.

I hear Oscar roar, and then the door is slammed shut.

The van drives away, and Locke and I are slammed into each other because of it driving away so fast.

"The needle! Get the needles into their necks!" The driver yells.

My hands find a man's arms, and I grab them, but it doesn't stop him from jabbing the needle into my neck and slamming down on the plunger.

And then everything goes out.

Epilogue

Kol

O scar and I run side by side, chasing the van through the city streets. There's no license plate on it. All I know is that it's a Mercedes. That's a start. We lose it somewhere near the riverfront.

"They were Legs's men, right?" I ask.

Oscar is too out of breath to answer. But the answer is yes.

I just watched Mads and Locke get taken right in front of us. They were maybe ten feet away. Oscar was on his phone ordering a car. I was trying to stop myself from going after Cadi and biting her exactly in the same spot Oscar bit Mads. They were talking about bites and marks, and I thought I was going to pass out. My ears have been ringing for the better part of an hour. I wasn't operating at 100%.

I wasn't paying attention.

My reflexes were non-existent.

I feel like I have no skin and all my organs are on display. I feel like I lost a limb. Two limbs. My beta and my alpha have been taken. I'm about to go feral.

I'm out of time.

It's happening.

I don't realize I'm screaming until Oscar shakes me.

"You need to breathe." He shows me how to do it. Suck in a breath and hold it. Slowly let it go. He guides me through until I'm calm. His hand is on my chest, and his other hand is on my shoulder.

"Think about it, Kol. We know where they are taking them. To Salt Port. We need to be smart. We have to bond with Cadi to make us strong. Then we will go get our brothers back. Do you trust me?" I have tunnel vision, and all I see are his earnest, sure eyes. I nod. Yes, I trust him.

Drool drips down the side of my mouth.

I'm not waiting any longer.

Even if I dark bond Acadia. I'm finding her, and I'm biting her. Right now.

"No, Kol!"

I hear Oscar yelling as I run from him.

I have no more time left.

She's mine.

Afterword

When I started writing Ondine, she was being published by the episode on Kindle Vella, and so her story developed in real time alongside my readers. I wrote Mads in secret. It was just him and me for a long time. His story is a lot more gentle and precious because of that. Mads is my refuge, and my hope is that he is for you, too.

I want to get down on my knees and thank my editor Kenzie, with Cupid's Inkwell. Meeting her at Romance Out West was a turning point for me as a writer. Thank you, Kenzie, for being so openly kind to me.

Next, I want to thank my brother Dustin and sister-in-law Jill, who are so supportive I could cry. I can't believe I have a family that doesn't shame me for writing Why-Choose, omegaverse romance novels.

All my beta readers, Jessica and Lorin specifically, you gave me gold. I will forever be in your debt.

I want to acknowledge the hundreds and thousands of readers of Ondine, who made me realize I am never going to stop doing this. I have one hundred more books inside of me, and I'm going to write all of them.

xx SHASTA

About the Author

Shasta has enthralled readers with her unique writing style and penchant for high-stakes tension. What she is most known for is her well-written and intense spicy scenes, bringing the action to life in the most toe-curling way. She started out as a Kindle Vella author then moved to indie publishing. She has 100 more books to write, so stick around to read more steamy romance from her.

www.shastadeleon.com